R

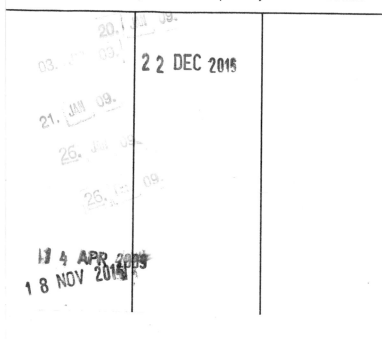
Library

community services

North Lanarkshire Council

Reap the
Whirlwind

By the same author

Windsong
Sand Against the Wind

Reap the Whirlwind

Book three of the
Cwmbran Trilogy

Catriona McCuaig

ROBERT HALE · LONDON

© Catriona McCuaig 2008
First published in Great Britain 2008

ISBN 978-0-7090-8670-3

Robert Hale Limited
Clerkenwell House
Clerkenwell Green
London EC1R 0HT

www.halebooks.com

2 4 6 8 10 9 7 5 3 1

Typeset in 11½/15pt Garamond
by Derek Doyle & Associates, Shaw Heath
Printed and bound in Great Britain
by Biddles Limited, King's Lynn

For they have sown the wind and they shall reap the whirlind.

Hosea 8:10

Chapter One

Warmer weather at last! May had come to their Carmarthenshire valley, bringing with it new hope for the future, for the war in Europe had just come to an end. Hard to believe, that was, after almost six years, Bessie Prosser thought as she trudged along, except that she had heard Mr Churchill on the wireless, saying it was all over and their side had won. And why not? The Lord was on their side.

She stopped for a moment, shifting her shopping bag to her other hand. She couldn't wait to get home and put the kettle on. She hoped that her stepsons hadn't finished off the tea ration again. When she'd first come into the house she'd tried to institute a system of keeping everyone's rations in separate containers in the larder, but Job had soon put a stop to that.

'There's silly you are, woman!' he'd sniffed. 'You'll be wanting extra teapots, next, I suppose, one for each of us to brew your precious rations in!'

'Only trying to be fair,' she pleaded, 'what with our Griff wanting a cup every five minutes and the rest not getting a look in.'

Her husband narrowed his eyes at that. 'Our Griff works hard down the pit, woman, and I'll thank you to remember that he brings in a good wage, unlike some I could mention.'

That meant her, of course. Never mind she spent all the daylight hours slaving away, looking after the eight of them, scrubbing the dirty pit clothes and all the rest! That didn't count.

Down at the end of the street, next to the sweet shop, the door to Merfin Jones's house was open, and Bessie could see that two women were seated on wooden chairs in the entrance, with their feet on the well-scrubbed step. One of them was Merfin's wife, Megan, and the other was that Ellen Richards, or Morgan, as they were supposed to call her since she'd married old Harry, who owned half of Cwmbran.

Bessie's lip curled in disdain. What was the world coming to, when the wife of the colliery owner could sit in the doorway of a miner's cottage, practically on the pavement, gossiping like any common housewife? Of course, Ellen Richards was no lady, never would be. She'd been nanny to Miss Meredith up at the House and then, when the child was grown, she'd stayed on as housekeeper. Then, three years ago, Mr Morgan had actually married the woman, which had caused plenty of talk around the town, no doubt about that!

The first Mrs Morgan, now, she was a lady. Bessie hadn't exactly known her, but as a child she'd seen Harry's wife in the town sometimes, beautifully dressed and walking with her nose in the air, always accompanied by a downtrodden sort of lady companion. Delicate she was, poor Mrs Morgan, and she'd died giving birth to Miss Meredith. That was during the last war.

Before Mr Morgan had stepped in with his proposal of marriage, Job Prosser had been paying court to Ellen Richards, but all his plans fell through when she married the owner of the colliery. He had come in for a fair amount of teasing as a result, Bessie remembered.

'No wonder you couldn't get a look in, boyo, when she had her sights set on the boss! Played you for a fool, she did!'

Bessie had been delighted. She'd had her eye on Job for a long time and she meant to catch him on the rebound. She'd squandered her week's fat and sugar ration to make him a cake, put on her Sunday hat, and arrived on his doorstep, full of sympathy.

After a moment's hesitation he had invited her in.

'Plenty more fish in the sea,' he grunted, when she finally ran out of steam. 'I didn't fancy her all that much, see. When our Myfanwy left us in the lurch I needed somebody to keep house, and Ellen Richards was experienced in that department. I thought she'd do.'

Bravado, Bessie thought, yet there was some truth in what he said. His only daughter, who was just a child when her mother had died, had fought an uphill battle for years, trying to take her place in the house, slaving away to look after her Dada and six brothers. No wonder she'd jumped at the chance to work up at Cwmbran House as nursemaid to Master Henry, Harry Morgan's grandson.

A cunning look had crossed Job's face as he stared at Bessie, all pink-faced and simpering beneath her Sunday hat. 'Don't suppose you'd fancy the job?' he remarked.

'Oh, I wouldn't want to give up my job at the greengrocer's,' she told him. 'They always let me have the leftover bits and pieces at the end of the week. Fruit that won't keep, that sort of thing. It does help to spin out the rations, see.'

'I'd marry you, if you'd come,' he muttered, and she hadn't needed asking twice.

'What a fool I was,' Bessie reminded herself now. She'd given up her little rented cottage, chucked in the job, and plighted her troth to Job Prosser in the Methodist chapel. She'd been lonely ever since her husband died, and was looking forward to being part of a couple again, but this had soon palled. Job was harshly critical, finding fault with all she did, and as for a word of praise, well, you might as well try to stop the sun from rising in the East as get him to commit himself.

Her expression turned sour as she approached the house where Megan Jones and Ellen Morgan sat in state. Why did some people get all the luck? It just wasn't fair. She crossed the street so she couldn't be expected to stop and chat.

'*Prynhawn da*, Bessie!' Megan called out.

'*Prynhawn da!*' Bessie muttered. She hurried on, wanting to get past before she was forced to acknowledge Mrs Lah-di-dah Morgan. Not that the other woman had bothered to greet her, stuck-up snob.

'Who was that?' Ellen asked, glancing up from the ribbons she was holding. 'She looks familiar.'

Megan laughed. 'Looks familiar? Surely you remember her? Bessie Harries she was. She married Job Prosser after you threw him over.'

9

'Now you come to mention it, I do know who she is, although I've only met her once or twice. And for your information, I did not throw him over! It's true we did see a bit of each other at one time, but I managed to cut him off before he got around to asking for my hand in marriage. I went out with him because I was feeling lonely, but I can honestly say I didn't lead him on. I was too much in love with Harry to contemplate teaming up with some other man, no matter how nice.'

'And you can hardly call Job Prosser nice. A proper dog's life he led that poor daughter of his. Treated her worse than a heathen slave, he did, and now he's got poor Bessie dancing to his tune.'

'I'm sure that Bessie is happy enough. From what Mariah told me at the time the woman was sweet on Job for years. She just about had forty fits when she thought he had designs on me. Now she's got what she wanted, so why wouldn't she be pleased?'

' "All that glitters is not gold",' Megan quoted, frowning at her handiwork. The two women were making rosettes from red, white and blue ribbons, meant to be worn at the VE Day celebrations on the eighth of May. 'Do you think this looks all right, Ellen? It's coming out all curved like a rosebud, instead of flat.'

Ellen grinned. 'You could always say it's supposed to be a tricolour buttercup or something.'

Megan said something rude in Welsh. 'I'll have to unpick it and start again. Why do things always go wrong when you want them done in a hurry?' She dug savagely at her stitches with the point of her scissors.

'Myfanwy dropped in to see me on her day off,' she remarked, when the rosette was once more in pieces. 'From what she's heard from her brothers, their father is still carrying a torch for you.'

'What? You're having me on!'

'It's true. Every time they fall out – Bessie and Job – he tells her she's not a patch on you. "Mrs Morgan would never serve me lumpy potatoes", that sort of thing.'

'That's horrible!'

'Nasty, yes, but I thought you ought to know. Mind, I'm not saying there's anything in it, as far as he's concerned. He knows you're a married woman now, and your husband is the one who pays his wages, so Job is not likely to do anything silly. He just wants to upset Bessie, I expect, though by all accounts she's a good enough wife to him. You had a narrow escape there, my girl.'

Ellen remembered what her daughter had said in the days when Bessie was in hot pursuit of Job. 'Mariah said something about Bessie's daughter from her first marriage going out with Llew Prosser. I would have thought that would make for family unity. Surely the girl would stick up for her mam?'

'Behind the times, you are! That may be all off by now. The silly girl started making eyes at some Polish airman she met at a dance in Llanelly and the chap turned up here in Cwmbran looking for her. Of course she sent him off with a flea in his ear, but Llew is acting like a bear with a sore head as result.

'But why are we wasting such a beautiful afternoon agonizing over those old Prossers? Tell me all about your Mariah. What's in the cards for her now that the war is just about over? She'll be moving away from Cwmbran, I take it?'

To Megan's amazement her friend put her head in her hands and began to cry.

Chapter Two

'Everything is bound to change now the war's over,' Ellen sobbed, dabbing at her eyes with a sodden handkerchief.

'I should jolly well hope so!' Megan retorted. 'Just imagine, no more bad news every time you switch on the wireless, no more worrying about when the invasion might come, and one of these days no more rationing! Mind you, we're not out of the woods yet. We still have to beat Japan.'

Ellen stared at the teacup which Megan had placed on the kitchen table in front of her. 'It's not that I don't want the war to end, Megan. Nobody in their right mind would want to see it go on. And my worries seem trivial compared with what other people have suffered, losing their homes and loved ones. We've been fortunate here, I know. No air raids, and few people have lost anyone at the war because all the men stayed here to work down the pit.'

'But?' Megan prompted.

'But before long we're going to have to face a different sort of upheaval. For one thing, when Aubrey gets demobbed he'll be looking for a job somewhere, and then he'll be off, taking my daughter with him. Goodness knows where they'll end up!'

'I'd say you've been lucky, *bach*, having Mariah at home all this time, see? "A man shall leave his father and mother and cleave unto his wife", the Bible says, and that applies to a woman, too.'

Ellen glared at her. 'Do you think I don't know that? They haven't had much of a married life so far. Of course I want them to set up home together and make up for lost time. I'm just going to find it a wrench, that's all. And that's not the only thing. We'll be losing the Swansea Six as well, and they've been with us so long I think of them as my own children. There again, I know I'm not unique. Evacuees from all over the country will be going back to their families, leaving their foster parents grieving for them.'

'That's if they all got on well together,' Megan remarked, her face grim. They had both heard horror stories of children who were badly treated by their hosts, or of kindly people who had suffered at the hands of incorrigible evacuees. The idea of sending children away from areas where they might be killed in the blitz was all very well in principle, but no doubt it had caused untold emotional damage to parents and youngsters alike.

'Have you heard anything about the boys, then?'

'Well, no, it's early days yet, isn't it? But I'm just trying to prepare myself for the inevitable. Young Evan has a mother in the services; I imagine she'll be turning up one of these days to collect him. It's the others I'm worried about. I only hope they won't be split up. They depend on each other, a real little band of brothers. And then there's

Dafydd. He's almost fourteen now and I have an idea that they don't keep them in the orphanage when they reach that age. What's to become of him, Megan? Can you tell me that?'

Her friend shook her head. 'It's a hard old life, Ellen. Surely Mr Morgan can put a word in somewhere. He was a magistrate, after all. He'll know the right way to go about it. You speak to him, see?'

'And speaking of Harry, I must be going, or he'll wonder what's become of me. Just give me the rest of that ribbon, will you? I'll finish up those rosettes this evening. Thanks for the tea, and say hello to Merfin for me.'

'I'll do that.' Megan smiled brightly, but deep inside she felt uneasy about her old friend. It was only natural that Ellen should be worried about her daughter and the boys moving on, but she sensed that there was something else on the woman's mind. If it had been anyone else, Megan would have probed gently, but it was impossible now that Ellen was married to Harry Morgan. If there was some sort of trouble between them and he learned that his wife had confided in the wife of one of his miners, the fat would be in the fire with a vengeance, never mind that the two women had been friends for a quarter of a century! Biting her lip, she followed Ellen to the door.

Ellen's thoughts were far away as she walked back to Cwmbran House. If only she could have confided in Megan, it would have been a great relief, but something told her it was best to say nothing to a soul, not even to her daughter. The trouble was Meredith, of course. Her step-daughter had always been difficult, but ever since she'd found out that Mariah was actually her half-sister, there had been no pleasing her. Foolishly, Ellen had hoped that something might change after she had finally married Harry Morgan three years ago, but if anything this had made matters worse. Meredith lost no opportunity to needle Ellen, taking care not to do it in her father's hearing, of course. And Ellen had learned that while her husband frequently grumbled about his daughter's shortcomings, he most certainly did not permit anyone else to do likewise.

Only this morning Meredith had put the knife in again. Ellen was in the flower room, arranging some fragrant spring blooms, when the girl had come up behind her.

'I hope things will soon get back to normal, now this beastly war is going to be over,' she announced, fixing Ellen with that wide-eyed defiant stare which usually meant that something unpleasant was coming.

'Surely we all hope that, my dear.'

'It would be lovely to do some real entertaining in this house, just like the old days.'

'I suppose it would. Food rationing has made that sort of thing difficult.'

'But there, I don't suppose you'd feel comfortable with putting on a big bash.'

'My dear girl, I've organized umpteen parties in this house over the years, including your own wedding!'

As soon as the words were out of her mouth Ellen realized that she had left herself wide open to her stepdaughter's malice.

'Oh, but you were just the housekeeper then, weren't you! How are you going to feel when it comes to mingling with my father's county friends, then? It's not exactly what you've been used to, is it?'

Count to ten, Ellen reminded herself, resisting the urge to hurl a vase at the girl.

'I expect we'll manage,' she murmured, concentrating on the flowers rather than meeting Meredith's triumphant gaze. It was only when the girl had flounced off that Ellen noticed the mangled blossoms she was holding in her clenched fist.

She sometimes thought that her situation was much like that of Jane Eyre, the heroine of Charlotte Brontë's novel. Each of them had started out in humble circumstances and had fallen in love with the wealthy man in whose house she was employed. Society women had looked down on the pair but in the end Jane had won her Mr Rochester and Ellen had married Harry Morgan. Unfortunately, Miss Brontë's book did not shed any light on what happened next, although as the orphaned Jane turned out to be an heiress, that fact might have endeared her to the county set.

Ellen was no heiress. Her father had been a hard-working stevedore on the Cardiff docks, and after leaving school she herself had been what Harry's first wife would have referred to as 'a little shop girl'. After that she had been nanny to Meredith, and later Harry Morgan's housekeeper, and what was wrong with that? She'd always worked for her living and had been proud to think that she'd given value for money. How dare society women look down on her for that? Nothing but drones, all of them.

'*Prynhawn da*, Mrs Morgan!'

Ellen whipped around to see who was greeting her. She had been so preoccupied by her bleak thoughts that it hadn't registered that a horse-drawn vehicle was coming up behind her.

'Oh, *prynhawn da* Mr Fredericks!' The old man and his equally ancient horse were well known in the district, where they went about collecting and delivering bundles for the Daffodil Laundry. He must be heading up to the House with their fresh linen.

'I'd offer you a lift, missus, only I don't suppose it would do for Mr Morgan's wife to be seen sitting up by here!' He grinned at her tooth-lessly.

'It's very kind of you, Mr Fredericks, but I'm enjoying the walk, and I haven't far to go now. Isn't it a lovely day?'

'And all the better for knowing that old Adolf Hitler has gone where he belongs. The good Lord must have had a few choice words to say to that evil man when he came before the Judgement Seat."Get down below with you and no argument. You'll be right at home there with all the other devils. Make sure you introduce yourself, because even that lot have done nothing to compare with your antics". What I don't understand, Mrs Morgan, is why it didn't happen sooner. But there, the Lord works in mysterious ways, see, and some day it will all be made plain to us. I just hope He'll have a good story to tell, that's all, for I'll be waiting to hear it.' He raised his battered hat and urged his horse into a trot.

Suddenly feeling better, Ellen began to giggle. The thought of the old man appearing before God and demanding an explanation for His actions struck her as funny. She continued on with a spring in her step.

Why worry about the future when the present was so good? The war in Europe was over at last, and they had all come safely through. They had much to be thankful for.

Chapter Three

VJ Day – celebrating victory over Japan – came three months later. On the 15 August 1945 Emperor Hirohito formally surrendered to the Allies, although the actual signing of the peace treaty did not take place until 2 September. At the same time, anyone at Cwmbran House who happened to overhear the row which had blown up between Meredith Fletcher and her father could be forgiven for thinking that Britain was still at war.

'I can't believe that you actually expect me to send my son to Cwmbran School!' Meredith spluttered.

'As far as I know it's a very good little school, *cariad*. The Swansea Six have been happy there, haven't they?'

'Good enough for children of their background I daresay, Daddy, but Henry will inherit all this. He needs to mix with other boys of his own class.'

'Granted, but he has three more years before he goes to my old prep school. What do you propose doing with him until then?'

'I'm going to advertise for a governess.'

'Don't be ridiculous.'

'How is that ridiculous? I had a governess, didn't I?'

Harry sighed. 'That was different, *cariad*. For one thing that was in the nineteen-twenties, a world away from how things are today. It was a different age, back then between the wars. And you have to bear in mind that small boys can be quite ruthless. A nanny is one thing, but if he arrives at his boarding school talking about his governess he'll be

16

teased unmercifully. Is that what you want for him? No, let him go to the local school, I say, where he can learn to fend for himself before he goes away.'

'I don't want him meeting nasty rough boys, Dad!'

'I'm sure that the Meistr is quite capable of keeping bullies in check, Meredith. And as for rough boys, Henry will come across those in any class of society. Better to get the corners rubbed off him now while he's young enough to take it all in his stride.'

Meredith glared at him without deigning to reply, so he blundered on. 'Let him start school with Lucas, then. They can look after each other, eh?' He was almost deafened by the loud scream which followed. Ellen, who happened to be in the next room, rushed in to see what was happening.

'Is everything all right? Harry, is something wrong?' Remembering the slight stroke he had suffered shortly before their wedding she had believed for one awful moment that he might have been taken ill again, and that Meredith had discovered him lying stretched out on the hearth rug.

'Just one of Meredith's tantrums,' he said sourly. 'Just a storm in a teacup.'

'That's a very unkind thing to say, Daddy! And if you must know, Nanny, he wants to send Henry off to the local school with Lucas, and I just won't have it!' With that she stalked out of the room, leaving Harry and his wife staring at each other in confusion.

'I do wish she wouldn't keep calling me Nanny!' Ellen burst out.

'What's wrong with that? You were her nanny.'

'That was years ago.' She waited for some spark of understanding but Harry merely shrugged. He'd never be able to see that Meredith used the term as a means of putting her stepmother in her place. Perhaps she couldn't be expected to think of Ellen as her mother, even though Antonia had died giving birth to Meredith, but requests to call Ellen by her first name had been ignored.

'You know what the worst part is,' Harry went on, 'Lucas is quite a decent little chap, actually. It's young Henry who needs taking down a peg or two. Attending the local school would do him the world of good.'

17

'Unless he decides to lord it over the other children because their fathers all work for you. They might be afraid to stand up to him for fear of what you might do.'

Harry laughed. 'I expect they'd all shake down together in due course. As I tried to tell Meredith before you came in, I know the Meistr and he's quite capable of sorting out a few juvenile squabbles.'

'Speaking of Lucas, shouldn't we be thinking of trying to find his mother, now the war is over? This situation can't go on much longer, and I must say that my sympathies lie with Meredith in this instance.'

'That's something new! You two are usually at loggerheads!'

Ellen ignored this remark. 'Surely you can see that poor little Lucas is a thorn in her side? She lost her husband in the war and naturally she wants to cling to any good memories she has of him. To her Chad was a hero, who died while helping to rescue our troops from the beaches of Dunkirk. That's something for young Henry to be proud of as he grows up.'

'What are you trying to say?'

'Honestly, Harry! Do try to put yourself in her shoes! Every time she looks at Lucas she's reminded anew that her idol had feet of clay. Her husband fathered a child on another woman, and what's more, she was forced to confront the girl.'

Ellen recalled how shocked they'd all been when this Dulcie Saunders had turned up at the house with her two-year-old son, determined to get something out of the Morgan family. At first she had claimed to have been Chad's wife, leaving poor Meredith with the impression that he was a bigamist, and that she herself might not even be his legal wife. That had all been straightened out but there was no denying the fact that the little boy was Chad's natural son, born out of wedlock.

When Harry had made it plain that he had no intention of being blackmailed into giving Dulcie a financial settlement she had disappeared in the night, leaving her son behind. Faced with a choice between placing Lucas in an orphanage or keeping him at Cwmbran House, Harry had decided to let him stay for the time being.

'Chad was a distant cousin of mine,' he pointed out, 'so I suppose we do bear some responsibility for the poor little chap. His grand-mother can't take him on; she's far too old to be able to cope.'

In actual fact Venetia Fletcher was not a great deal older than Harry, but unlike him she did not have a houseful of servants to share the burden.

Meredith was against the plan, of course, but as Ellen pointed out, it wasn't as if she had to care for the boy herself. They had a nanny to do that, and as Henry was an only child, and much of an age with his half-brother, they could be playmates. Dulcie was never heard from again, and as a sop to his daughter's feelings Harry had promised to try to trace her when the war came to an end. That time had now come.

'So do you think we should set the wheels in motion?' Ellen asked. 'Meredith is not about to let this drop, you know. And what's going to happen now that the boys have to start school?'

Harry frowned. 'Not you as well! I've just been through all that with Meredith.'

'I don't think you have, Harry. It seems to me that she flounced off before you had the chance to get down to brass tacks. Those little boys are as much alike as two peas in a pod, at least in appearance. They look more like twins than half-brothers. If they go to the Cwmbran School people are sure to remark on it, and then the rumours will start to fly. Up to now people have believed that Lucas is just another of our evacuees, like the Swansea Six; that is, if they've thought about it all. The gossip that is sure to circulate after people put two and two together is going to be extremely embarrassing to Meredith. And what about the boys themselves? So far they haven't asked any questions, but all that will change when the other children start teasing them. No, Harry, a decision has to be made, and made soon.'

'I don't know what you expect me to do.'

'Isn't it obvious? Hire a private detective, or get your solicitor to deal with it. Dulcie has to be found, or failing that, someone from the Saunders side.'

Harry grunted. It seemed to him that the women were making a mountain out of a molehill. Why not let sleeping dogs lie? The boy would have to face the truth of his birth sooner or later and he'd be in good company. There must be a great many fatherless children in Britain as a result of the war, either as the result of irregular unions or because their fathers had been killed in battle or in air raids.

As for Meredith, what did she have to be ashamed of? It was nothing to do with her that her husband had gone off the rails; in fact, Lucas had been conceived even before she and Chad were married.

He became aware that his wife was fixing him with a gimlet eye. 'Oh, all right, I'll get on to it right away. Don't fuss, woman!'

'See that you do, then!' Ellen said, getting up to leave. 'But if you ask me there's not much hope of getting this sorted out before school starts. Perhaps you should let Meredith hire a governess after all. That will solve the problem in the short term.'

But Harry was adamant. 'Better to start as we mean to go on. What if we can't find the boy's family? Once I let a governess into the house we'll never get rid of the wretched woman. No, the boys must go to the local school like everyone else, and that's my last word on the subject.'

'It'll bring trouble,' Ellen warned.

He shrugged. 'We'll cross that bridge when we come to it.'

Chapter Four

'Please, Mrs Morgan, we want to give in our notice.'

Ellen stared at the trio in disbelief. Mrs Edwards, the cook, stout and red-faced; Ruth, the parlourmaid, short and wiry; Rosie Yeoman, housemaid, the youngest of the three. She herself had worked in the house with them, during her tenure as housekeeper, before she married Harry Morgan. That was why none of them could bring themselves to address her as madam.

'What do you call this, then, a mutiny?'

'It's my legs,' the cook explained. 'I've got veins, see? And the doctor says I've got blood pressure as well.'

'We've all got blood pressure,' Ellen snapped, but the older woman merely looked puzzled.

'I've made up my mind, Mrs Morgan. I'm going to live with my daughter, in Llanelly.'

'I thought she was in the ATS, Mrs Edwards.'

'So she was, but she's been demobbed, hasn't she? But for her joining up, I would have left sooner, but that being the case I thought I might as well stay by here, doing my bit, like.'

'And we've appreciated that very much, Mrs Edwards,' Ellen countered. No harm in a bit of flannel, if there was any chance of getting the old girl to change her mind. She turned to Ruth. 'And what's brought all this on, Ruth? You've been here forever. Why, you were already in the house when I arrived in 1918.'

'It's my old auntie in Lampeter, Mrs Morgan.'

'I suppose she's being demobbed from the ATS too, is she?'

'What? Oh, she was too old to join up, Mrs Morgan. Not that they'd have taken her on if she wasn't, her with her gammy leg and all.'

'That was a joke, Ruth.'

'I wouldn't call her leg a joke, Mrs Morgan. Nasty ulcers she has on it, and nothing the doctor can do. The district nurse comes in once a week and dabs ointment on it. Stings like the devil, Auntie says. Well, a nice little wool shop she has in Lampeter, and she wants me to help her with it now the war's over. Trade has been off these past few years with this old rationing, but now things will be looking up, won't they? Auntie Gwladys has been hinting that if I play my cards right she'll leave me her little shop when she goes up to glory, so I'd be a fool to miss my chance, wouldn't I?'

'I suppose you would,' Ellen sighed. 'And what's your problem, Rosie? You don't have a grown-up daughter, or the promise of a snug little billet in Lampeter. Hoping for a pay raise, are you?'

'Na, na. Leastways, I wouldn't turn it down, but I just thought it's time for a change, with these two leaving. I wouldn't want to work under some stranger, see.'

'We could think about promoting you to head parlourmaid, Rose. That would mean a room of your own and a higher wage,' Ellen suggested. She noticed a flicker of interest in the girl's eyes and decided to postpone the subject.

'Just give me some time to work on this, will you, please? I shall have to discuss this with my husband.'

Mrs Edwards's face took on a stubborn look. 'I don't see what there is to discuss, madam. I've had my say, and that's all there is to it.'

So it was madam now, was it? Time to appeal to higher authority, then. 'Even so, it is not for me to accept your resignation. Mr Morgan is your employer and at present he knows nothing about all this. You may go, all of you. I'm sure you have work to do.'

The trio marched out of the room, heads held high. Mariah, who was coming down the stairs, saw them go and wondered what was going on.

'Problems, Mam? Have you been reading the riot act? I just saw half the staff dashing off looking like they've just had their pay docked for impertinence, or something.'

Ellen sank down on the nearest chair, looking defeated. 'I'm afraid the shoe is on the other foot, *cariad*. They've all three handed in their notice. I don't know what Harry's going to say, I'm sure.'

'But why on earth? Have they all taken umbrage, or what?'

'Mrs Edwards is pleading poor health and she wants to join forces with her daughter, who is about to get out of the army. Ruth is going to help her aunt with her wool shop. Apparently she has expectations there. As for Rosie Yeoman, I can't imagine what's got into her. Not enough life in Cwmbran, I suppose. Not a dance hall in sight, and just the one mouldy picture palace. The next thing we know, Myfanwy will be giving in her notice as well, saying she wants to go back to Dada.'

'There's not much likelihood of that, Mam. Old Job Prosser is married to Bessie Harries now. Whatever else she may be, she's a good enough housewife, I hear. Myfanwy isn't needed there, and she knows which side her bread is buttered on. She's told me more than once that she's never been so happy in her life as since she's come here to work. There's gratitude for you.'

'Yes, well, I'm glad to know somebody's satisfied. I must go and break the glad news to Harry. We'll talk later.'

Unfortunately, Harry Morgan was no help.

'The staff are your province, *cariad*. Servants are ten a penny. Just send them packing and replace them with new ones.'

'It's not as easy as you make it sound, Harry. Take Ruth, for example. She's been here for twenty-seven years. She may be expecting an annuity, or something. Didn't you pension off that old companion of Antonia's, for instance?'

'I believe I did give the old girl something when Antonia died. At her age she had no chance of landing another job, but it wasn't a pension, as you put it. And back in my grandfather's day he did provide for old servants who had spent all their working lives here, rather than see them end their days in the workhouse. Mind you, that was more than many employers would have done, even then.'

'I know.'

'But Mrs Edwards hasn't been with us all that long. One can hardly class her as a faithful old retainer. Now, don't look at me like that, for goodness' sake. I'll give the two of them a few quid to speed them on their way. Not that cheeky young Rosie, though! She's only trying it on, as far as I can see. You give her a good reference and let her go. Let Mariah go down to the labour exchange and ask them to send up a few women for interview, all right?'

Mariah pulled a face when she heard this. 'Of course I'll go, Mam, but don't expect a rush of applications.'

'Oh, I don't think we'll have any trouble finding a few willing workers, do you?'

'Yes, I do, actually.'

'I don't see why. With the men coming back from the forces, all the women who took their places in civilian jobs will be out of work again.'

'Perhaps so, but from what I've read in the papers nobody wants to go into service any more, especially women who've proved their worth in offices and factories.'

'That remains to be seen. In a place like this with good wages and all found, a girl would be far better off than she would be living in cramped quarters in a miner's cottage, two up and two down. Ask Myfanwy if I'm not right.'

As it turned out, Mariah was correct, and Ellen and Harry were definitely behind the times. There were only two applicants for the position of cook. One of them arrived smelling of drink and was unsteady on her feet with it. Ellen showed her to the door, trying not to breathe in the fumes and praying that the woman would make it back to the main road without falling on her face.

The other was a starchy individual who reminded her of the trained nurse who had come to the house when Meredith and Mariah were new babies. This alarming person, who was known as Mrs Watson, took over the interview as if she were the lady of the house and Ellen in search of the job.

'How many servants are employed here, madam?'

'Er, four at present.' Six, if you counted the gardener and the old dodderer who kept the stables going.

'Four! In a house this size! I hope I shouldn't be required to do the work of a kitchen maid! It's not at all what I've been used to.'

'We had sixteen servants at one time,' Ellen told her, feeling very much on the defensive. 'It's the war, you see. People were called up and we were unable to replace them.' Somehow she didn't want to explain that throughout much of the war she had worked extremely hard here in her role as housekeeper, while her own daughter had slaved away outside with the help of their young evacuees. Longing for this interview to be over she struggled to think of some more questions to put to this Mrs Watson. She knew that if she took her on the situation would quickly become impossible.

'Thank you for coming,' she said at last, extending her hand to the awful woman. 'I do have other applicants to see. I'll let you know what I've decided.'

'That won't be necessary, madam. I've already decided. Good day to you!'

Chapter Five

In the night nursery at the top of the house, a little boy lay awake, too anxious to give himself up to sleep. In the bed beside him Henry Fletcher was snoring softly, one arm tucked behind his head, half hidden by his bright curls. On top of a chest of drawers a night light burned, a small, squat candle, standing in a saucer of water, for safety's sake. Lucas did not need its light in order to make out the other furnishings in the room because everything there was as familiar to him as his own hand.

He had lived here forever, it seemed. He had no memory of anything that might have happened at an earlier stage in his life; his whole world was bounded by this suite of rooms, supervised by Myfanwy Prosser. Vanny, they called her; she was more than a nurse-maid but not quite a nanny, just a young woman who watched over them with loving care.

The door to the day nursery was firmly shut, but it didn't matter. In his mind's eye the child could see everything in the room. The fire-place, with its brass-topped fender; the rocking chair; the table where they ate their meals; the cupboards filled with toys and books. It was a secure place; a happy place. Now Lucas Saunders knew that he was going to lose his grasp on that world which meant so much.

It wasn't the idea of school that was bothering him. The older boys had told him all about that. The teachers at the Cwmbran School were strict, but fair. If you did as you were told, that was all right. If you were naughty you got the cane, a crack on the hand, and if you were really bad you went to the Meistr, but that seldom happened. Yes, Lucas quite liked the thought of school, where he might play with other children, boys who were less bossy than Henry.

The other thought, so terrible as to be thrust to the back of his mind each time it reared its ugly head, was that he, Lucas Saunders, did not really belong here, as Henry did, and so one of these days he

25

would have to leave. And where would he go? Who would look after him? It was a terrifying concept for a five-year-old.

His fear had first overtaken him on the day when Mrs Fletcher had come into the nursery to measure Henry for a pullover she was making him, knitted from wool that had been pulled down from an old jumper of her own. Henry had broken into a spate of excited chatter as soon as she entered the room.

'Look, Mummy! I've painted this picture of a puffer train!'

'Very nice, darling. Shall Myfanwy pin it up on the wall?'

'I've drawn a motor car, Mummy,' Lucas said, not wanting to be left out.

'I'm not your mummy,' Meredith said, her voice cold. 'Lift your arms, please, Henry.' She turned back to her son, placing her tape measure around his chest.

'What did she mean, Vanny?' Lucas asked when Meredith had gone away again. 'She is Mummy. She is!'

Myfanwy sighed. This had been bound to happen some day, of course, but now the day had arrived she found that she wasn't prepared for it at all.

'Come and sit on my lap, Lucas, and I'll tell you all about it.' She glanced at Henry, but he was absorbed in his painting and seemed not to be tuned in.

'Sometimes ladies have two names,' she began.

'Do they, Vanny? Why do they?'

'Sit still and listen, there's a good boy. Well, we all have names, don't we? The lady who was in here just now is Mrs Fletcher. You knew that, didn't you?'

'Um.' Lucas popped his thumb in his mouth, and Myfanwy gently pulled it out again. 'Don't do that, dear, it's dirty, and if you do that when you go to school they'll call you a baby, and we don't want that, do we?' Lucas shook his head.

'When ladies get married and have little boys of their own, that means they are mothers then, so we have to think of a special name for their little boys to call them. Some people say Mam, or Mum, or Mummy. Henry says Mummy. What I mean is, Mrs Fletcher is Henry's mother, but she's not your mother, do you understand what I'm saying?'

Lucas stared at her blankly. 'Oh dear, I'm not explaining this very well, am I?' Myfanwy thought. The child's lip trembled.

'Don't I have a mummy, then, Vanny?'

'Of course you do, *bach*.'

'Where is she, then?'

'She had to go away for a while because of the war.'

'Isn't she coming back, then?'

'Of course she's coming back,' Myfanwy said, smiling. And may the Lord forgive me if I've told a lie, because it's been three years now, and not a word from the woman.

Unconvinced, Lucas had gone to ask Ceri Davies, who was one of his main allies in the house, being just a few years older than himself. 'Do you think my mummy is coming back, Ceri?'

'I dunno. Depends, I s'pose.'

'What does it depend on?'

'She may be dead, see, like my mam. If she is, she won't be back. But if she's only been away helping to fight the war, like Evan's mam, then she'll be back soon, cos the war's over now, see?'

'Who looks after you then, Ceri if your mam is dead?'

'Told you all about it before, haven't I? Me and the rest of the Swansea Six lived in the orph'nage till the war came, and then we got 'vacuated here. Mrs Mortimer and Mrs Morgan, they look after us. We'll be leaving soon, I 'spect. Don't know where we'll go next, though. The orph'nage may have got bombed. Flattened, see?' Ceri ran off with outstretched arms, making aeroplane noises as he went.

Lucas trudged back to the house, with his eyes on the ground. Watching from an upstairs window, Myfanwy thought she knew what was bothering him. Smoothing down her apron, she went in search of Ellen.

'Could you come back later, Myfanwy? I'm in the middle of something here.' Ellen was down on her hands and knees, trying to pin a paper pattern on to some pieces of fabric. 'I thought it would be a simple matter to unpick my old frock and make it up into a skirt, with the faded side in, but it's not wide enough. What do you think?'

'I think you need to buy a different pattern, Mrs Morgan. That one seems to be for quite a full skirt.'

'Patterns are as scarce as hen's teeth these days, Myfanwy. Never mind, I'll put it away for another day. What was it you wanted to ask me?' She struggled to her feet, assisted by the nursery maid.

'It's young Lucas, Mrs Morgan. He's started asking questions, and I don't know what to say for the best. Mrs Fletcher snapped at him when he called her Mummy in all innocence, and then of course he wondered what he'd done wrong. He doesn't seem to have any memory of his own mother, or how he happened to come here.'

'That's not surprising, considering he was only two years old when he arrived.'

'I know, but it looks to me as if his poor little mind is working overtime, and I'm dreading what he might come out with next.'

'I don't know what to think, Myfanwy. Perhaps we should have said something to the child sooner, but what? He's so young. Rightly or wrongly it seemed easier just to let things drift.'

'But what about school, Mrs Morgan? I hope you'll pardon my saying this, but are they brothers? I mean, they look awfully alike.' She put her hand over her mouth and stared at Ellen, wide-eyed.

'I'm afraid you're quite correct, Myfanwy, but I hope you'll be a sensible girl and say nothing outside this house. Remember those posters we used to see everywhere? "Be like Dad, keep Mum"? And in particular, do guard your tongue in front of Mrs Fletcher.'

Myfanwy gasped. 'Wild horses couldn't make me breathe a word, Mrs Morgan.'

'That's all right, then. It seems that Chad Fletcher – Meredith's husband – had a roving eye and the upshot was that Dulcie Saunders found herself in trouble, and poor little Lucas is the result. I don't know if you were aware of all that went on when she came here with the child, but she did a moonlight flit, leaving her child here with us. As you can imagine, all that was most distressing for Mrs Fletcher, and that is why she tends to be a bit abrupt where the boy is concerned.

Not that he's to blame in any way, poor little chap.'

For the next few minutes there was silence in the room, broken only by the ticking of the clock. 'As far as everyone knows,' Ellen went on at last, 'Lucas is a young relative who has been evacuated here for the duration of the war. And of course that is all quite true! Cousins often do resemble each other, so it isn't surprising that he and Henry look alike. I really don't think you need to worry so much, my dear.'

'But I can't help it, madam. What's to become of him now the war is over?'

'As it happens, my husband is about to set the wheels in motion to try to trace Miss Saunders. Until then, things must continue as they are.'

'But what if she can't be found? What will happen to him then?'

'We'll deal with that when we come to it,' Ellen told her, but Myfanwy was not convinced. She returned to the nursery with a thoughtful frown on her pretty face.

Chapter Six

Ellen stared down at her friend in exasperation. 'What on earth were you doing up a ladder in the first place? Couldn't it have waited until Merfin came home?'

'Are you out of your mind? I can just see him finishing a long shift down the pit and then coming home to wash windows! He'd be the laughing stock of the whole neighbourhood. No, as far as people round here are concerned, that's women's work, unless of course you're a professional window cleaner like Jacko the glass, and he seems to have disappeared.'

'Actually I was suggesting that he might have held the ladder steady for you, but perhaps it needn't have come to that. I've seen other women leaning out of their upstairs windows when they wanted to wash the outside, not going up ladders. You were lucky to get away with just a sprained ankle, my girl! How did it happen, anyway?'

'I was just putting my foot on the third rung when two dogs came chasing around the corner and bumped into the ladder, and down I came. Got a very nasty bruise in an unmentionable place, I have, never mind the twisted ankle. Merfin fetched the doctor to me and a fat lot of good that was! "You'll have to keep your leg up on a stool for a few days, Mrs Jones", he says. What does he think this is – Liberty Hall? Who does he think is going do the work round here while I'm laid up?'

'You'll just have to let the dust gather until your daughter gets here, then.'

'Never mind the old dust! It's the meals I'm worried about, and carrying the water for Merfin's bath, see. No servants in this house to wait on me hand and foot; not like some.'

Was Megan having a dig at her? Surely not, when they'd been friends for so many years. All the same, Ellen felt uncomfortable. As the wife of a miner, Megan lived in a tiny terraced house, while Ellen had a mansion to call home, and several servants to look after her.

'Tell you what, I'll send Rosie Yeoman down this afternoon to give you a hand. I'm sure she'll be glad of the excuse to get out for a bit.'

'There's kind of you, *bach*. What's going on up there, then? Managed to set on some new staff, have you?'

Ellen sighed. 'No such luck! There are a couple of local women who say they'd come in by day and do a bit of cleaning, and we may have to consider that if all else fails. The problem is that Harry is pretty set in his ways. He's not what you'd call a demanding man, yet he's used to having servants at the other end of a bell, so to speak. I'd be happy to wait on him myself, but it's the idea of cooking that bothers me. I've never had to do much more than making tea up in my room. I suppose I could learn, but to suddenly go from that to preparing three square meals a day for more than a dozen people might be more than I could manage! Speaking of tea, shall we have a cup?' She leaned forward and moved the kettle to the side of the hob, where it immediately began to sing.

Back at Cwmbran House, Meredith Fletcher was feeling very pleased with herself. She had managed to solve the problem of a replacement for Mrs Edwards without making much of an effort. Everything had fallen into her lap quite nicely, and it would be good to put one over on Ellen for a change.

She'd been in her bedroom, frowning over a tired old blouse which might possibly be improved by being dyed a different colour, when she heard voices in the corridor. One belonged to Myfanwy Prosser, her son's nursemaid cum nanny; the other she failed to recognize.

'I can't stand it a moment longer!' the unknown woman was complaining. 'There's no pleasing the man at all!'

Meredith had to strain to hear Myfanwy's reply. 'I know Dada can be a bit difficult at times.'

'Difficult!' the visitor's voice was shrill. 'Difficult I can cope with. It's this constant criticism I cannot take. I pride myself on being a good housekeeper and cook, none better. I have been married before, you know. I know what is expected of a wife, but with your father I can do nothing right. And those younger brothers of yours! Like wild animals they are. Won't listen to a word I say, and he does nothing to support me.'

'I'll speak to him if you like, Bessie, but I doubt if he'll listen to me. I'm likely to get a thump round the head for interference.'

'Na, na! That's no good. I'm off, see, and you'll have to come home and look after things. You'd be looking for a new job in any case, once the young master starts school.'

'Oh, no, you don't!' Meredith thought. She had plans for Myfanwy. She wasn't about to have her whisked back to that hovel where Job Prosser held sway. She flung the door open and confronted the pair.

'What's going on here? Who are you, might I ask?'

Bessie stared at her, dumbfounded. Her mouth opened, and closed again.

'Um, this is my stepmother, madam. Mrs Prosser.'

'I don't care if she's the Duchess of Windsor! I won't have people walking into my home and upsetting the household.'

'No, madam.'

'And have you any thought of going home to your father, girl?'

'Oh, no, madam! I'm happy here, see.'

'So I should hope. Very well then, off you go. As for you, Mrs Prosser, I have something to say to you, but we can't have a civilized conversation standing here in the corridor. We'll go to my sitting-room. Follow me, if you please.'

Meek as a mouse now, Bessie followed in Meredith's wake and seemed relieved when she was invited to take a seat. Perched on the edge of an antique sofa she waited for something to happen in much the same way as a rabbit watches a predatory stoat.

'Well, Mrs Prosser? What is all this about?'

'It's my husband, madam. Been married three years, we have, and that is three years too long.'

'Does he beat you?'

'Not exactly. He's threatened me with a thick ear once or twice, but he's never taken his belt to me, madam, not like some, if you can believe everything you hear round the doors. It's just him going on at me all the time I cannot take. I thought if our Myfanwy was to come back home I could get out with a clear conscience, see.'

'Where will you go? Have you thought about that?'

'I can't go back to my old house. That's been let long since. I suppose I'll have to try for a job somewhere, living in, for preference.'

Meredith took a deep breath. 'Well, if you've made up your mind . . . can you cook, Mrs Prosser?'

'Cook? I'm the best cook in Cwmbran, though I says it as should-n't. Why do you want to know?'

'Because our Mrs Edwards is leaving to go to her daughter in Llanelly, and we need someone to replace her. Would you care for the job, Mrs Prosser?'

'Me? Come here? Oh, I don't know as I could do that, madam. It would be a bit awkward, see, with my hubby living so close by. Kick up a stink, he would. He never stops grumbling about how Mr Morgan stole his daughter away from home, begging your pardon, madam! He wouldn't like it if it happened again with his wife!'

'He's not going to like it anyway, when you leave him,' Meredith pointed out. 'I do think you might consider it. You'd have a nice room, all to yourself, and a good wage so you could put something by for the future. What's the alternative? Working long hours on your feet in some shop and then coming home to a dreary room with only a gas ring to cook on?'

'I'm not sure. . . .'

'Wouldn't it be nice to stay in Cwmbran, where all your friends are?' Meredith wheedled.

'How many will I have left if I leave my husband, I wonder? A big man in the chapel, he is, see. They'll all side with him when it's known what I've done.'

'Never mind that. You won't have to see much of them once you're settled in here. Why not give it a try?'

'All right, then, I will! When do you want me to start, madam? I could go and pack now, if you like, while Job is at work. I don't fancy telling him to his face that I'm leaving him. I'll leave him a note. That would be for the best.'

'We don't need you right away, because Mrs Edwards is still here. We'll have to find out when she means to go, and let you know when to come. Will that be all right?'

'Oh, yes, madam! *Diolch yn fawr!*'

Bessie marched away from the house, feeling very pleased with herself indeed. She'd left home with no set plan, other than trying to persuade Myfanwy to return, and now a good job had fallen into her lap. She had no qualms about taking it on because she knew her own worth. That was what upset her so much about Job's carping. If she was a lazy lump she'd deserve it, but she'd done her best and got no thanks for it.

Chapter Seven

Anyone who might have been watching the private road leading up from the town to Cwmbran House might have observed a well-padded woman hopping and skipping on her way to the gate. Bessie Prosser felt like a child again. She'd gone up to the house to plead with her step-daughter to return to the family fold, and now was corning away with the promise of a good job, all found!

She'd need to think carefully about this one. After leaving the Morgan girl, who'd hired her on, she'd gone round the back and rapped at the kitchen door.

The red-faced woman who answered must be the cook she was meant to replace; who else would answer the door swathed in a starched apron, with a wooden spoon in her hand?

'Yes?'

'I'm Bessie Prosser. Mrs Job Prosser, that is.'

'Oh, yes?' The name seemed to mean nothing to the cook.

'You'll be Mrs Edwards, I suppose. I've just been taken on as cook here. After you leave, see.'

Mrs Edwards brightened at once. 'You better come in then, *bach*.'

Fifteen minutes and three cups of tea later, Bessie had found out everything she wanted to know, including the fact that the cook was 'working out her month' and then would be off to stay with her daughter.

'I remember now,' the cook said suddenly. 'You married that miner who was sniffing round after Madam!'

Bessie didn't care for that expression, but she held her peace. No point in having a row before she'd even set foot in the house on a permanent basis.

'Funny, that,' Mrs Edwards continued. 'She knew what she was doing when she turned him down. Married Mr Morgan instead. Well can you blame her? No comparison, is there? Went up in the world, eh? Still, it left the way open for you, didn't it? A bit of luck, that was.'

'Aye,' Bessie said grimly.

'And what about your man, then? Doesn't he mind you going out to work? Most men would.'

'He doesn't know anything about it yet. I'll have to tell him when I get home.'

'Good luck to you, then,' the cook told her, giving her custard a final stir.

'And luck is what I'll need,' Bessie told herself, as she reached the gate at the end of the long drive. Perhaps she wouldn't put him in the picture right away. She'd leave it for a bit and see if he sweetened up at all. If he did, she could always change her mind and let the Morgans know she wouldn't be coming. Or, if Job continued to be awkward, then she might tell him what she had in mind, which would give him the chance to change his ways. She decided to stop at the shop on the way home and discuss the matter with her daughter. Gwyneth had a vested interest in what she did, since she was walking out with Llew Prosser, Job's eldest son.

Gwyneth was serving behind the counter, wearing a mob cap and a flowered overall.

'Hello, Mam! What you doing out at this time of day, then?'

'I've got myself a nice little job,' Bessie burst out, unable to hold back her news any longer.

'Whatever for? Don't you have enough to do as it is? And what's Job going to say? He's not going to like it, Mam! I wouldn't be surprised if he puts his foot down. Anyway, where is it? Going back to the green-grocer's, are you?'

'I'm going up to the House, as cook there.'

'You're never! A long old walk that'll be, coming and going every day.'

'Oh, I'll be living in, see. No travelling involved at all.'

Gwyneth's jaw dropped. 'O, *Duw*! You're leaving Job! Have you thought this through, Mam? What about the old cats down the chapel? Think of the scandal!'

Bessie said a rude word under her breath. 'That lot don't have to put up with Job and his miserable ways. I don't know what I ever saw in the man, our Gwyn, I don't really.'

'And what about me, Mam? Have you thought of that? Llew is bound to side with his Da in this, and that could put paid to him and me.'

'And maybe a good thing, too, my girl. Going out together for three years, you've been, and never a sniff of a ring on your finger. And where does he take you when you do go out? Just to some old rugger game. When was the last time he treated you to the pictures, or tea in a caff?'

'We're saving to get married, Mam. Llew can't afford to splash money around.' A sudden thought struck her. 'When we do get married I'll probably have to move in with the family. With you gone – if you do go – all the work will fall on me. I'm not afraid of hard work, Mam, as you know, but I'm not cut out to be the old man's skivvy.'

'Neither am I, *cariad*. Neither am I.'

The bell over the shop door pinged and Gwyneth had to attend to her customers. Bessie seized the chance to escape. She hoped that her daughter had seen the writing on the wall. If the girl did move into the house to take her mother's place, she wouldn't put it past Job to make life difficult for her, out of pure spite. And, come to that, Gwyneth could do better than to wed a man who kept her hanging about for three years before making a commitment.

Meanwhile, Mrs Edwards was rubbing her hands in glee. Young Rosie Yeoman was fascinated to see the cook looking so pleased with herself and decided to take advantage.

'Any chance of a cup of tea, Mrs E? I'm that parched I can hardly swallow.'

'Plenty of water in the tap, my girl.'

'Aw, just a small cup. Please?'

'Oh, all right, you've twisted my arm. But be quick about it, mind. We don't want the mistress coming down and finding you lazing about. Not that I'd care if she did. I'll be leaving in another three weeks.'

'Oh, does that mean they've found somebody?'

'It does, and you'll never guess who.'

'Who, then? Come on, spit it out!'

'Bessie Prosser!'

'Oh, is that Myfanwy's mam, then?'

'Step-mam. But that's not all, see. Remember when Myfanwy's da was courting the mistress? Mad with jealousy, that Bessie was. That's what I heard. Wanted him for herself, see. Even spoke to Miss Mariah about it, asked her to find out if they was serious.'

'She never!'

'Yes, she did. I heard Miss Mariah telling her mam about it. I remember thinking at the time, it was like one of them romances you bring home from the library. Two men trying to woo the heroine. Which one will she choose?'

'Two men? Who was the other one, then?'

'Mr Morgan, of course. She married him, didn't she?'

'I didn't see Mr Morgan doing no wooing, Mrs Edwards.'

'He must have done, mustn't he, if he put a ring on her finger.'

'He was a long time thinking about it, then, if you ask me. She worked in this house since before I was born, and all those years she was nothing but the Widow Richards.'

But Mrs Edwards was not to be done out of her romantic dream. 'He was in love with his poor young wife, you see, who died when Miss Meredith was born. It was years before he could look at another woman in that way.'

Rosie raised her eyes to the ceiling. Mr Morgan had never struck her as a lovesick widower, although no doubt he had grieved for a time. But that was years ago and a lot of water had gone under the bridge since then.

'If you stay on here, girl, you must write and let me know what happens.'

'How d'you mean?'

'For goodness' sake, haven't you been listening? There's going to be high jinks when that Bessie moves in here. It might almost be worth me staying on to see what happens.'

'If you did, then she wouldn't be here,' Rosie pointed out.

'That's true. Well, to start with, if she's taking on this job, living in, then she must be leaving her hubby. The whole of Cwmbran's going to be talking about it, laughing behind his back and wondering what's been going on behind closed doors. I shouldn't be surprised if the man doesn't follow her here and drag her back by the hair, caveman style! Or what if she lets him have it with the rolling pin? She's hefty enough. I imagine she could hold her own in a fight.'

Rosie listened to this flight of fancy, completely enthralled.

'Do watch what you're doing, girl! You're spilling that tea all over my clean scrubbed table! While you're at it, I may as well have a cup, too! Thirsty work, talking!'

Chapter Eight

'You've done what!' Ellen was aware that she was shouting in a most unladylike manner, but she was too shocked to care. What she really wanted to do was to wipe the smug look off Meredith's face, but somehow she managed to restrain herself.

'I told you; I've found us a cook and she can start right away. I thought you'd be pleased.'

'Then you thought wrong!'

'I see what it is. You're always nagging me to do more in the house, but now I've taken the initiative that doesn't suit you either. You're jealous, of course. You like to think that this is your house now, and nobody else must get a look in. Just because my father was fool enough to marry you doesn't mean that you really belong here, Nanny.'

'Stuff and nonsense! And I've asked you before to stop calling me that. It's a good many years since I worked as your nanny, even though you do seem to revert to your childish tantrums far too often!'

'Girls! Girls! Has war broken out again? I could hear you all the way outside. What on earth is the matter now?'

Meredith looked as if butter wouldn't melt in her mouth. 'Oh, Daddy! I tried to do something nice for your wife, and now she's all upset, and I don't know why!' She dabbed at a non-existent tear with a tiny lace-edged hankie. Harry turned a stern look on his wife. Ellen was too cross to choose her words with care.

'Meredith has engaged a cook, Harry! Behind my back, I might add.'

'But that's splendid, isn't it? You keep saying that you don't know how you'll cope now that the Edwards woman has given notice, and, thanks to Meredith, you'll have nothing more to worry about.'

'That's all you know! Go on, Meredith, tell your father who this marvellous new cook is.'

'It's Bessie Prosser, Daddy. Bessie Harries as was.'

'Prosser? I seem to know that name from somewhere.'

Ellen groaned. 'And so you should!'

'She's Myfanwy's step-mother, Daddy,' Meredith chipped in before Ellen could get the words out. Harry nodded and smiled. It was obvious to Ellen that the penny hadn't dropped. She took a deep breath and soldiered on.

'Job Prosser is one of the miners you employ, Harry. Two or three of his sons also work in the pit. Job Prosser was also the man who, er, came courting me, back in the days before you proposed and I accepted you. He then married this Bessie, but it now seems as if their marriage wasn't made in heaven. Bessie is about to leave the poor man and move in here, with all of us. Now do you understand?'

Harry frowned at his daughter. 'Were you aware of these circumstances, Meredith?'

'Of course she was, and this has just provided her with a marvellous opportunity to embarrass me.'

'Come now, Ellen, I won't have that! I'm sure that Meredith acted with the best of intentions, didn't you, *cariad*?' Behind her father's back Meredith smirked. Ellen realized she'd gone too far by criticizing Harry's daughter to his face. In for a penny, in for a pound, then.

'Your name will be mud in Cwmbran with the chapel lot if they think you're coming between husband and wife, Harry. And no, I'm not suggesting that anyone will get the wrong idea. But people of that sort take marriage seriously and if Bessie walks out on Job they'll think that we encouraged her. Just look at all the fuss there was when Myfanwy came here to work, and that was all above board.'

Harry scratched his ear, saying nothing for a long moment. 'I suppose you're right, Ellen. That's that, then. We won't take her on after all.'

'But Daddy, I promised her!' Meredith wailed. 'I'll look such a fool if I have to say I've changed my mind! I said she could have a month's trial. That's the usual thing with servants, isn't it? How can I tell her she can't even have that? She might sue us or something!'

'Highly unlikely when her whole family depend on us for their livelihood, *cariad*. I tell you what we'll do. She can come for her precious month, and if it causes as much of an uproar as Ellen suspects, then we'll tell her that it hasn't worked out. What do you say to that?'

'Thank you, Daddy,' Meredith simpered.

Fuming, Ellen went in search of her daughter. 'You should have put your foot down, Mam,' Mariah said, only half listening. She had just received a phone call from Aubrey, telling her that he was being sent to Germany, for goodness knows how long.

'It's because I studied German at university,' he explained. 'The army needs interpreters and I suppose I fit the bill. There's not much I can do about it, I'm afraid.'

'But you're in the RAF, darling.'

'That little problem doesn't seem to bother the powers that be. I've got my orders and I'll have to go. Unfortunately that means that my demob will be deferred for the foreseeable future.'

'Oh, Aubrey!'

'I know. It's pretty rotten, isn't it. Nothing else for it, we'll just have to be patient for a while longer. Look, I've got to go. There's a whole line of chaps waiting to use this phone. Write to me, OK? Love you.' The phone went dead.

'Was that Aubrey?' Ellen asked. 'All right, is he? You simply must help me to think of something, *cariad*. I can see big trouble ahead, and I'm not talking about Job Prosser here. It's that woman. You know how she hates me. If we end up under the same roof we'll be at daggers drawn the whole time.'

'Aren't you exaggerating a bit, Mam?'

'I don't believe I am. As she sees it, we were rivals for Job's hand, such as it is, and look what happened. She won, as she thought, and the marriage has turned into a disaster. I married what amounts to the lord of the manor, and now she'll have to take orders from me. She'll resent me, Mariah, you mark my words. I wouldn't put it past her to put poison in the soup.'

'Now you're being silly!'

Ellen was hurt. Was nobody going to support her in this? She couldn't understand it when Mariah walked out of the room, without saying anything more.

At that moment there was a gentle rap at the door. Ellen tried to control her emotions. 'Come in!'

Myfanwy Prosser sidled into the room. 'Begging your pardon, Mrs Morgan.'

'Yes, Myfanwy; can I help you?'

'Oh, madam, is it true that you've taken her on to do the cooking here?'

'Mrs Fletcher wishes to give her a trial, yes.' Ellen was blessed if she was going to take all the blame for this.

'She told me she was leaving Dada but I never thought she'd go through with it. Just hot air, that's all I thought it was. Dada won't like it, madam. He won't like it one bit.'

'No, I don't suppose he will.'

'A terrible temper he has, when he's roused.'

'I suppose that has something to do with it,' Ellen agreed. 'Whatever has been going on in that house has proved to be too much for your stepmother, and now she's making other plans for herself.'

'I just want to warn you, madam, that's all. You don't know Dada like I do.'

'I actually believe that I know him quite well, Myfanwy. I did see

41

quite a bit of him before I married Mr Morgan, remember.'

'Begging your pardon, madam, I'd say you only saw him on his best behaviour.'

Ellen had to laugh. 'I expect that men are all the same, my dear. It's only natural that they want to show themselves in their best light when they come a-courting. At least I've had no surprises with my present husband. We've lived under the same roof since the end of the last war!'

'But he's a gentleman, madam. They're different, aren't they? My da's only an ordinary working man, see.'

'Believe me, child, a great many gentlemen aren't all they should be. No, indeed. There's good and bad in every class, and you'd do well to remember that if you ever go out into the world when you choose to leave here.'

Myfanwy wasn't convinced. 'My da's a good man, really, and I love him as a daughter should. Only he truly believes that men are supposed to be the head of the household, like the Bible says, and we womenfolk are supposed to accept that, and do as we are told. That's why he was so angry when I left home to come here to work. According to him I wasn't only wilful but sinful as well, in disobeying my father.'

'As far as I know, Myfanwy, that isn't all the Bible says. Husbands are supposed to cherish their wives in return for their allegiance, not threaten them with a thick ear when something doesn't meet their expectations.'

'Yes, madam. But Dada won't see it like that if Bessie forgets herself and comes up here to work. There's awful it will be if he does something stupid.'

Chapter Nine

'You'll be glad to know I've made a start on tracing Dulcie,' Harry said, looking up from his desk as his wife entered the room, carrying a tray of tea.

'What's that, dear? Dulcie, did you say?'

'I telephoned Verona, to see if she's had any news of the girl, but she knows no more than we do. She was glad to hear from me, though, and she sends her love to you, and to her grandson, of course. In a way, having Lucas has, in some small measure, made up for losing her son, even though she was sorely disappointed in Chad when she learned what he'd done.'

'Carrying on with Dulcie when he was about to marry Meredith,' Ellen nodded. 'What else have you done?'

'I've spoken to my solicitor and he will hire a private detective he knows of in London. He feels, as I do, that the best place to start is by finding Dulcie's parents. She may well be living with them, or if not they surely must know where she is. Lucas is their grandchild too; they have a vested interest in seeing that the child is all right.'

'Then I suppose that's all we can do until we hear back from him.'

'There's something else, cariad. This letter arrived in this morning's post. Do you want to have a look?'

'Read it for me, will you? I can't do two things at once and I want to pour out your tea before it gets stewed.'

'Well, it's signed by a Mavis Dolski, who says she's Evan Phillips's mother.'

'That's odd! Do you think she's married again?'

'How do I know? Dolski. Perhaps he's a Pole. Anyway, she says that she's just writing to let us know that she'll be coming to collect him next month, only will we please not tell him anything, as she has a lovely surprise for him.'

'It sounds to me as if she's about to present him with a new papa.

Let's hope he thinks it's a lovely surprise and not a horrid shock. You know how he's always talking about his father, who was killed early on in the war. That's why she put the child in the orphanage for the duration so she could go off to join up. Honestly, what sort of mother would do a thing like that?' Ellen pulled a wry face.

'What's the difference between that and the thousands of very loving parents who had their children evacuated, for the sake of their safety?'

'I don't know. It just feels different, that's all.' Her own daughter, Mariah, was a married woman now, yet Ellen still shuddered to think about what might have happened to the baby if things had turned out differently. Having given birth to her child out of wedlock, Ellen had come to Cwmbran House as wet nurse to Harry's daughter, Meredith, bringing Mariah with her. They had been invited to stay on, so that the child had grown up with the best of everything. Otherwise she would probably have ended up in an orphanage, for back at the time of the Great War it was next to impossible for a single mother to be able to support herself and a little one.

'Do you remember the state those boys were in when they came to us from Swansea?' she asked.

Her husband shrugged. 'They seemed cheerful enough to me, *cariad*. A bright little bunch of chaps, hoping that the Luftwaffe would bomb their school, not to mention the orphanage!'

'But the state of them, Harry. I was horrified when I undressed little Ceri to give him a bath. He was so skinny that his ribs were showing.'

'Not many fat people around nowadays,' he replied, patting his stomach. 'It's this rationing that's keeping us all fighting fit. That and the vegetables that Mariah and the boys have produced all through the war.'

But that wasn't what she had meant, exactly. The children had been neglected. No doubt the matron and her helpers had done their best but with too few resources at their disposal they had not been able to provide all the comforts of home that were accorded to more fortunate youngsters.

'What's going to happen to them when they leave here, Harry?' she cried, suddenly overwhelmed by the thought of losing them.

'You've asked me that before, *cariad*, and my answer's the same now. If the orphanage can't take them back they'll be farmed out some-where by the authorities. Nobody's going to let them starve.'

Ellen felt like hitting him. Harry had served as a magistrate for many years and he still saw life in shades of black and white. Added to that, he was very much a product of the Victorian age, having been born in 1876. In his view, people were born into varying social circumstances and had to make the best of it. The better-off people, such as himself, had a moral duty to do what they could for the poor, but beyond that there was no point in fretting over what could not be changed. Ellen, having been born into vastly different circumstances, saw a different side of the picture.

When the Swansea Six had first arrived, one of the boys had told her that some of the little chaps in his dormitory had been shipped out to Canada to work on farms, and before the war broke out he had been next on the list to go. This was supposed to be a great adventure and a chance for orphaned children to make a new life for themselves. They would receive a wage, and be allowed to continue with their schooling in the new country. Perhaps this was a good idea if it had all worked out as the authorities planned, but what if the children fell into the hands of unscrupulous people who treated them like slaves? And what would happen to a little chap like Ceri, alone and far from home if he ended up in such a situation?

Fortunately for Ellen's peace of mind there was a knock at the door at that moment and Meredith peeped in. 'Do you have a minute, Daddy?'

Ellen stood up and left. She obviously wasn't going to get any satis-faction out of Harry, so she might as well give it up as a bad job. For now!

Mariah was waiting for her in the sewing room. This had been Ellen's sitting-room in the days before she'd married Harry, and although she now, of course, had access to the main rooms of the house, she had kept this cosy little retreat as her own private domain. Here she sat at odd hours, contentedly knitting, or stitching away on her old Singer treadle sewing machine.

'I wondered where you'd got to, Mam!'

'Is everything all right?'

'Of course it is. Why do you ask?'

'Oh, you know! I can't quite grasp the fact that the war is over, and we shan't be seeing the telegraph boy pedalling up here with bad news.'

'Thank goodness for that! But you look as if you've lost a shilling and found sixpence! What's on your mind?'

Ellen put her finger to her lips and closed the door softly. 'Treat this as hush-hush for the moment, but it seems that we're losing young Evan.'

'His mother is coming back to claim him, then?'

'Apparently so, but it looks as if she's remarried. In any event she's signing herself as Mavis Dolski now, not Phillips.'

Mariah frowned. 'Don't tell me she's gone and married a Russian!'

'Harry thinks it's a Polish name. As you know, we've had quite a few Poles serving in the RAF and so on. He's probably some chap she met while she was in the services.'

'I hope they don't mean to take the poor boy back to Poland with them, then. From what I read in the papers the country is pretty well devastated after the Germans and the Russians have done their worst there.'

'Surely it can't be much worse than what happened to London during the blitz? The Luftwaffe even had a go at Buckingham Palace. It's a wonder to me that anything is still standing. What do you suppose Lucas is going to find when he gets there?'

Mariah's eyebrows disappeared under her fringe. 'Lucas is being sent to London?'

'For goodness' sake keep your voice down! We don't know anything yet. Harry has put his solicitor onto it and we hope to hear something soon. Even if Dulcie can't be found, she does have family down there, and they'll have to take responsibility for him, Harry says.'

'Poor little chap. It's a great pity he can't stay here. Blood is thicker than water, and all that.'

'I doubt if Meredith would stand for it. She can barely tolerate having him in the house as it is. And Dulcie is his mother, when all is said and done. Why should she get off scot-free?'

'Nobody is getting off scot-free,' Mariah said soberly. 'This rotten war has affected us all in one way or another. Didn't you hear the vicar's text last Sunday? "They have sown the wind and they shall reap the whirlwind". They were cheering in Trafalgar Square on VE night, and we're all joyful because the war is over at last, but it's not over for a lot of people, and never will be.'

'Like that poor chap with no legs I saw sitting on a bogie in the arcade on Broad Street,' Ellen murmured. 'Just sitting there, shaking a tin can and begging for coppers. He went off to fight for king and country, and where did it get him? What does he have to look forward to now? You tell me that!'

Chapter Ten

The new term began, and the eight boys from Cwmbran House went more or less willingly to school. Against her better judgment Meredith had allowed Henry to enrol, although she was heard to mutter that if things hadn't worked out by Christmas she would take steps to hire a governess. Ellen didn't know just what she meant by things not working but she made no effort to find out. Any breath of criticism was likely to set Meredith off, and Ellen had enough on her plate as it was.

Being in the infants' class, Henry and Lucas had Mariah's friend, Luci Adams, as their teacher. Friendly but firm, she had the ideal personality for dealing with tearful youngsters who were separated from their mothers for the first time. Not that Henry Morgan was tearful. Far from it!

'How are the boys settling in?' Mariah asked, when she happened to run into Luci while doing some Saturday shopping.

'All right, I suppose. Want to join me in the Copper Kettle? I could do with a hot drink; it's nippy out this morning.'

Mariah knew her friend too well to be put off with a casual assessment. 'Only all right? That sounds like trouble to me. Out with it, Luci!'

'I meant it about that snack! Let's get in out of the wind and I'll tell you all about it.'

When they were seated at a corner table, partaking of some watery coffee and a penny bun apiece, she took up her tale again.

'Don't think I'm complaining, Mariah, will you? The first term with the new intake is always a bit difficult until they manage to make the adjustment. I have to make allowances, you see?'

'But?'

'But your Henry is a bit of a handful.'

'In what way?'

'I'm not saying he's a bad boy, mind you, but he's too full of himself by half. My class is where the children learn skills to prepare them for Standard One next year, and I don't just mean the three R's. Things like putting up your hand when you want to speak. Sharing equipment with other children. It takes a bit of doing, but they all learn eventually.'

'And Henry is taking longer than usual to fit in, is that it?'

'Well, it's early days yet, of course.'

'I could ask Myfanwy to have a word with him if that would help. What exactly has he been up to?'

Judging by the pained expression on her face, Luci was struggling to find the right words to get her point across without sounding too critical. Henry was, after all, Harry Morgan's grandson, and that lofty personage was one of the governors of the school, and as such had some say in whether Luci remained there as a teacher.

'Part of the problem is that he wants everything for himself,' she said at last. 'When the children come up to my desk for supplies, he always has to have the longest pencil, the nicest box of crayons, or the tin drum when we have music. I've tried making him go to the back of the line to give the shyer ones a chance, and then he sulks and kicks out at the furniture. I tell you, Mariah, at times he makes a thorough nuisance of himself. I'm on the point of sending a note home to Mrs Fletcher, asking her to pop in to see me.'

'For goodness' sake don't do that! Let me have a go first.'

'But she's his mother. Surely she wants him to succeed at school?'

'It's a bit more complicated than that. As you know, his grandfather is a very wealthy man.'

Luci nodded, licking one finger before mopping up the crumbs from her plate.

'Mr Morgan's estate is entailed, you see. That means that the house and the land, with all the farms, has to be passed down to the nearest male heir after his death. And, of course, he also owns the colliery and the miners' houses in Cwmbran, as well as having shares in a number of big concerns, such as the railway.'

'And Henry inherits all that in time?'

'You've got it in one. And Meredith is fully aware of that and she treats him like a little prince as a result. Heaven help us all if the child finds out about it before he's old enough to take it in his stride, but so far she's had the good sense to keep him in the dark. At the same time she dotes on the boy – the widow's only son and all that – and she simply won't allow him to be corrected. The nursemaid we had before Myfanwy got the boot because she dared to smack him for some piece of mischief, so he's been thoroughly spoiled. He's king of the nursery, used to lording it over little Lucas, and now I'm afraid that behaviour is spilling over into school life.'

Luci groaned. 'And I'm left to pick up the pieces!'

Later, Myfanwy listened carefully to what Mariah had to say. 'In my day you did what the teacher said, or else! And when you got home you had another thrashing for showing the family up while you were at school!'

'Surely not when you were only five years old?' Mariah gasped.

'Na, na, we were all too scared of the teacher to step out of line at that age. I was talking about later, see? What is it you want me to do, then, Mrs Mortimer? I will talk to Henry, but I doubt it will do any good. I've tried to teach him his manners but every child needs a bit of a tap now and then to make him take heed, and his mother does not allow me to do that. She is my employer, so what can I do?'

'Other than having a word with the boy there's not much you can do, unless you want to get on the wrong side of Meredith,' Mariah replied, with a sigh. 'Nor can I get involved to any extent, other than to mention it to mam and let her go to Harry with the problem. Oh, dear, I do hate all this underhanded business, and all over a five-year-old child! I prefer to deal with problems directly.'

Myfanwy looked thoughtful. 'I remember when our Micah was small, and grieving over the death of our mam. He started playing up at the school but luckily for him Miss Williams – that was the teacher then – Miss Williams said he was suffering from lack of someone to pay attention to him, that was all it was. It hurt me when she said that, for I was only twelve years old, you see, and doing my best to take Mam's place where I could. Dada was grieving too, of course, and had enough to do, trying to earn a living down the pit to keep us all.'

Mariah's heart bled for the little girl that Myfanwy had been, keeping house for her father and six brothers, and going to school as well.

'I left the school as soon as I turned fourteen,' Myfanwy remarked, as if she had read Mariah's mind. 'I couldn't keep it up, you see. Not all the washing and the cooking and doing my lessons as well.'

'What became of Micah at that time, Myfanwy?'

'Oh, Miss Williams made him blackboard monitor, see. He liked that. Made him feel a somebody. He loved to take the erasers outside and bang them against the wall to get rid of the chalk. Miss Adams is your friend; do you think if you asked she would make him blackboard monitor? He'd love that!'

'I daresay he would, but he already believes he's king of the castle. He'd be unbearable if he thought he was his teacher's pet.'

'I suppose so. What's to be done with him, then?'

Mariah shrugged. 'Time will tell. Meanwhile, is there something else bothering you? You've been looking rather strained, and I'm sure it's not all due to Henry's difficulties.'

Myfanwy hesitated. 'I suppose you've heard that my father's wife is coming here to work as cook, when Mrs Edwards leaves.'

'Mam did mention it. Is that what's worrying you? I don't see why. She'll be down in the kitchen and you spend most of your time up here in the nurseries. You'll hardly ever come into contact with each other.'

'I'm not overly fond of Bessie, but that's not it. It's my father, see. He's bound to kick up a stink when he finds out she's left him – you can hardly blame him – and then he'll come looking for me.'

'It's not your fault if he and Bessie don't get on.'

'In a way it is. You remember how furious he was when I came here to work; leaving him in the lurch was how he put it, although all that was really worrying him was having nobody there to keep house for him. If Mam had been alive he'd have been glad to see me go out to work, like anyone else my age. I might even have joined the forces and helped to win the war. Always fancied myself in uniform, I did.

'So that is it, you see. Oh, they do say around the doors that Bessie was that keen to marry him, and she was the one in hot pursuit, especially when he was courting your mam, but I don't believe he was ever in love with her. As I say, it was a housekeeper he was after, not love, like it was with our mam. If Bessie goes, then who will fill her place? He cannot marry again, with her still living, and that only leaves me. He'll insist that I go back to the house, and I couldn't bear it. I have everything I need here, all lovely, and a nice wage, paid regular. I don't want to go, Mrs Mortimer!'

'And for that reason you certainly don't want to offend Mrs Fletcher and risk getting the sack, so that leaves me to deal with Henry,' Mariah said grimly.

Chapter Eleven

'Please, Mrs Morgan, there's a woman at the front door, calling herself Mrs Doughsky. She says she's come to fetch Evan Phillips!' Rosie's eyes were alight with excitement as she waited for Ellen's response.

'That will be his mother, Rosie. I hope you invited her in and didn't leave her standing on the doorstep! It's nippy out there this morning. And her name is Dolski, by the way.'

'Yes, madam. Shall I bring her up, or will you come down?'

'Show her into the morning-room, please, and say I'll be there in a minute.'

Rosie disappeared and Ellen looked at her daughter, biting her lip. 'This is it, then! The first of the Swansea Six to leave us. I don't know if I can bear it, Mariah.'

'Buck up, Mam! He's being reunited with his mother. That's what you want, isn't it?'

'Of course it is! Now, do I look all right, or should I go and change my jumper first?'

'Just get downstairs, Mam! This is an ordinary woman like ourselves, not the Archbishop of Canterbury come to pay us a visit! Anyway, she'll only have eyes for her son, and she won't care what we look like!'

'Mrs Doughsky!' Rosie announced, waving a hand with a dramatic flourish as Ellen entered the morning-room.

'Thank you, Rosie. How do you do, Mrs Dolski? Did you have a good journey?'

'How do you do? And the name's Doherty. I had to change trains twice, but I'm here at last.'

'Do sit down. Would you care for a cup of tea?'

The formalities dispensed with, Ellen was able to take a good look at Evan's mother. She was quite smartly dressed, although her navy blue suit was rather shabby. Was that a contradiction in terms? Very few people could manage to buy new clothes nowadays, when all garments cost coupons as well as money. An adorable little hat with a feather in it was perched on the side of her head and she had obviously had a perm recently rather than wearing her hair in a victory roll, such as Ellen had.

There came a sudden flurry of activity as the Swansea Six burst into the room and came to a stop, staring at the visitor.

'Steady on, boys!' Ellen brought them to order by the simple expedient of raising her hand, like a traffic warden on duty in the High Street. 'This is Mrs Doherty, Evan's mother. Say how do you do, nicely.'

Mrs Doherty seemed bewildered. 'Which one of you is my Evan, then? You're all such tall boys I can't make him out.'

Evan appeared to be equally befuddled. 'You're not my mam! She's called Mrs Phillips!'

For a moment Ellen was lost for words. It was almost four years since the pair had seen each other and Evan had shot up in the past few months. He was no longer the little chap that his mother had left behind in the orphanage. And she'd forgotten that the boy had no idea that his mother had remarried, and had introduced the woman by her new name. What was she supposed to do now? Fortunately Mrs Doherty moved forward and took her son in her arms.

'Don't you know your mam now, Evan? And look at you, all grown-up. I was expecting to see a little chap like you were the last time I saw you!'

'Why did Mrs Morgan call you that funny name, Mam? Doesn't she know you're Mrs Phillips?'

His mother cleared her throat. 'Um, I have a surprise for you, Evan *bach*. I've married again, see. Jimmy Doherty, his name is, so I'm Mrs Doherty now.'

'But you can't have married him. You're married to Dada!' Evan burst into tears and turned to Ellen for comfort.

'I think the rest of you better go outside to play,' Ellen murmured. 'Evan and his mam need to have a little talk, all right?'

Reluctantly the other boys shuffled out. Mavis Doherty stared at Ellen rather pointedly, but Ellen stood her ground. After all, she had been the child's foster parent all these years and she was not about to desert him now. The absentee mother did indeed have some explaining to do, although it was hardly her fault that the beastly war had invaded her family unit and torn it apart.

'You know that Dada is dead, Evan *bach*. I wish he was still here, but he is not, and life must go on. I've met somebody new, and he asked me to marry him. He will be your Dada now.'

Evan buried his face in Ellen's lap and refused to look at his mother.

'We thought you had a Polish name now, and might be planning to live in Poland. Dolski, that's what you said in your letter, wasn't it?' Ellen asked, trying to fill the conversational gap.

Mavis stared at her before bursting into laughter. 'That's a good one! It must have been my handwriting. I dashed off that letter in a hurry, that's what it was. No, Jimmy Doherty is Canadian, of Irish descent, actually.'

Ellen felt foolish, although it was Harry who had made the original mistake. Perhaps he needed to get his eyes tested! Dolski, indeed!

'Will you be going to live in Canada, then?'

'Of course. Jimmy will be going back on a troopship quite soon now and me and Evan will follow on later, with all the other war brides.'

Evan's head came up at that.

'Jimmy owns a ranch in a place called Saddle Landing,' Mavis said. 'You'll love it there, Evan.'

'I don't want to go to any old ranch!' he stammered. 'I just want to stay here in Cwmbran with the Morgans. And I don't want a new da!'

'You've never been on a big ship, have you, Evan?' Ellen wheedled. 'That will be something to look forward to, won't it? And imagine going to live on a ranch! Perhaps there will be real cowboys and Indians, and all sorts of wild animals to see.'

Evan wrenched himself away from Ellen and raced out of the room.

'Better leave him,' she murmured, as Mavis took a step towards the door. "This has all come as a shock to the child. Look, you're welcome to stay the night with us, if you don't have to rush off again immediately. By the time he's slept on this news he'll be seeing things more clearly.'

'I don't understand it,' Mavis frowned. 'I thought he'd be delighted to see me. And surely any boy would give his eye-teeth to go to Canada with all that it has to offer!'

'Of course he's pleased to see you, Mrs Doherty. He'll be as right as rain by tomorrow, you'll see.'

In the end it was the other boys who managed to calm Evan down. By showing their envy of what lay ahead for him, they innocently made him realize that he was very fortunate indeed.

'Cor! Wish I was going to Canada!' Huw cried.

'Will there be wolves and bears?' That was Ceri Davies.

'I expect they'll teach you to ride a horse, and you'll go out roping steers,' Dai Jones put in.

Little by little Evan saw himself as a denizen of the Wild West. 'I'll come with you, then, Mrs Dubusky,' he said at last.

'I'm your mam!' she corrected. 'And you must learn to say Doherty. That's your name now, you know; Evan Doherty. Come along, say it after me. Evan Doherty.'

But on that point Evan refused to budge. 'I'm Evan Phillips,' he insisted, and no matter how hard his mother tried to force it, he could not be persuaded to pronounce the name.

Ellen wasn't sure if this was because he was too young to understand the significance of what Mavis was proposing, or because he wanted to hang on to his own name.

'He'll have to learn,' Mavis protested, 'because he's down on my passport as Evan Doherty. What's going to happen if he pipes up with this nonsense when we land in Canada? The authorities may wonder if I've kidnapped the child!'

'I'm sure it will all work out,' Ellen soothed. 'You won't be the only war bride travelling with a child. Besides, once you get over there he'll be so excited by all the new sights and sounds he won't have time to worry about what people are calling him. In any case, I understand from what you've said that it may be weeks before you board your ship. He'll have come to terms with it all by then, I'm sure.'

The next morning it was a sad little party which gathered to wave Evan off. Mariah was driving him and his mother to the railway station, and Ellen helped to stow his pathetic little bundle of clothing in the boot, along with Mavis's own travelling gear. She had longed to go with him to the station but Harry had persuaded her not to.

'You don't want any last-minute scenes, do you, *cariad*? It will be hard enough for the boy, without you weeping all over him.'

So now the first of the Swansea Six, the little wartime family she had come to love, was gone. The cheers of the other boys followed the car as it swept down the drive. Ellen took a deep breath and turned to go indoors.

Chapter Twelve

'Come in!' Harry looked up from his desk as five boys crowded into his study.

'What's this, then, a deputation?'

'Please, sir, we need to know what's going to happen to us.'

'What do you mean, Dafydd?' Harry countered, stalling for time. He knew what they were going to ask, and he didn't have any ready answers.

'Well, sir, the war is over and we were only staying here for the duration, weren't we? Evan has already gone but the rest of us don't have parents and we were wondering where we'll be sent.'

'I've heard nothing about that yet, but you can rest assured that a place will be found for you somewhere. You will certainly be looked after.'

'Excuse me, sir, but I don't think that will happen. At least, not in my case. I'm fourteen, you see. They kick you out of the orphanage then. You have to go to work and fend for yourself.'

'Perhaps you haven't heard, my boy, that the government passed a new Education Act last year. The school-leaving age has been raised to fifteen so you'll have to stay in school for a few more terms after all.'

Dafydd shifted from one foot to the other. 'I was wondering, sir, if I could stay here. Oh, I don't mean here at the House. I was hoping that p'raps you'd give me a job in the colliery; down the pit, see?'

'You mean you want to become a miner, boy?'

'Yes, sir.'

Harry managed to swallow the grin that threatened to spread over his face. The lad's expression was akin to one that might have been worn by a Christian martyr, about to face the lions in the Coliseum.

'We no longer employ children in the mines,' he told the boy. 'You'll have to wait a while before we can take you on, although if you like to come and see me when you're a bit older, I'll see what can be done. But are you sure you wouldn't be happier working above ground? I know that you did a good job of growing vegetables under Mrs Mortimer's supervision. What about taking a job as an under-gardener here after you leave school? There will be plenty to do to get the grounds back to their pre-war state.'

'Oh, yes, please, sir!' Dafydd's face lit up.

'That's all right, then. Anything else?'

Huw raised his hand. 'It's the eleven plus, sir!'

'What about it?'

Once again Dafydd took up the story. 'Huw is clever at the school, sir. His teacher wants him to sit the exams in the spring to try for the grammar school.'

'Then what's the problem?' Harry knew that when children reached the age of eleven they were eligible to take examinations which, if passed, would provide them with a scholarship to attend the grammar school, which provided a secondary education for bright youngsters. This in turn would fit them for good jobs, or even for a university place later on.

'There isn't much point, sir. Nobody at our orphanage ever went to the grammar school, just the primary school down the street. There was no money for the books and the uniforms and the games equipment you see.'

'Education is never wasted, Dafydd. Would you like to sit these exams, Huw? What is involved, by the way?'

'English comprehension, Welsh comprehension, English composition, Welsh composition,' Huw rhymed off. 'And arithmetic problems. You can choose whether to do those in English or Welsh, see.'

'You seem to have it down pat, boy. Well, I advise you to get on with it, then. Even if it turns out that you can't take up your place at the grammar school, the very fact of your having won a scholarship will be a point in your favour when you apply for work in the future.'

Huw nodded, bright-eyed.

'What about you, then, Dai? Jones, isn't that your last name?'

'I think so, sir.'

'You think so! Don't you know your own name, boy?'

'Not really, sir. I was left on the church steps when I was a baby, see, and they didn't know where I came from, or what my name was. Matron picked my name out of the telephone book, see.'

Harry winced. 'And you, Trevor Pritchard?'

'My parents died, sir, and Mamgu couldn't keep me cos she had arthritis awful bad. They were going to send me and some other boys to Canada to work on farms, but then the war came and the Jerries were sinking our ships all over the place, so they changed their minds.'

'And would you like to go to work in Canada, my boy?'

Trevor shrugged. 'It won't make much difference, I s'pose. They'll send me out to work as soon as I'm old enough and when you're an orphan they don't give you any say in the matter.'

Little Ceri Davies had been listening to all this with his eyes opening wider and wider.

'I'm not going back to the orph'nage,' he blurted, 'and I won't go to that Canada place, neither! I'm going to stay here with Mrs Richards, see!'

'She is called Mrs Morgan now, Ceri,' Harry said gently. 'Can you remember that?'

'Yes. That's who I'm going to live with, forever and ever, amen!'

Four pairs of eyes swivelled in Harry's direction. Suddenly he felt as if he'd had as much as he could take for one day. 'You've given me a lot to think about, you chaps,' he told them. 'Cut along now, will you? I have a lot of work to get through this morning.'

But when they had gone he found himself quite unable to concentrate. When his wife came in search of him some time later she found him standing at the window, staring into space.

'I've had a rather distressing interview with what's left of the Swansea Six,' he began.

'What have they been up to now?'

'Nothing in particular, *cariad*. Evan's departure has left them feeling rather anxious about their own future, of course. Dafydd wanted me to send him down the pit to work, of all things, and as for young Ceri, he's determined to stay here with his beloved Mrs Morgan!'

'Bless him!'

'It's going to be a wrench for both of you when he has to go, *cariad*. I saw how unhappy you were when you had to say goodbye to Evan, and he has a mother to take care of him, and an assured future in Canada. But you'll have to face up to it one of these days, you know, and so will Ceri.'

'Couldn't we keep him, Harry? We've plenty of room here and it would only be for a few years.'

'Quite impossible, *cariad*! Even if we wanted to keep him, the authorities would never permit it. I'm pushing seventy, far too old to adopt a small boy.'

Ellen bit her lip. But I'm not, she wanted to say, but to put this into words would not be tactful. She was in her late forties and she knew better than to remind her husband of the age gap between them, especially now, when he was already feeling despondent about reaching this worrisome milestone. The stress of the war had been hard on him, and he had already had a slight stroke. Whereas many other men of his age were hale and hearty, looking forward to another ten or twenty years of life, Harry had to live with the knowledge that he could be taken at any moment.

'No need to worry,' she said now, trying to sound bracing and cheerful. 'We may not hear from the authorities for some time to come. I imagine that the school system is in complete turmoil at the moment, with thousands of evacuees being returned to their original homes. And there must be a lot more orphaned children nowadays than there were before the war, what with people being killed in action, or wiped out during the blitz, and what are they going to do with them? The poor kiddies, I mean.'

'Build more orphanages, probably. Although where the materials or the manpower are to come from I can't think. So many people have lost everything in the bombing and housing is desperately needed. As far as I can see the work of reconstruction will take years.'

'That's what I mean!' Ellen sounded triumphant. 'Why would anyone want to remove the boys from our care if there's nowhere to put them?'

'Speaking of which,' Harry interrupted, 'a letter came from my solicitor by the first post. He's heard from his contact in London and wanted me to know the result of his enquiries there.'

'He's found Dulcie, has he?'

'Yes and no. Apparently she was killed in the blitz.'

'No! How dreadful!'

'Her parents are still alive, though, but they've expressed not the slightest interest in taking on their grandchild.'

'Poor little Lucas! So what now?'

'There's nothing for it, but I'll have to go there myself and have a word or two with this Albert Saunders.'

Chapter Thirteen

The great conker caper was to have repercussions that went far beyond a childish game. But in the beginning nobody could have foreseen what was to happen as a result of such an innocent pastime.

One good thing about the playground games in which the local children indulged was that they did not create a gulf between rich and poor, for the youngsters derived a great deal of pleasure from activities which cost nothing. The nurseries of Cwmbran House were filled with expensive toys, including a magnificent miniature railway set, complete with all sorts of lead trees, signals and other accessories. There was also a fine dapple-grey rocking horse which had served generations of Morgan children, but Henry Fletcher seldom played with that, considering it beneath his notice. The only time he showed an interest was when Lucas climbed onto its back, and then he claimed ownership, forcing the other boy to get down.

Other children had to rely on the items they could provide for themselves. A stub of chalk made it possible for girls to play hopscotch in the school playground, and a length of old clothes-line lent itself to all sorts of skipping games. The boys played five-stones with suitably sized pebbles, and at the right time of year they had conkers.

'Where are you off to, boys?' Mariah came upon the remnants of the Swansea Six as they were setting off across the grounds.

'To get conkers, miss!'

'All right, but try to find some which have fallen on the ground. Use sticks if you must, but no throwing stones up into the tree to try to dislodge the unripe ones. Remember what happened last year, when Trevor ended up with a black eye!'

'Did you play conkers when you were a little girl, Miss?'

'Not like you do, Trevor. That's a boys' game. Mrs Fletcher and I did use the chestnuts to make doll's furniture, though. We stuck pins into them for chair legs and so on.'

But the boys had no interest in dolls' furniture, and off they ran, whooping and calling.

'What's a conker, Auntie 'Riah?' Henry asked, wondering if he was missing out on something.

'Haven't you heard the boys in your class at school talking about them? A conker is the fruit of the horse chestnut tree. You peel off the green prickly pod and inside there is a lovely brown nut. This is the time of year when people collect them to play with.'

'But what do they want them for?'

'To play a game, Henry. When the boys come back you'll be able to watch them making a hole in each of the conkers with a skewer. Then we'll thread a piece of string through the hole and make a knot under-neath so it doesn't fall off.'

'And then what?'

'One person holds his conker on the end of the string and some-body else tries to hit it with his own conker, to break it.'

'That's silly,' Lucas lisped.

'I suppose it is,' Mariah agreed, wondering what a visitor from a foreign country might make of it all. 'A lot of people enjoy doing it, though.'

'I want to do it, too!' Henry shouted.

While Mariah was doing her best to explain what the game was all about, Harry and Meredith had come up behind her, and were now looking on with interest.

'I don't want you playing with conkers,' Meredith told her son. 'You're far too young for such a dangerous game.'

'Don't baby the child, Meredith,' Harry laughed. 'Playing conkers is the birthright of every red-blooded little boy. I was a dab hand at conkers when I wasn't much older than him. I tell you what, why don't we hold a contest in the play room this evening? I'll referee the thing to make sure nobody gets hurt, and it will give the chaps some prac-tice before they turn up at school to take on all corners! Cwmbran House versus the rest of the world!'

Mariah went out to the toolshed in search of a hammer, in case the skewers needed help in boring through the chestnuts. Her next stop was her mother's store cupboard, which was a veritable treasure trove of string, used wrapping paper and half-used sticks of sealing wax. Every parcel that came into the house was opened very carefully so that the wrappings could be used again and again; no knot was ever cut apart but had to be gently worked apart, no matter how long it took.

'I hope you don't mean to hand over that whole ball,' Ellen grumbled. 'You can dish out one piece of string per boy, and that's it.'

'Why, you're not expecting another war, are you, Mam?'

'Waste not, want not. That's what I've always taught you, my girl, war or no war!'

Mariah laughed. Then she collected Henry and Lucas and accompanied them to the edge of the park where the older boys were already filling their pockets with the best conkers they could find.

That evening the whole family gathered in the playroom, where Harry announced that he would first outline the rules of the game.

'Yes, you older boys know all about it, I'm sure, but we have some first-timers here, so I shall explain for their benefit. Now, this game is for two players at a time. One man holds up his hand, letting his conker dangle on the end of its string. Have a look at Dafydd, Lucas; he's showing us what to do. His opponent is going to swing his own conker, as hard as he can, and will try to hit the first man's conker as hard as he can. Got that, Lucas?'

Lucas nodded.

'If he scores a hit he gets another go. If he misses it's the first man's turn. Are we all ready? Right, Dafydd will challenge Trevor. Stand well back, everyone. We don't want any accidents.'

After some spirited play, Dafydd managed to smash Trevor's conker. 'Now mine is a oner,' he explained to the onlookers. 'That means I've defeated one enemy conker, see? Trev's conker was new, otherwise I could have added his score to mine.'

'I don't understand that,' Meredith frowned.

'Oh, if somebody smashes my oner, his will be a twoer then, see.'

'No, I'm afraid I don't.'

'For goodness sake let's get on with it!' Harry fumed. 'No need to get everybody tied up in knots! You'll see what happens as the game gets on. Now, Dai and Huw, are you ready to have a go next? And after that you youngsters can have a turn if you think you know what you're supposed to do.'

Lucas was encouraged to take part, with Ceri Davies as his opponent. 'And mind you take it easy, Ceri," Ellen warned. 'Just remember, he's only half your age!'

Much to everyone's surprise, Lucas turned out to be a natural at the game. Whether it was beginner's luck, or perhaps that he was unusually well coordinated for a child of five, he managed to defeat Ceri at once. Ceri took it in good part and stepped aside to thread up a new conker.

'It's my turn! Let me! Let me!' Henry thrust himself into the circle, clutching his weapon. Smiling, Dafydd held out his conker, eager to give the little boy his chance. Henry's swing went a mile wide. When Dafydd's turn came he made a half-hearted effort, not wanting to spoil the younger boy's fun. Henry swung again, this time managing to make contact, but it was his conker which split apart, while Dafydd's shiny brown beauty reclaimed intact.

Henry's lip quivered. 'This one was no good!' he bawled. 'I want another one!'

'There are plenty on the table, dear,' Ellen pointed out. 'Come and choose one of those.'

'No! I want his!' Henry snapped, pointed at Lucas. 'He's got a twoer. Give it here, Lucas!'

'No!' Lucas insisted, made unusually bold by the presence of so many grown-ups. Just to make sure he sidled behind Mariah, clutching his property.

Henry dashed forward and snatched it away. Lucas promptly burst into tears.

'That's not sporting, old man,' Harry said at once. 'Hand it over, there's a good boy.'

The hammer was still lying on the table where Mariah had left it. Henry grabbed it and attacked Lucas's conker with full force.

'Here, be careful of that table!' Ellen cried, as the hammer missed its target and made a gouge in the polished wood, but Henry was not to be stopped. Panting, he attacked the nut again until it fell to the floor, where he knelt to hammer it again. At last the poor conker lay crushed at his feet and he glanced around triumphantly. The room fell silent.

Lucas stood watching him, white-faced, with his thumb in his mouth. His other hand clutched Mariah's skirt until she feared that the worn fabric might tear. Aghast, Harry Morgan stared down at his defiant little grandson. What an exhibition! His mind registered the expressions on the faces of the older boys. What he saw there wasn't hard to read. Scorn, disgust, even fear. He had spent years sitting on the magisterial bench, and he knew that justice had to be done, and had to be seen to be done.

Chapter Fourteen

Meredith made a move towards her son, but her father stopped her with an impatient gesture.

'Myfanwy, I want you to take Master Henry back to the nursery and put him to bed. And there will be no supper for you, young man! It's time you learned how to behave in polite company.'

Myfanwy stepped forward and took the boy by the arm but he shook her off and darted from the room, wailing loudly. She ran after him, letting the door swing shut behind her.

'Dad! I won't allow you to treat Henry like this! He's my son, and I decide what's to be done with him. He's done nothing wrong!'

'That's a matter of opinion,' her father snapped. 'We can't discuss this here. Kindly come up to my study and you can say your piece there. Mariah, keep an eye on things here, will you? There's no reason why the competition can't go on for the rest of the boys.' He shepherded Meredith out of the room as a babble of talk broke out behind him.

'Come on,' Mariah encouraged. 'Whose turn is it next? Dai Jones? Do you want to pick a partner?' The two contestants got into position, and the fun went on. Only Lucas hung back, sucking his thumb. Ellen bent down and gently removed it from his mouth.

'I don't like that Henry!' he whispered. 'He's nasty, and he busted my conker.'

'Conkers are meant to be busted – er, broken – you know. We'll find you another one, never fear.'

'But mine was a twoer, Auntie Ellen.'

'That's all right. You'll soon have another one, perhaps even a fiver!'

A shout went up as Trevor's conker shattered.

'There, you see, Lucas? Trevor isn't crying, is he? Now try to be a brave boy like him.'

'I don't want to sleep in the nursery tonight,' Lucas snivelled. 'Henry jumps on my bed and hits me. He'll be worse now if he doesn't get his supper.'

Ellen didn't doubt that this was the case. 'Then you shall sleep in the boys' dormitory, just for tonight. You can have Evan's old bed. You'd like that, wouldn't you? Now, go and pick out another conker and I'll help you with the string.'

In Harry's study, Meredith was red-faced with fury. 'How dare you humiliate me in front of those horrid little boys!'

'If anyone caused you to be humiliated it was your own son. I've seen this coming for a long time, Meredith. Henry has the makings of a nasty little bully and he has to be curbed before he's very much older. That scene downstairs just now was utterly disgraceful. I was ashamed to call him my grandson.'

'Stuff and nonsense! All this fuss over a nut!'

'Come now, my girl, that's not the point, and well you know it! What Henry did was unsporting behaviour, not to mention having a full-blown tantrum.'

'Don't you think you're making too much of this, Dad? He's just a little boy.'

'A little boy who has to learn, Meredith. And I'm afraid that this is more than a bit of sibling rivalry between him and Lucas. Mariah tells me that he's been playing up at school as well.'

'Pshaw! What does she know about it?'

'As you know, Miss Adams is her friend, and naturally she's dropped a hint or two in her direction.'

'So now Mariah is carrying tales, is she?'

'She happened to mention something in passing, that's all. Miss Adams is concerned because the boy is disrupting the class.'

'Huh! That's just an excuse because the woman can't keep order. I knew this would happen if you forced me to send Henry to the local school. If you'd let me hire a governess as I wanted to, we wouldn't be having this conversation now. And I blame Myfanwy. She should be teaching him right from wrong. Why else do we pay her?'

'Myfanwy's hands are tied because you refuse to let her chastise the boy in any way. He knows he can do as he likes and there's not much she can do about it. Thanks to you, the boy is being ruined. That has to change, Meredith, or I won't answer for the consequences.'

Meredith's eyes filled with tears. 'You're very harsh, Dad. Poor little Henry doesn't have a father and I have to make it up to him for that.'

'I'm well aware of his fatherless state, my girl. Perhaps you've forgotten that there are a number of young boys in this house who are in the very same situation. Despite having no parents in their lives they are growing up to be decent people, even though the odds are stacked against them. Henry, now, he's the most fortunate of boys. He can look forward to a life of privilege, which has been handed down to him from past generations. It is up to us to make sure that he grows up to be worthy of that heritage, can't you see that?'

Unfortunately, Harry's mood was spoiled when his daughter made a rude noise in response to this stirring speech. He struggled to hold down the rage which boiled up inside him. He had to keep his blood pressure under control before he had another stroke. The problem of dealing with Henry was one thing, but the destruction of a child's conker was not worth dying for.

'What that son of yours needs is a good, smacked bottom!' he snapped, 'and that should occur before he's very much older.'

'Don't you dare lay a finger on that child!' Meredith yelped.

'Keep your voice down, girl! Do you want the servants to hear you? You sound like a fishwife!'

Meredith gave him a look of loathing and flounced out of the study. Harry sat down on his leather armchair, feeling slightly sick. Almost at once he got to his feet again and went to pour himself a stiff drink. By the time his wife came in search of him he had calmed down somewhat but to her way of thinking he still looked thoroughly upset.

'Is there anything I can do, Harry.'

He squeezed her hand. 'No, no, *cariad*. I do wish I could get Meredith to see sense, though. As far as she is concerned the boy can do no wrong.'

'That's a mother for you,' Ellen said, laughing. 'Even I like to protect my one ewe lamb!' Any fool could see that Henry was riding for a fall, so spoiled was he by his doting mother, but she knew better than to express an opinion on that score. Harry knew quite well that his daughter was no angel, but just let anyone else remark on that, and they would feel the rough side of his tongue!

'But why can't she see what she's doing to the child, Ellen? He's turning into a holy terror. How is young Lucas now? Has he got over the shock?'

'Oh, he'll be all right. If he meets nothing worse in life he'll do well. I've found him another conker and once again he's ready for the fray. I'm not letting him go back to the nursery tonight, though. I'm going to let him sleep in the boys' dormitory, and he's looking forward to that as if it's the world's greatest treat, funny little chap.'

'Just as well,' Harry grunted. 'It will do Henry good to be sent to Coventry for once. I hope that Myfanwy managed to get him into bed. It would be just like him to resist her, tooth and claw!'

'It's only a storm in a teacup,' Ellen said, rubbing the tight muscles in his shoulders. 'Being sent to bed without supper will give him some-thing to think about. An empty tummy will make more of an impres-sion on him than all the scolding in the world.'

Harry gave a long sigh. 'I wish that something would make an impression on that daughter of mine, *cariad*. Trouble is, the poor girl is lonely. What she needs is a new husband, but how is she to find one? She never meets anyone of her own class, and I don't have any more eligible cousins to parade in front of her. It's a bit of a lost cause.'

'Nonsense. She'll meet someone nice once of these days, now all the boys are coming home from the war. Perhaps Aubrey can intro-duce her to somebody suitable.'

Henry Fletcher was indeed in his bed, decked out in red, white and blue striped pyjamas. He had cooperated quite meekly when Myfanwy stripped him of his shorts and pullover, and wiped his face and hands. While he had no compunction in defying her, he was in awe of his grandfather, and that gentleman had roared at him like a bear. Henry wasn't sure what might happen if his nursemaid reported any disobe-dience and he had no desire to find out.

He lolled in his bed, listening to the voices which drifted up from Grandfather's study. The sound was too far away for him to make out what was being said, but he was able to identify the speakers. That low rumble was Grandfather. He sounded cross. And that was Mummy, who seemed to be in a rage. He chuckled. Myfanwy was cross, too.

'There's spiteful you were, Master Henry!' she'd gasped, dragged his jersey over his head, none too gently. 'Showed me up good and proper, you did. Serve you right, your *Tadcu* saying you have to go hungry until morning. Teach you a lesson that will!' As if that was likely to happen! Mummy would come up after a while, bringing him something nice to eat to make him feel better. Perhaps it would be a sandwich with homemade strawberry jam, or even a Bourbon biscuit.

Chapter Fifteen

By the next morning the fuss over Henry's little misdemeanour had calmed down, overtaken by the daily panic involving missing socks and lost homework as the boys prepared for school. When they had left the house, jostling and shouting, Ellen sat down to have a leisurely breakfast with her husband.

'I wonder if I should let Lucas sleep in the dormitory from now on,' she remarked. 'He quite enjoyed himself last night and I know he's still in awe of Henry.'

Harry smeared marmalade on his toast. 'Best to go back to normal, *cariad*. Otherwise Henry will have an inflated idea of his own importance. As for Lucas, he's too timid for his own good. Let him face up to the boy if he can.'

Ellen looked doubtful. Harry hadn't seen the child shaking with fright, as she had.

'Anyway, the situation may resolve itself before too long. I've decided to go up to London today and see what I can find out from the Saunders family. I'll catch the afternoon train, so if you could pack a few things for me I'll be grateful.'

'I'll do it right after breakfast. You hope to verify that Dulcie is dead, is that it?'

'Oh, I believe that, all right. Higgins, the man in London, appears to be quite thorough. No, I want to see for myself what the situation is there. I'm not about to hand over a five-year-old child to anyone who seems less than ideal.'

'I don't suppose you'll have much choice in the matter, will you? Blood relatives and all that.'

'We shall have to see. Is there any more tea in that pot? This national loaf, or whatever fool name they've tacked on to this bread, is absolutely foul. I need something to wash it down!'

Ellen filled his cup once more.

*

After registering at the Grosvenor Hotel, Harry had a quick wash and then sallied out to find Dulcie's family. Peering out of the window as the taxi sped through the East End he was horrified to see the piles of rubble left behind after the blitz. In some cases whole streets seemed to have been destroyed. He wondered what had happened to the people. Had most of them been wiped out, too? Of course he knew about the carnage which the air raids had wrought, but surveying the scene at first hand brought it all home to him in a thoroughly unpleasant way. He was glad that he hadn't brought Ellen with him. She would have been greatly distressed by all this.

Number 65, Blossom Street, was one of several dwellings in a terrace, whose doors fronted directly on to the pavement. He paid off his driver, adding a substantial tip, and rapped on the door.

It was some time before it was flung open, and he was confronted by the unlovely sight of a man who had not been expecting company, or who perhaps didn't care what others thought of him. His grubby singlet had egg stains down the front, and his feet were thrust into brown plaid slippers which had holes cut in them to accommodate bunions. By contrast Harry, in his homburg hat and pre-war overcoat, looked as if his photo should be gracing the cover of a glossy magazine.

'Yeah?'

'Mr Saunders?'

'That's right. Who wants to know?'

'I'm Harry Morgan. I believe that you've had a letter from my solicitor, concerning your grandson, Lucas Saunders?'

'Huh!'

'May I come in?'

Wordlessly Saunders stood aside, and Harry took that as an invitation and followed him in, closing the door behind him.

'Sit down if you can find a place,' Saunders said, lowering himself into the sagging armchair which he'd probably just vacated. Harry pulled out an upright chair from beside the table, resisting the urge to dust it for crumbs.

Clearing his throat, he began his prepared speech. Saunders listened without interruption.

'So you see,' Harry concluded, 'we've looked after the boy for the past three years, and now it's time to hand him back. The war is over, and all the evacuees are being returned to their families now.'

The man ran his hand over the stubble on his chin. 'Seems to me he should stay where he is. He's your grandson, ain't he, and from what our Dulce had to say, you're pretty well fixed. There's nothing for him here.'

'I'm afraid you've been misinformed, Mr Saunders. I'm not denying that Chad Fletcher was the boy's father, but he was not my son.'

'Related to you, though, eh? Cousin or summat, and wed to your girl.'

'True, but you are the child's grandparent. Look, perhaps I should have a word with your wife. Is she at home?'

'She's in the san, mate. She's got TB, hasn't she? Tuberculosis,' he added, as if Harry might have misunderstood.

Harry thought that he might have known this was a house without a woman in charge. There was a thick layer of dust on the cheap furniture and a pile of newspapers a mile high stood on a chair in the corner. He could not imagine Lucas thriving in such a place. No wonder Dulcie had been delighted to go down to Wiltshire to help her ailing aunt, and Chad Fletcher, the product of a comfortable home, must have seemed like her passport to paradise.

'Is there anyone else who might take the boy?' he asked.

'You can try our Doreen if you want, but she's stuck with five of her own and one on the way. P'raps if you make it worth her while?' Saunders scratched his palm in the universal gesture of one seeking money.

Dulcie's sister lived within walking distance, so within minutes Harry had arrived at another house which seemed to be a duplicate of the one he had just left. Before he could knock the door was flung open and he was confronted by a blowsy woman in an advanced state of pregnancy.

'Whatever it is you're trying to flog, we don't want none!' the harridan screeched.

'May I come in? I've come about your nephew, Lucas Saunders. I'm his foster parent, Harry Morgan.'

Once again he found himself in an untidy room, reeking with the smell of boiled cabbage. A toddler with a jam-smeared mouth was sitting on the hearth rug, playing with a battered Dinky toy. The child was wearing nothing but a shrunken pullover that was in sore need of darning, and Harry could only hope that the boy was potty trained. The mother seemed to be waiting for her visitor to say something.

'It's time that Lucas was returned to his family,' he began, but she interrupted him in a loud voice that caused the toddler's lip to curl in fright.

'Then I hope you don't think you can palm him off on me, mister! Where do you s'pose I'm going to put another kid, hey? This place is bursting at the seams as it is. And what about that bloke what got our Dulce in the club, anyway? Let him do something about it. You chaps are all the same. Get a girl into trouble and then it's goodbye and nice knowing yer!'

'Surely Dulcie told you that Chad was killed at Dunkirk, Mrs–er—'

'Chappell. I'm Mrs Chappell.'

'Mrs Chappell. He went over there in his friend's boat to help rescue the troops who were stranded on the beaches there, and unfortunately he didn't make it back.'

Doreen shrugged. 'Our Dulce was never one for letting us know what was going on in her life. We knew about the baby, of course, because she had to come home to have it. Dad was all for kicking her out but Mum talked him round. After a bit Dulcie got sick of looking after the kid so she told me she was off to join the ATS. Do her bit for the war effort, she said. She went down to that place in Wiltshire where the boy's granny lives, and when she come back she was on her own, so we thought the old girl had taken him in.'

'Mrs Fletcher is an elderly woman. She couldn't possibly have looked after a toddler, as Lucas was then. That's when your sister brought the boy to us. His father happened to be my son-in-law, you see.'

'Didn't know nothing about that.'

Harry decided that there was no point in telling this slatternly woman that her sister had dumped her child on them and flitted in the night. 'So Miss Saunders joined the ATS, did she?'

'No, not her. Serving in the greengrocer's down Emily Street was as far as she got. Went down to her friend's one night to try out a new hair-do, and that's when the Jerries got her. Direct hit on the Marshalls' house, and everyone killed.'

'I'm sorry.'

'Yeah, well, that's war for you, innit?'

Harry could think of nothing more to say so, reaching into his pocket he took out half-a-crown, which he pressed into the toddler's hand. The child immediately put it in his mouth and his mother gave a stifled cry and snatched it from him. Harry noted that it disappeared into the pocket of her grubby apron.

Chapter Sixteen

So that was as far as I got,' Harry confessed, when he reached home two days later.

'Poor dear!' Ellen told him. 'Mind you, I could have told you it wouldn't do any good, your going to see those people, but I suppose you were bound to go through the motions.'

'What on earth do you mean, you could have told me? What do you know about it? You haven't even met these people.'

'To start with, no decently brought up girl would have left her child with complete strangers and run off in the night. Letting your children be evacuated is one thing, and heartbreaking it must have been for all those thousands of women who had to send their children off into the blue. But I'm sure most of them kept in touch with their children and tried to visit them when they could. But did Dulcie send Lucas so much as a birthday card? She did not.'

'She could hardly do that when she was dead, *cariad*.'

'Of course not, but surely the parents could have let us know about that when she was killed.'

'According to the sister, they didn't know about us,' Harry said.

'Oh, do stop making excuses for them, man! They knew enough to be able to find Verona Fletcher, by all accounts. They just didn't bother. And now see what's happened. Instead of welcoming Lucas with open arms they're full of excuses. All right, so his other grandmother is in the sanatorium, and the husband can't cope. The sister is probably at her wits' end with a house full of children. I suppose the law says that the family has to take him in, but what chance would he have in a situation like that? Lucas will have to stay with us, Harry!'

'It's all so irregular,' he frowned. 'As long as the war was on the boy was only one evacuee among thousands. Now we're giving house-room to someone else's child, to whom we have absolutely no legal right.'

'I suppose we could just let things stay as they are for now.' Ellen sounded hopeful, knowing as she spoke that her husband was not one to let matters slide. 'I mean, the country is bound to be in a bit of a mess at the moment, what with families being reunited and the government trying to house them all. It could be years before the authorities find out about Lucas being here, if indeed they ever do. Will they even care? He has a good home with us.'

'You know how I feel about things being done by the book, *cariad*. Besides, we could be leaving ourselves wide open to some kind of blackmail by that Bert Saunders.'

'Blackmail? What on earth do you mean? We haven't done anything wrong!'

'I wasn't a magistrate all those years for nothing, you know. I got his measure at once. Saunders is the sort of lazy lump who'd do anything to make a dishonest shilling. I wouldn't put it past him to try to sell the child to us.'

'Now you're being silly.'

'You think so, do you? Perhaps he wouldn't go so far as to ask for hush money to stop him reporting us for keeping his grandson from him. It's more likely to take the shape of a pathetic plea, along the lines of "I can't provide for the boy when I can barely keep myself". In other words grease my palm and I'll let you keep the lad.'

'That won't wash, of course. You'll tell him where to get off and he won't have a leg to stand on.'

'Except that if he carries out his threat and goes bleating to the child protection services, poor little Lucas will be placed in foster care somewhere and that's the last we'll see of him. Is that what you want?'

'Of course it isn't! What do we do now, then?'

'I think we'll start by getting Verona to sign a solicitor's letter, stating that, as his grandmother, she wishes Lucas to remain in our care for the moment. I'll have to take advice on that, of course, because Bert Saunders is also the boy's next of kin. Under the law, I don't know who would have the greater claim; the child's maternal grandfather or Verona, since Chad was never married to Dulcie. I'm afraid it could be Saunders.'

'I see.'

'Then I'll have some sort of document drawn up, outlining what happened when Dulcie left Lucas with us. It's a great pity that she didn't leave a note when she ran off in the night. That would have strengthened our position considerably. We must get a copy of the birth certificate, which names Chad as the father, and I shall dig up documentation showing that Chad was, in fact, related to me, as a distant cousin.'

'And all that will allow us to keep Lucas here?'

Harry shook his head. 'I doubt it would stand up in a court of law, but at least we'll be prepared if Saunders tries any funny stuff.'

'Perhaps he won't bother,' Ellen decided, but Harry was not so sure.

Meredith Fletcher suddenly felt that she couldn't stay indoors a moment longer. The walls seemed to be closing in on her and she had a desperate longing for some fresh air. Pulling on an old tweed jacket and wrapping a cashmere scarf around her throat, she left the house at a trot and went out into the gardens. It had rained earlier in the day and the vegetable plots, with their winter cabbages and collapsed onion tops, looked dank and uncared for. She longed for the day when the grounds of Cwmbran House would be restored to their pre-war splendour, with velvety lawns and beds of sweet-smelling roses.

Spurred on by the need to get away from the house, she turned into the park. The sight of a splendid horse chestnut tree, with its fruit littering the ground beneath it, roused her to fury. All that fuss over a bit of childish nonsense! Her father was making far too much of it. Why couldn't people understand that Henry, poor, fatherless boy that he was, needed special care and attention? It disgusted her that Lucas was pampered and petted so much by Ellen and the rest, when he was nothing but a little changeling. The sooner he was sent back where he belonged, the better for all concerned. At least Dad was doing something about that. He had returned from London without having achieved his purpose, but it was a step in the right direction.

Deep inside herself, Meredith knew that it was wrong of her to dislike Lucas so much. He was an innocent child who could not be held responsible for what his father had done. What stuck in her craw was the fact that Chad had carried on an affair with another woman when he was engaged to marry her, Meredith.

According to Dulcie, he had deceived her as well, but the girl could have been lying. She had certainly attempted to pull the wool over their eyes by insisting that she and Chad had actually been married! That had given Meredith a few sleepless nights, living with the fear that she herself had, all unknowingly, entered into a bigamous marriage. Luckily, Dad had been able to prove otherwise, but the feeling of impotent rage had remained with her for a long time.

If only Lucas could be taken away from Cwmbran, she could start to heal. Chad had died while performing one last, selfless act, attempting to rescue his fellow countrymen from the beaches of Dunkirk, and she so much wanted to remember him as a man who might have gone on to do great things, had he lived. Perhaps it was not his fault that he had become embroiled with Dulcie. He would not have been the first man to be seduced by a loose woman, and as for Dulcie's claim that the affair had lasted for some time, and that Chad had promised to marry her, that was another of her lies.

Trudging along, hardly taking in her surroundings, Meredith had to admit that she was lonely. She had friends, of a sort – women of the better class in the surrounding district, such as the bank manager's wife – but she only met them at the meetings of the various organizations to which she belonged, such as the Red Cross. Several of them had hinted that they would welcome an invitation to Cwmbran House, but she had managed to fob them off. The last thing she wanted was for Lucas and her son to be seen together, when awkward questions might be asked or, worse, sly looks given.

Ellen had tried to help, which only made things worse. 'You're a young woman,' she'd murmured, pointing out the obvious. 'You'll remarry some day. Look at me if you don't believe that! Alone for years and now a bride in my forties!'

Meredith had rewarded her with a glare. In one way she hoped it might be true, but on the other hand remarrying might mean that she would have to leave Cwmbran House, and that she never wished to do.

Her reverie was interrupted by the approach of a stout figure, tacking along on a bicycle: Bessie Prosser, bursting out of a shabby brown overcoat, with her hair done up in a turban.

'*Prynhawn da*, Mrs Fletcher!'

'Hello, Mrs Prosser.'

'Just going up to see Mrs Edwards. I'd like to know when she's going to be moving on. Haven't heard nothing about that, see. Has she said anything to you?'

'I'm afraid not. You might ask Mrs Morgan, though.'

'Na, na. I don't like to bother her. I'll just slip round to the kitchen door and get the news from the horse's mouth, see.'

She laughed and remounted her machine.

Chapter Seventeen

'Oh, it's you.' Mrs Edwards grimaced as she waved Bessie inside. 'I suppose you want to know when I'm leaving. Soon, I hope. My daughter got herself demobbed all right, and she even has a job lined up in civvy street, but getting somewhere to live is the problem. She's found herself a room in a boarding house, but that won't do for the pair of us, not at my time of life. As I said to Mrs Morgan, if that's where I'm going to end up, I might as well stop on here. As a matter of fact I had a letter from her this morning.'

Bessie looked puzzled. 'Mrs Morgan wrote you a letter?'

'Na, na! There's stupid you are, Bessie Prosser! My daughter, see. She's the one who wrote to me. She says she's heard of a few flats going but somebody else always beats her to it. When she gets there to see about a place it's already taken. Never mind, she has a plan, she says. She's going out with this reporter chap, from the local newspaper. Sweet on her, he is, although she thinks he's not much cop. The thing is, him being on the staff, he can get a look at the paper before it comes out on the street, and he knows what's in the classified ads. That way she'll have a better chance of finding somewhere.'

Bessie grinned. 'I hope she doesn't have to give him more than she's prepared to pay!'

Mrs Edwards raised her rolling pin in a threatening manner. 'Here, I hope you're not insinuating what I think you are, Bessie Prosser! She's a good girl, my Marged, never mind what some nasty folks have to say about young women in the services.'

Bessie backed down in a hurry. 'I only meant I hoped she didn't have to slip him a few bob to hear about the places to rent, Mrs Edwards.'

'Bribes, is it! Then I hope she doesn't think about doing that, either. She's been brought up Methodist, has Marged, and she'd better keep to the straight and narrow, or she'll hear about it from me!'

Giving it up as a bad job, Bessie sat down heavily on a three-legged stool. 'I hope you'll give me a bit of notice when the time comes,' she remarked, 'so I can sort things out at home.'

'Your hubby don't mind you taking this job, then? I was sure he'd kick up a fuss, 'specially as it's living in. Or is Mrs Morgan letting you go home at night? I don't know, I'm sure. Everything's gone to pot after this old war.'

'Job can make all the fuss he likes. I'm fed up with his miserable ways. As soon as this job comes up, I'm off out of it, and he's not changing my mind.'

Mrs Edwards's jaw dropped. 'That's what you said before, but I thought it was just talk. So you've really made up your mind, then? What's brought all this on?'

'Part of it's his penny-pinching ways. He doles out a little bit of housekeeping – not enough to manage on – and when I complain he tells me I should learn to make do. Honestly, it's like that book we done at school, about that little boy who wanted more porridge in the work-house! Or was it an orphanage? I never can remember. *All of a Twist*, it was called. There's four wages coming into that house, Mrs Edwards: Job and his two oldest each bring in three pound five a week, and the next boy not as much, on account of his age. And their Myfanwy sends something home as well.'

'She never does!'

Bessie nodded. 'Oh, yes. When she left home to come to work here she started doing that so Job could pay a woman to do a bit around the house, the washing and that. You'd think that after we were married he'd tell the girl to keep it for her bottom drawer, but no! He said it was her duty to help support the family she'd left. That will tell you how mean that man is, Mrs Edwards. And then there's his constant carping. Never satisfied with anything I do.'

'That's a man for you!' Mrs Edwards had lost interest, having heard a similar tale of woe from other women of her acquaintance. 'Just let me leave this blancmange to set and I'll make us a nice cup of tea, and then I'll tell you all about the work here. There's things you'll need to know when you're doing it on your own, see. You'll be cooking for fifteen people, remember.'

'I'm cooking for eight of us now. What's a few more? The Morgans have to make do with their rations, same as the rest of us, I daresay.'

'Ah, but the trick is to get it all served up at different times and not letting the hot food dry out. There's the Morgans themselves, and Miss Mariah and Miss Meredith. Then there's them boys, coming in from school wanting their tea. There's the nursery supper, which is wanted earlier than the rest, on account of the little ones' bedtime. Last, but not least, there's us, the servants. We eat after everyone else has been waited on. Oh, yes, Mrs Prosser there's knack to catering in a big house like this!'

Far from being intimidated by this, Bessie decided that it sounded wonderful. She would not have to sit and watch while ungrateful lumps of men gobbled down their food and then complained because there were no second helpings. There would be no more struggling home with bulging shopping bags after queuing for ages at one shop after another, because the weekly order was delivered to Cwmbran House by a boy on a boneshaker bicycle, with a loaded basket in front of the handlebars. Best of all there would be Rosie Yeoman to tackle the washing-up. Needless to say the Prosser men never did a hand's turn; it was beneath their dignity as masters of the household. Bessie felt ambivalent on this last point; men who put in a hard shift down the pit should not have to come home to do household chores; that was why they had wives to look after them. Nevertheless there were times when she would give anything to put her feet up at the end of the day, instead of scrubbing a mountain of crockery.

Her resolution to say nothing to Job until she was given the green light to start work at the House collapsed that very evening. She had a request to put to her husband but she knew she had to pick her moment. The evening meal was over, and her elder stepsons had gone out, one of them to chapel and the others to some unspecified meeting with friends. The smaller boys were out in the street, where their voices mingled shrilly with those of other youngsters as they kicked a tin can to and fro. Job himself was sitting in the kitchen's one armchair, glancing over the sports page in the evening paper.

'I'd like a word, Job,' Bessie said softly, preparing to butter him up. 'Can I get you another cuppa while we talk?'

'Eh? What's that? Can't you see I'm trying to read the paper? Isn't it enough that I slave all day to support you, without you nagging me when I'm taking a few minutes to relax?'

'This won't take long, Job.'

'Oh, all right! Let's get it over with, then!' He folded his newspaper with exaggerated care.

'I happened to be in the draper's today when Miss Cooke received a delivery of women's knickers.'

Job swore softly. 'I don't want to hear about no woman's knickers, *merch*! I've just had my supper!'

'I'm in desperate need of some new ones, Job.' Bessie had two pairs – one to wash and one to wear – which she had bought before the war. 'I've mended mine so often there's more patch than anything else. I must have these. I've got enough points for a couple of pairs, and Miss Cooke doesn't know how long it might be before she can get hold of any more. I've asked her to put some aside for me, but she says if I don't take them within a week, she'll have to let them go to somebody else.'

'I don't know why you want me to hear this, Bessie.'

'Because I need the money to pay for them, that's why.'

'I give you your housekeeping, don't I? Take it out of that.'

'It's barely enough to feed the lot of us, let alone anything else.'

Her husband looked at her severely. 'You have no cause for complaint. I give you the same amount I used to give my Siwsan, and she managed on it.'

Mentally, Bessie counted to ten. His first wife had been dead for a good many years. Prices had gone up considerably since then and the war had made it more difficult to cope because rationing and shortages limited one's choice of menu.

'I would like to have a dress allowance,' she said bravely, thinking that pigs might fly. Perhaps making an extravagant demand would trick him into paying for her more modest request. He looked at her as if she'd spoken blasphemy.

'Have you forgotten you're the wife of a coal miner, Elizabeth Prosser? You're not one of them Morgans up there. You've got clothes on your back this very minute, and a good Sunday dress hanging in the wardrobe. Why, I've made the one good suit do me ever since the end of the Great War. I won't have a wife who's a spendthrift, and that's all I have to say on the subject.' He picked up his newspaper and began to read.

Bessie glared down at him. 'There's mean you are, Job Prosser!' she shrieked. 'More than ten pounds a week there is, coming into this house, and you begrudge me decent clothes on my back. Well, I'm not going to stick it no more. I'm leaving you, Job, so put that in your pipe and smoke it!'

'You'll soon come running back,' he grunted.

'No I won't then. I've got a job! Up Cwmbran House, see! What do you say to that?'

Chapter Eighteen

'I got a gold star at school today, Auntie!'

Lucas beamed at Ellen, obviously very pleased with himself.

'That's lovely, dear. What was it for, getting all your sums right?'

'No, it was for being a good boy, Miss said.'

'Can I see it?'

'No. Miss licked it and put it on the chart on the wall. It has all our names on it, and each week miss is going to give a star to all the best-behaved boys and girls. She wants to see who can get the most stars by the end of term.'

'And will that person get a prize, do you think?'

Lucas shrugged. 'Dunno.'

'Never mind. I have a choccy biscuit here for a good boy, if you'd like one.'

'Cor, yes, please!' After great deliberation he took a biscuit from the tin she held out to him, and began to nibble his prize very slowly, as if to make it last. 'Henry won't be getting one, will he?' he asked, through a mouthful of crumbs.

Ellen wondered what was coming. 'He didn't get a star, Auntie. Miss was cross with him this morning. He left the room without asking, and you're supposed to put up your hand first.'

She was aware from her own school days that saying you needed to leave the room was a polite euphemism for wanting the lavatory. It usually took beginners in the infants' class a few weeks before they cottoned on to the fact that they couldn't wander in and out of the classroom whenever they felt like it.

'That wasn't so bad, was it, Lucas? I expect he'll know what's expected next time.'

'Yes, only then he went to the washups and stayed there a long time.'

'But hasn't Myfanwy told you to wash your hands after using the lavatory? I expect that's what delayed him.'

She deplored the sanitary arrangements at the Cwmbran school, which she had heard about from the older boys, but they were lucky to have even those in the old Victorian building. The lavatories were in separate enclosures, one for girls, the other for boys, while the shed-like edifice known as the 'washups' was across the playground, equipped with several wash basins and a couple of grimy roller towels. Some rural schools had to manage with an outdoor privy and water from the pump.

'He didn't come back, and Miss had to send a monitor to look for him. Henry made the soap all soft and shoved it down the bung-hole, and then he let the tap run and the water went all over the floor.'

'So that's why he didn't get a star this week,' Ellen agreed. 'I should jolly well think not, after that piece of work!' She said no more. There was enough trouble between the two boys as it was, without her making it worse by seeming to side with Lucas. While this was another example of Henry's wayward behaviour it wasn't up to her to stir up trouble. Let the teacher and the child's mother sort out between them. After a moment, however, she asked 'I wonder what Miss Adams said to him about that?'

'She said, 'Any more of that, boyo, and I'll send you to the Meistr!'' and then she made him stand in the corner until playtime. Can I have another biscuit, please, Auntie?'

'You've had your ration for today, Lucas, you'll spoil your appetite for tea. Why don't you run along and see what Ceri is up to? He might let you play with his marbles.' Lucas ran off, happily enough, and Ellen returned the biscuit tin to the high shelf, where it was safe from marauding little boys.

Lucas found Ceri giggling with Huw in the old stables. Henry was the hero of the hour because of the mayhem he had caused at school. At playtime they had gone to the washups and found the fierce old man who worked as the school caretaker angrily mopping up.

'I hope it wasn't none of you what caused this mess,' he grumbled, squeezing out his mop into a tin pail. 'I've got enough to do without cleaning up after you young devils every day of the week!'

'Wasn't us, sir!' Huw told him.

'So you say! But somebody pushed a lot of soap down the plug-hole and now the drain really is plugged!'

'You could try shoving a bit of old wire down it,' Huw suggested, but the old man ignored that sensible suggestion.

'That won't work, son. The soap's all hard now and blocking the S-bend. I'm going to have to unscrew the pipes underneath and dig at it from there. If that don't work the plumber will have to come, and the Meistr won't like that! If you find out who played this daft trick, just you let me know, and I'll give him a piece of my mind!'

'It could be a her.'

'What's that? None of your lip, boyo! This is a boys' trick, see. Girls can cause enough trouble on their own account, but blocking plug-holes ain't one of them. Now get out of here before I wash you down the drain!' he waved his mop threateningly in their direction. They swaggered out, laughing.

The news flew around like greased lightning. The whole school knew that one of the tiddlers had done it and were impressed. Had an older child done this, and been found out, he'd have received six of the best from the headmaster, but they were all convinced that Harry Morgan's grandson was untouchable.

Listening to all the talk, Lucas was bewildered. He didn't like Henry, who frequently bullied him. The episode of the stolen conker was still very much on his mind. Good boys were praised and given gold stars; bad ones deserved to be punished. He knew that because Henry had been sent to bed after destroying the conker and now, today, Miss had made him stand in the corner, which was a terrible disgrace. Lucas knew that he wouldn't be able to bear it if such a thing happened to him.

Now the other boys all thought that Henry was a hero. Some of the pupils from Standard Three had patted him on the back as the children streamed out of the yard at the end of the school day, and he'd been offered sweets as well. What did all this mean?

When it was time for nursery tea, Myfanwy remembered that she had left her scissors in Mrs Morgan's sitting room. 'I just have to run down the hall for a minute,' she told her two charges. 'Be good now, and wash your hands while I'm gone.'

She sped off, confident that all would be well while she was away. When they were little it was a firm rule that the pair were never to be left unattended for an instant, in case some dreadful accident befell them, but they were schoolboys now and that rule had been considerably relaxed.

Lucas looked around him. Henry was deeply immersed in a copy of the *Rainbow* and showed no sign of obeying the girl. Lucas sidled into the bathroom and began to wash. The Pear's transparent soap made a fine lather as he rubbed it between his fingers. The bar was used up to the point where he was able to break it in pieces. It occurred to him that if he kept working at it he might be able to duplicate Henry's feat with the coarse soap they used at the school. Eventually he succeeded

in his task and then, leaving the tap running, he went into the day nursery, where he selected a book from the shelf and began looking at the
pictures, the picture of innocence.

'All ready for tea, boys? I can hear the dumb waiter coming. We're
having cake today, and fishpaste sandwiches. A meal fit for a king!'

They were just finishing their meal when Myfanwy remarked that
she could hear something dripping. 'Did one of you boys leave a tap
running in the bathroom?'

'Not me,' Henry replied. Lucas shook his head. It wasn't a fib if you
didn't say anything, was it?

When a shriek came from the bathroom the boys rushed to the
door where they found their nursemaid standing ankle-deep in water,
trying to turn off the taps. She snatched up the blue toothbrush which
Lucas had used to jam the pieces of soft soap into the drain.

'This is your toothbrush, Henry! Are you responsible for this?'

'No!' Henry shouted, red-faced. Had his sins somehow followed
him home?

'You, Lucas?' Lucas shook his head again.

Later that evening Ellen, having been called to the nursery to
inspect the damage, had a quiet word with Myfanwy. 'I didn't mean to
say anything, but now I feel I must. Henry was in trouble at school
today, for doing the very same thing in what the children refer to as the
washups.'

'How do you know about that?'

'Lucas let it slip, and then I overheard the other boys discussing it.
Apparently Henry had a good talking-to, and was made to stand in the
corner.'

'And I suppose he was so pleased with himself that he thought he'd
try it again at home. Well, Mrs Morgan, I can't let this go, can I? I'll
have to report it to Mrs Fletcher, but she's not going to like it.'

Lucas, hidden from view behind the door, smiled softly to himself.
He had got even with Henry the bully, and he was glad. Serve him right
if they gave him a smacking. And flooding the bathroom had been
fun. He felt quite pleased with himself.

Chapter Nineteen

Job's response was predictable. 'No wife of mine is going out to work, and that's flat!'

Bessie took a deep breath. 'I'm not just going out to work, Job, I'm leaving you.'

'Don't talk silly, *merch*!'

'It's true. Mrs Edwards is going to stay with her daughter, and I've been given her job.'

'You never have!'

She nodded. 'Miss Meredith – Mrs Fletcher, that is – she took me on. Cook to the Morgans, I'll be.'

'And I'm supposed to be kept waiting for my meals until you come tripping back at night, dog-tired, is that it?'

'You don't get it, do you, man? I'm leaving, as in going away and never coming back. It's not a day job, it's living-in. I'll have a nice room, all to myself, without listening to you snoring all night, and I'll get a proper wage.'

'I've said no, and I mean no. Now shut up and let me get on with my reading.'

'You can put your head in the sand all you like, Job Prosser, but my mind is made up. As soon as Mrs Edwards moves on, I move in. So there!'

'If you do, they'll put you on a stool in the chapel, I'll see to that!'

'What?' For a moment Bessie couldn't fathom what on earth he meant, and then it dawned on her. She remembered hearing her old granny talk about the bad old days, back in Queen Victoria's time, when sinners had to sit on a stool under the eyes of the congregation, while the minister ranted on about their disgrace. The victim was usually some poor woman or girl, who had become pregnant out of wedlock, or left her husband because of ill treatment. Real sinners, such as the occasional conman or adulterer, usually fled the district before they could be brought to book.

'They don't do that no more,' Bessie stammered.

'Then it's time they did. And even if the minister won't do anything about you, you know what you'll get from the other women!'

Bessie did. Half the women might secretly sympathize with her, wishing that they, too, could escape a difficult situation, while the rest of them would act as if God had appointed them judge, jury and jailer, all rolled into one. She decided that some conciliatory tactics might be in order.

'I won't leave you in the lurch, Job. I did go up to the House to see our Myfanwy, thinking she might come home to take my place. In fact, that's when Mrs Fletcher saw me and offered me the position as cook.'

'And no doubt Myfanwy wouldn't give you the time of day!'

'Well, she did say she was settled up there, so long as they still need her,' Bessie admitted. 'She's been there over three years now. But then there's my Gwyneth. She's not a bad little cook, and when she and Llew get married, she'll move in and look after you all.'

'My Llew married to your Gwyneth? Over my dead body, *merch*!'

'But they're engaged. He's bought her the ring!'

'Engagements can be broken. Do you think that I'll allow their wedding to go forward after that girl's mother has brought shame on me and mine? Like mother, like daughter.'

'That isn't fair!'

'I'll tell you what isn't fair, you Jezebel! I make an honest woman of you, give you my name, provide a decent home for you, and you disgrace me before the whole of Cwmbran. No need to wait until Mrs Edwards leaves. You can pack your things and go now! I won't keep you under my roof a moment longer!'

Bessie winced. 'No need to get worked up, man! Can't we discuss this sensibly?'

Throwing his paper down in a crumpled heap, Job leapt up and grabbed his cap and muffler from the hook behind the door.

'Where are you off to now?'

'Much you care, woman! If you must know, I'm going down the

allotment.' The door closed behind him and Bessie sank down on the chair he had just vacated, feeling shaken.

Now she'd done it! Too late, she realized that she'd been hoping for some sort of overture from her husband, something to make her feel loved and wanted. It didn't need to be anything grand. Her first husband had occasionally slipped her a bob or two, telling her to get herself some wine gums. Even when they were courting Job hadn't made any romantic little gestures. Not for her the traditional bunch of flowers – even wild ones – the nearest he'd come to that was a string bag full of sprouts he'd grown himself.

Why, oh why, had she ever fancied him? He was quite good-look-ing, in that rugged, Celtic sort of way, but he was no Tyrone Power. He could sing like the angels, but that was confined to the chapel choir. He hadn't come to serenade her underneath her window. The plain fact of the matter was that she'd been lonely, and Job was the only unattached man around, at least, in her age group.

It wasn't too late to change her mind, of course. She could grovel and say she didn't know what came over her, and he would probably agree to let her stay, if only because he needed a woman to keep house. But after all that had been said her life wouldn't be worth living. Better to go while the going was good.

Job did not go to his allotment. Instead, he plodded on to the edge of town and began to climb the hill leading up to the *gorsedd*. He was more shocked by what had just taken place than he would ever admit to his wife. The ingratitude of the woman! According to his lights he had indeed provided her with a good home but apparently it wasn't good enough. He thought he knew what this was all about. Bessie was at a funny age. Women started behaving irrationally when they reached the 'change of life,' whatever that meant!

At last he reached the standing stones on the top of the hill, and stood leaning on the flat one in the middle. Long ago, when he was a boy at the Cwmbran school, the teacher had brought them up here for a walk and explained that the stones had been placed there by the old druids, and that the flat one that Job was resting against now was where they performed their pagan sacrifices.

That had been a romantic tale, designed to gladden the hearts of bloodthirsty small boys. Job had since learned that the stone circle was of modern origin, put there in the past century by men who had nothing better to do than to commemorate their ancient heritage. His lip curled at the thought. How many horses must have struggled and strained to cart all those tons of stone up the mountainside? And what would such an operation have cost, while miners like himself slaved away for a pittance?

Most likely those Morgans were behind it, Harry Morgan's grandfather, perhaps, or even his great-grandfather. More money than sense! Living off the backs of the miners, that's how some of his workmates had described the family which was the nearest Cwmbran came to the aristocracy. Ought to have been drowned at birth, the lot of them. And now the Morgans were trying to lure his wife away from him. Harry had already stolen Ellen Richards from under his nose. The man must not be allowed to take Bessie as well. He would prevent that, or die in the attempt.

By the time he reached the outskirts of the town he felt better. The steep climb to the *gorsedd* had exhausted him in body and mind, and with that release of tension came a certain amount of peace. Bessie could go, and good riddance to bad rubbish! He had no fear that his workmates and neighbours would scorn him or poke fun; he was the innocent party in all this.

He must tread warily when it came to dealing with the Morgans, though; his whole family depended on the colliery for their livelihood. Deprived of their several pay packets, as well as the terraced house they lived in, they would have to leave the district in order to find work elsewhere, and that might be hard to do. Job kept up with the news and was well aware of all the unemployment there was now, with men coming home from the war.

'*Nos da,* Job!'

He came to with a start, surprised to find himself addressed by the minister. He hadn't even been aware of the man's approach.

'*Nos da!*' he called in return, hurrying past. Better not let the man know what was in his mind. The minister would urge him to turn the other cheek, and that was not what was called for in this case. Better to fetch Bessie a clip round the ear to bring her to her senses!

'Hello, Dada! Been out for a walk, have you?'

Rounding the corner at the end of their street he had come face to face with his boy, Llew, with that Gwyneth Harries hanging on to his arm.

'Na, I've been driving my Bentley!' he retorted, and swept by, with Gwyneth's laughter ringing in his ears. Stupid girl! That reminded him, he had to have a serious talk with Llew before matters went too far. If Bessie was leaving home, her daughter was definitely not coming into the house in her place!

Chapter Twenty

That first Christmas in peacetime was celebrated in a relaxed atmosphere, and Ellen had made up her mind to enjoy it. While the new year might bring the changes she feared, she meant to put her worries in the back of her mind, if only for the sake of the others in the household.

Henry Fletcher, at five years of age, still believed in Father Christmas, a fact which caused him to behave like an angel, both at home and at school. He expected to receive his presents via one of the several chimneys which Cwmbran House boasted, and as for Cwmbran Infants, that was where lessons had given way to many exciting projects, from which he had no wish to be excluded. The children were making paper chains, cutting out Christmas cards and learning to recite the Christmas story by heart, as it appeared in the Bible. On the last day of term there was to be a performance of this same story by the pupils of Standard Five, accompanied by carols performed by the whole school. After that the children were to return to their own classrooms, where they would indulge in a feast while sitting at their own desks.

All that was old hat for the remnants of the Swansea Six, but they had their own ideas as to how they wanted to celebrate the season. Dafydd came to Ellen with what seemed a reasonable enough request, and she was sorry when she had to squelch it.

'But what's wrong with going carol singing?' he asked, looking so downcast that she wanted to hug him. 'Everybody does it.'

'Nothing wrong with it at all – for most children. It's only that I can't let you go singing from door-to-door and have people giving you pennies, not when they know you're our boys. It wouldn't be right.'

He plainly could not follow her reasoning.

'Mr Morgan is a wealthy man, Dafydd. Most of the people you'd be singing to are employed by him.'

'You mean, he's their boss?'

'That's right. It might look as though he was sending you down in the town to take their money back off them.'

As soon as the words were out of her mouth, Ellen realized how silly she sounded. Of all the lame excuses! It wasn't all that far-fetched, though. Ever since Bessie Prosser had left her husband to come to work at Cwmbran House there had been rumblings of discontent in the town. On several occasions when she had gone into the shops in search of Christmas gifts all conversation had stopped when she came through the door, and one or two women had turned their backs on her pointedly. How would those same women react if confronted by a party of carol singers from the Morgan place?

'You can sing for us, if you like,' she told Dafydd. 'Turn up at the front door when we least expect it, and perform for us. When you've finished we'll let you in and serve you mince pies and cocoa. Will that do?'

'Yes,' the boy answered, hanging his head.

'I did feel awful turning the child down, but I felt I had to nip that in the bud,' Ellen told Mariah later. 'Don't you think it would be asking for trouble if I let them do it?'

'Who knows? I see your point, Mam, but I have an idea. Dr Barnardo's!'

'I don't know what you mean.' Like many people, Harry Morgan kept a collection box on his desk, the contents of which were meant to benefit the Dr Barnardo's homes for orphaned and needy children. Fashioned out of prettily painted papier mâché, the boxes were made in the shape of little houses. Ellen couldn't for the life of her imagine what they had to do with carol singing.

'Wait there a minute and I'll show you.' Mariah sped off, returning a moment later with a brightly coloured sheet of paper. 'Luci gave me this. They'll be giving them out at the school for the children to display at home.' The sheet showed a Christmas tree, laden with gaily wrapped presents.

'What is it?'

'It's an extra effort in aid of Dr Barnardo's. You ask people to donate something, and they write their names on the gift with the amount donated. Mariah Mortimer, sixpence, that sort of thing. Why not let the boys take one of these with them, Mam? People will feel virtuous because they're giving to charity and nobody can say that the cash is going to line Harry's pockets.'

'That's a wonderful idea, Mariah, and it will add poignancy when people realize that they've opened their doors to local orphans who are singing on behalf of other orphans! Yes, I think that will work out very well. I'll mention it to the boys, and tell them to make sure they pick up one or two of these sheets to bring home.'

Bessie Prosser, now installed in the kitchens of Cwmbran House, was looking forward to cooking up a real dinner on Christmas Day, no expense spared. She had already done some baking, as far as rations allowed, and had hidden these items away in cake tins, tightly sealed.

'I was thinking of sending some of this lot down to the house,' she told Myfanwy. 'What do you think? The boys would enjoy them.'

'I'm sure they would, that's if they ever got a sniff of them.'

'I don't know what you mean!'

'Don't you? If Dada found out where these cakes had come from, they'd go straight into the pig bucket. I'd forget it, if I were you. No point in wasting good food.'

'I suppose not,' Bessie agreed sadly.

Henry, Lucas and Ceri prepared letters to Father Christmas, with Ellen's help. Lucas became tearful when Ceri remarked that if you showed your list to anyone, or told them what you wanted for Christmas, you wouldn't get the presents you hoped for.

'That's only for big boys,' Ellen said tactfully. 'Father Christmas knows that little people, who haven't learned to read and write yet, may need a bit of help. You whisper in my ear, Lucas, and then I'll tell you the letters to print.' After a struggle he managed to compile a respectable list, and then it was time to send their letters up the chimney.

'If it doesn't go up, Father Christmas won't get it!' Ceri warned. Ellen gave him one of her famous looks. Fortunately nobody noticed that she opened the door to create a draught, and all three letters sailed up the chimney with no problem.

Mysterious parcels began to arrive in the post. Some of these were items that the Morgans had ordered from the big stores in Cardiff; while the Cwmbran shopkeepers had done their best their stock was limited. One package came from Verona Fletcher, who had knitted a jersey for each of her grandsons, one in red and the other in blue. During the summer she had prudently written to Ellen, asking for the boys' measurements, so with any luck the garments would do them for a couple of years.

It was the parcel addressed in Henrietta Meredith's copperplate handwriting that caused some consternation. Meredith had taken off the brown paper – carefully smoothed out and saved for another time – and found a large, soft package inside, done up in holly-patterned wrapping.

'Gran hasn't put a label on this,' she remarked to Ellen.

'I'm sure it must be meant for either you, or Henry,' Ellen replied, too absorbed in what she was doing to pay much attention.

'Yes, but which of us? If I put it at the foot of his bed on Christmas morning, and he opens it up to find a shawl or a nightie, or something, he'll be disappointed.'

'Oh, give it to me! I'll open it very carefully and see what's inside, and then we'll tape it up again, and no harm done!'

Both women looked puzzled when the contents were revealed. Ellen held up a red velvet dress with a white lace collar. It was a pretty garment, the sort of thing an eight-year-old might wear to a winter party.

'She can't have meant this for Henry,' Meredith murmured.

'Obviously not, and I doubt it will fit you, either!'

Meredith made no response to Ellen's little joke. 'I don't understand. It must be a mistake.'

'Of course it is, but it's no great mystery. She's got her presents mixed up, that's all, put the wrong addresses on them. Some little girl has probably received a toy car meant for Henry.'

'But Henrietta only has one grandchild.'

'She probably has a godchild or two. That's what it will be.'

After fussing for a few moments, Meredith wrote a polite little note of explanation to include with the frock, and parcelled it up again, ready to return it to Hereford.

'I hope that Grandmamma won't take umbrage, though. You know what she's like.'

'Do stop worrying, Meredith. If she's got any sense at all she'll be grateful. There's nobody here who can wear it, and it would be a crime to let it go to waste, especially when she's had to part with some of her on clothing coupons to buy it. Why don't you run down to the post office now, and send it on its way? With any luck it will reach the rightful owner in time for Christmas. And while you're there, will you pick up some stamps for me, please? Our Christmas card list seems to be getting longer every year, and I really ought to get some in the post soon.' Ellen had too much to do to worry about one misdirected parcel, but Meredith was pensive as she went to put on her coat.

Chapter Twenty-one

Rosie Yeoman had decided to stay on at Cwmbran House, rather than striking out on her own, and Ellen had accepted this change of heart with no more than an absentminded, 'That's good, then.' Although part of Rosie's decision was based on a 'better the devil you know' way of thinking, she also wanted to be around to see what became of the Prosser business.

In any case the Morgan household was an interesting place to work, made lively by all the little chaps who lived there. Rosie had no brothers of her own and she regarded boys as an alien species, one she would have to learn to understand if she was ever to snare a man of her own.

As a result she had written to her cousin Wyn, a slightly older girl, who was in service at Chepstow with a retired dentist and his ailing wife. Wyn wrote back at once to say that she'd like a change, and Ellen, who was worrying over how to replace Ruth when she left in the new year, was willing to give the girl a trial, sight unseen. Rosie was careful to explain that she herself would be *head* house parlourmaid and Wyn her junior and, that being understood, Wyn packed her few belongings and headed for Carmarthenshire.

Accordingly, Rosie turned up at the station to meet the newcomer, who stepped off the train muttering about the length of time it had taken the local to come from Cardiff, where she'd had to change.

'Talk about a slow boat to China! And not even a dining-car to get a cup of tea! If I'd known about that I wouldn't have come!'

'Never mind, we'll soon be home, and they'll give you a cuppa there.' Rosie was well used to the other girl's extravagant way of talking and knew she could safely ignore it. Once you encouraged that sort of talk there was no stopping Wyn Matthews. She could be a bit spiteful at times, could their Wyn.

A slight drizzle was coming down as they emerged from the station, and Rosie adjusted her head square to protect her Christmas hair-do. 'Just a bit of Welsh mist,' she remarked cheerfully, as they set off together on foot.

Used to working in a compact Victorian villa, Wyn was over-whelmed when Cwmbran House first came in sight.

'This is it? This great barracks of a place? Don't tell me there's just you and me to keep the whole bally lot clean? If you tell me that I may as well turn round and head back right this minute!'

'There will be just the two of us, when Ruth goes,' Rosie admitted, 'but it won't be as bad as you think. A lot of the rooms is shut up ever since the war started, and Mrs Morgan and Mrs Mortimer – that's her daughter – they do quite a bit as well.'

Wyn sniffed. 'Funny, that, the ladies of the house turning to and getting their hands dirty! Not my idea of gentry, not by a long shot!'

'P'raps they won't have to, much longer. Madam says she'll see about getting a couple of daily women in the new year. Anyway, here we are! I'll take you up and see you settled, and then I'll let Mrs Prosser know you've come. Never off the hob, her kettle isn't, so you'll soon be drinking that tea you've been looking forward to.'

Later, in the kitchen, Bessie and Wyn took a long look at each other and then, finding nothing to complain of, Bessie told the girl to sit down.

'A long distance to come, all the way from Chepstow,' she remarked. 'Never been further than Carmarthen, me. They speak Welsh there, do they?'

'English, mostly, leastways the Grants and their friends. That's who I worked for, see, Mr Grant and his wife.'

'Oh, aye? A big place, was it, a lot of staff?'

'Only me and Agnes. Cook-general, she is. I was glad to get away from her, always mumbling on about how hard it was in the old days, when she first went into service as a girl of twelve, back when old Queen Victoria was alive. A shilling a week she was paid as a mother's helper, and glad to get it, and plenty willing to take her place if she didn't want to stay. I suppose it was true; she said it often enough.'

Wyn looked appraisingly at Bessie. 'You've just started here an' all,

Rosie tells me. Do you think you'll like it?'

'I expect so. Of course, I'm no stranger to this place. Our Myfanwy, that's my stepdaughter, she works upstairs. Nursemaid to Master Henry.'

'Who's he when he's at home?'

'Mr Morgan's grandson.'

'Do his parents live here too?'

'His father was killed at Dunkirk, but Mrs Fletcher is here.'

'And what about your hubby, then? Is he the butler, or something?'

Rosie had outlined the situation to her cousin, but Wyn wanted to get the story from the horse's mouth. Bessie's cheeks turned pink.

'He works down the pit, but I've left him.'

'Never! Knock you about, did he?'

'I don't care to discuss my private affairs, thank you very much!' Bessie's tone was harsh.

'No offence meant, I'm sure!'

'And there hasn't been a butler here for a couple of years,' Rosie put in. 'The last one got pensioned off. Mr Morgan said they had to cut back while the war was on.' Ruth had told her that, since Rosie had hardly been in a position to overhear their employer making any such pronouncements, her activities being confined to the household's more menial tasks.

'Huh! Who needs butlers?' Bessie demanded. 'This is nineteen-forty-five, not the dark ages. It's a kitchen maid I need! I don't mind doing my own vegetables, mind. It's a good washer-upper I need! To give her credit, Mrs Morgan has tried to find one, but girls nowadays don't want to go into service. I said to her, I don't know how I'm going to manage over Christmas, madam, I don't really. All the extra crockery and saucepans there will be, and me standing at that old sink all night long, scrubbing away. "You leave it to me, Mrs Prosser," she says, "and I'll see what I can do".'

'She's never going to roll up her sleeves herself!' Rosie gasped.

'There's stupid you are, Rosie Yeoman! Na, na, she's going to let the Swansea Six do it all. They older ones are willing, and it will give them the chance to earn some money, she says.'

'What's a Swansea Six, then?' Wyn wondered.

'Them orphans upstairs. Evacuees. Madness, that is, letting boys do the washing-up, especially with good quality dishes like they have here. There'll be a few breakages before we're all very much older, you mark my words. Still, I'll say nothing! So long as I don't have to do it all, I'll keep my mouth shut.'

'This place sounds more like a zoo than a stately home,' Wyn grumbled, as she and Rosie made their way upstairs. 'Not enough servants to do the work, and little boys being made to do the chores. I'm beginning to wish I'd never come. The Grants were a pain in the neck to work for, but at least you knew where you were with them. I've a good mind to turn round and go straight back where I come from!'

'I never said it was stately home,' Rosie muttered, 'and the Morgans are good people. It's not their fault the war upset everything. Lovely here it was before that, so Ruth told me. She was here when Mr Morgan's first wife was alive. A bit of an invalid she was, with a companion and a lady's maid to wait on her. And Mr Morgan kept horses, and a smart car, and when they went travelling he had a private coach hooked up to the train.'

'Bit of a comedown now, then. Sounds like the coach turned back into a pumpkin!'

'What is the new girl like, Ellen? Do you think she'll be satisfactory?' Harry Morgan was not normally interested in the workings of the household, but he knew that his wife had been worried about how they were going to manage, and he felt that some comment was called for.

'It's hard to say. I've only seen her for five minutes. I got the impression that she's a bit too full of herself, but time will tell.'

'If it doesn't work out, send her packing and bring in somebody else. No need to put up with impertinence, if that's what it boils down to.'

Dear Harry, Ellen thought, bestowing an affectionate glance on her husband of three years. When it came to household matters his mind was still firmly stuck in the pre-war era, and by that she meant the

Great War, not the one they'd just come through! She was amazed that he'd given in without a struggle when she'd told him that the boys had volunteered to tackle the washing-up!

'Won't people think we're exploiting the poor little chaps?' she wondered, but he'd pooh-poohed this suggestion.

'Not when you're paying them.'

'Bribing them, more like.'

'It's good for boys to take on some responsibility, and they'll enjoy having some ready cash. You worry too much, *cariad*. Learn to take life more as it comes.'

Chapter Twenty-two

The celebration of Christmas had to be orchestrated carefully at Cwmbran House. The older members of the family planned to go to the midnight service at All Saints' Church, and this year some of the Swansea Six would be allowed to go with them. Ceri Davies was in a whirl of delight at the thought of going out in the middle of the night and not coming back home until two o'clock in the morning! Ellen gave him permission to go on condition that he and Huw went to bed at the usual hour for an extended nap.

'But what if I don't wake up in time?' he wailed.

'One of us will wake you up, never fear, but if you start any nonsense, I shall change my mind. No pillow fights or creeping down the hall to see what's going on downstairs, do you understand?'

The child nodded, bright-eyed. Henry and Lucas were to stay home with Myfanwy in charge. 'We'll lock up when we leave,' Ellen explained, so you need have no fear of being alone. In any case, Bessie and the girls will be in the house.'

This met with Myfanwy's approval because she would not have

crossed the doorstep of All Saints in any case. Staunchly chapel in her beliefs, she was pleased to be given Christmas Day off so she could attend the morning service there, and spend the day with her father and brothers. Rosie and Wyn would also be attending chapel, with Wyn looking forward to an introduction to Myfanwy's brothers.

Bessie, meanwhile, had turned down Ellen's offer to arrange the times of their meals so that she, too, could attend the Christmas service; it would have taken a woman with a much thicker skin than Bessie possessed to walk into the chapel with dozens of pairs of censorious eyes on her.

It must be admitted that she had been indulging in a foolish fantasy of late. Job would turn up on Christmas Eve – or perhaps on Christmas morning – carrying a small, prettily wrapped gift in his hand which he would present to her with downcast eyes. He would mumble something about being sorry for his past neglect of her, and then he would beg her to come home. After a moment's hesitation she would respond favourably to his plea and all would be forgiven.

Sometimes there would be a variation on this tale. Job would say his piece and then she would turn him down with as much hauteur as she could muster. You should have thought of that before, she would snap, as she showed him the door.

'There's stupid you are, Bessie Prosser!' she'd tell herself in her more rational moments. 'Job Prosser, admitting he's in the wrong? Pigs might fly!'

The evening of 23 December was the date chosen by the Swansea Six – or Five, as they now were – to descend on the town to do their singing. Ellen made sure that the carols chosen were suitable, not too many, nor too few. For if they didn't give value for money, she warned them, people would be annoyed and not inclined to open the door.

'Who is doing the last bit?' she wanted to know. The boys pointed at Ceri.

'Let's hear you then, boyo.'

Her heart went out to him as he stood in front of her, feet apart, hands clasped behind his back. In his clear little voice he piped:

Christmas is coming, the goose is getting fat,
Please put a penny in the old man's hat.
If you haven't got a penny, a piece of cake will do,
If you haven't got a piece of cake, then God bless you!

'Very nice,' she told him, wiping away a tear. The dear little chap deserved parents and a good home, yet he would have neither when the evacuees were taken away from Cwmbran. It just wasn't right.

Meanwhile, nothing could spoil Myfanwy's pleasure in the Christmas celebrations to come. She was looking forward to settling down beside the fire in the day nursery, listening to the wireless while dipping into her bag of sweets. On her last day off she had managed to buy a quarter of chocolate toffees, her favourite, and she had taken good care not to leave them lying about where the boys could find them. There should be something good on the wireless, it being Christmas Eve; carols perhaps, or a comedy. No more terrible news from the war, thank the good Lord.

For once, her two charges would go willingly to bed, knowing that the earlier they fell asleep the sooner Father Christmas would come. Usually she had a bit of trouble with them. Henry was inclined to keep popping out of bed, while Lucas called for a drink of water until she was tired of explaining that if had one, he would wet the bed. She wished she had the knack known to old-time nannies, whose firm insistence that their children behave was always listened to, or so she'd been led to believe by Mrs Fletcher's *mamgu*. But there, why scold herself for failing, when it would have taken an angel to make young Henry toe the line, first time of asking!

Harry Morgan had problems of his own. At almost seventy years of age he had been forced to realize that his eyesight wasn't quite as good as it had been, especially since he'd suffered a slight stroke which had robbed him of partial sight in the right eye. His doctor had urged him to invest in a pair of spectacles and Harry had stoutly denied the necessity for these. Now he found himself peering closely at his news-

103

paper, which annoyed him no end.

'The vicar wants me to read one of the lessons tonight,' he complained to his wife, 'but I don't think I can manage it.'

'Why ever not?'

'You know why not! What are people going to say when they see me squinting down at the Bible? It's not as if I can lift that great heavy thing closer to my face. They'll nudge each other and whisper that poor old Harry Morgan is getting past it.'

'What rot!'

'It's nothing of the sort!'

'Then take a magnifying glass in your pocket.'

'It's not funny, Ellen!'

'I never said it was, but how long have you been doing this at Christmas time?'

'I don't know; close to fifty years, I suppose.'

Ellen laughed. 'There you are, then! You must know the passages by heart now. I do myself, actually. "Now there were in the same country shepherds abiding in the fields, keeping watch over their flocks by night." You see? All you have to do is stand up there, looking as handsome as usual, and repeat the words we all know so well. Problem solved!'

He grinned at his wife, suddenly looking ten years younger. He had done well to marry her, he told himself, after all those years as a solitary widower. Ellen would be a comfort to him in his old age, no doubt about that.

The lady in question went off to supervise the opening of the old drawing-room. It was seldom used nowadays, except on special occasions when the whole family gathered together. In good weather the windows were left open, to give the place a good airing, and in winter a fire was left on occasionally, to rid the place of damp.

'This is a huge room,' Wyn marvelled, as she helped Rosie to remove the dust sheets from the sofas and armchairs. 'A whole family could live in a place this size, especially now, with all them people bombed out up London.'

'Swansea, too, where our evacuees were from,' Rosie reminded her.

'What do they usually give you for Christmas, them Morgans?' Wyn asked, as she folded a sheet into squares, ready for taking away.

'A nice tip, usually. Why? Are you expecting something? You haven't been here two minutes.'

'Just wondering, see. Mrs Grant used to give us each a new apron. That's not what I call Christmassy.'

'Better than a kick in the head,' Rosie quipped. 'Anyway, they supply our uniforms here, so there won't be no apron for me.'

Soon after dusk had settled in the older boys went off to sing at the houses they hadn't had time to reach the evening before. The women of Cwmbran House were going about their various preparations when a spirited version of 'Hark, the Herald Angels Sing' was begun outside the front door.

'I say, that chap has a good voice,' Ellen remarked, leaning over the banisters. 'The chapel must have some new blood. I wonder why he's singing a solo, though? Usually the men come in a group.'

Mariah seemed to be listening intently, and all of a sudden she gave a glad cry, and flew down the stairs to wrench open the door.

'Let them finish their performance before you invite them in,' Ellen called, but she was too late.

'Aubrey! Oh, Aubrey! Why didn't you let me know you were coming?'

'I wanted it to be a nice surprise,' he told her, but the words were lost as she flung herself into his arms, sobbing as if her heart would break. Ellen tiptoed away to her husband's study.

'Aubrey's here,' she remarked. 'Now Mariah will have a happy Christmas after all. I don't know yet, but I hope he's been demobbed at last.'

Chapter Twenty-three

1946

'I simply must do something about finding a job,' Aubrey said. 'I can't just laze around here living on someone else's charity.'

'Charity, my foot!' Ellen told him. 'You're our daughter's husband and very welcome to stay as long as you wish. Besides, after all you've been through, you deserve to relax for a while.'

'I couldn't agree with you more,' Aubrey grinned, 'but I must get on with it. With so many men coming out of the services and looking for work, good jobs will be at a premium. I can't sit here and let others beat me to it.'

'Don't listen to him, Mam!' Mariah put in. 'He's not as hopeless as he makes out. He's already sent off dozens of letters of application and he should be hearing from some of those employers soon.'

'What sort of posts are you applying for, then?'

'Everything and anything, Ellen. Teaching jobs, clerical posts. As I see it, I should take almost anything to help me get a foot in the door. I can get choosy later, when I've got a bit of money behind me. When *we've* got money behind us,' he amended, smiling at his wife.

'But what would you really like to do? I mean, you were at university before the war, so you must have had something in mind?'

'My degree is in modern languages, as you know. I suppose I had some vague idea about the diplomatic service or even schoolteaching, but unfortunately German isn't high on anyone's list right now. It might even work against me in some way.'

'What on earth do you mean?'

'Let's say I took up a post in a school. I could of course teach French – I'm qualified in that – but what if word got out that I speak German as well? The parents might kick up a fuss, possibly even put it out that I have German ancestry or connections. The war is only just over and feelings are still running high in some quarters. I'm not so sure I wouldn't agree with them, after spending so many years in the RAF, fighting against those chaps.'

'You've always said you'd like to go in for farming,' Mariah reminded him.

'True, but I've no experience in that line of work, and certainly no capital to speak of. Unless you'd like me to work as a farm labourer, which wouldn't bring in much of a wage, I'm afraid that's a non-starter.'

'Oh, well, let's not talk about it any more tonight,' Ellen decided. 'You're sure to hear something soon from those places you've applied to, so there's no point in worrying yourself silly until you do.'

This made good sense, Mariah thought, but as the days went by and she watched her husband becoming more and more despondent she began to worry too.

'Anything in the post?' she asked one morning, seeing him with a bundle of envelopes which he had torn open in his haste to see what they contained.

'Nothing along the lines of what I'm hoping for, old girl. Listen to this. "Regret to inform you ... position already awarded to another candidate ... nothing to offer you at this time, but we will keep your particulars on file". I've sent off forty-seven applications to date, and so far I haven't even been summoned for interview! Is this all a grateful country has to offer me after I've put my life on hold for years?'

'Something is bound to turn up soon, Aubrey.'

'Is it? I wish I shared your optimism, Mariah!' Throwing the sheaf of paper down on the table he banged out of the room, not bothering to say where he was going.

'I can't think what to do, Mam!' Mariah said later. 'He's so discouraged. I ought to be helping him through this, but nothing I can say is of any help at all!'

'The two of you just have to be patient, *cariad*. These things don't happen overnight. And I don't understand why you're so worried. You can stay here as long as you like, and as far as I'm concerned, the longer the better! Tell me truthfully, you don't really want to leave Cwmbran, do you?'

Mariah scratched her chin slowly. 'In one way, of course I don't. I've never known any other home. But I'm married to Aubrey now and I've been looking forward so much to setting up a home with him, and having a family.'

'I know, *cariad*, and that will happen one of these days, I promise. No sign of anything happening on that front yet, I suppose?'

'No, Mam, and I've been so disappointed about that. It's probably a result of the stress of knowing Aubrey has been in such danger all along, but that's all over now. In a way, it may be just as well that we don't have a baby coming. If that was the case Aubrey would be even more upset, knowing he had someone else to support.'

Ellen patted her daughter on the hand. 'It will all come right in the end, you'll see. And as for children, you've plenty of time for that.' But despite her brave words, she was as worried as Mariah seemed to be. As time went on, with no luck on the job front, Aubrey began to talk about being a burden, and not wanting to live off his in-laws.

'Just because your father is a wealthy man it doesn't mean that it's fair or right for us to leech off him,' he explained to Mariah one evening, when they were tucked up in their double bed. 'I was thinking that perhaps we should go down to Kent, and move in with Mother. She has a spare room, and I know she'd welcome us there. The advantage would be that I could get up to London quite easily and do the rounds of the businesses and government offices there. I'd have a better chance of finding something.'

Mariah sat bolt upright in bed. 'I do wish you'd be consistent, Aubrey. You moan about living off Harry but you're quite prepared for us to batten on your mother!'

'I've explained that, Mariah! We'll be close to London. . . .'

'But you haven't asked me how I'd feel about living there! I'm a country girl, born and bred, and from what I've seen on the newsreels at the cinema the place has practically been reduced to rubble. How do you expect me to adjust to that?'

'I expect you to follow wherever I lead,' he countered. 'If I remember rightly you promised to love, honour and obey!'

Mariah rolled over with a thump, and after a moment Aubrey followed suit, facing in the opposite direction. The room was quiet but the air seemed to be full of tension. Down the hall, Ellen stirred uneasily in the bedroom she shared with her husband.

'Raised voices!' she exclaimed in a stage whisper.

'I know. I heard.'

'You know what it's all about, don't you? The poor boy can't find a job, and he's too proud to live off his wife's family.'

'So I should hope.'

'What? Whose side are you on, anyway? What a thing to say about my daughter's husband!'

'No, no, *cariad*. All I meant was that I respect the chap for feeling that way. I'd feel the same if I were in his position.'

'I suppose you would, but that doesn't help Aubrey. Can't you do something for him, Harry?'

'Such as?'

'You have friends in high places. Couldn't you pull strings somewhere? It doesn't have to be a very grand job, not to start with. Something to give him a leg-up, that's all I'm asking.'

'If you promise to stop talking and let me get to sleep, I'll see what I can do in the morning.'

'I love you!' Ellen cried, giving him a resounding kiss on the cheek.

The following morning Harry invited Aubrey to join him in his study. 'There's something I'd like to explain to you, my boy,' he began. Wondering what was coming next, Aubrey crossed his ankles and waited.

'I imagine you know that the Cwmbran estates have been in the Morgan family for generations.'

'Mariah has told me something about that, sir.'

'This house and the estate, not including the colliery, are entailed, which means of course that after I die they must be passed on in the male line. I have no sons, so my heir was your friend Chad Fletcher, a distant cousin of mine. Chad died, of course, so young Henry, his son

109

and my grandson, will inherit in due course.'

'Ah,' Aubrey thought. 'I see where this is going. He wants to let me know that Mariah can't expect anything much in the way of an inheritance when he passes on. Well, he needn't have bothered. I already knew all that. I fell in love with Mariah, not her expectations.'

Although Mariah was in fact Harry's first child and elder daughter she'd been born out of wedlock and that fact effectively put her out of the running when it came to inheriting anything automatically. If Harry chose to leave her anything out of his private income that was a different matter. Aubrey was aware that Harry had stopped speaking and was regarding him with a quizzical look in his eye. The older man leaned forward in his seat and cleared his throat noisily.

'So to cut a long story short, Aubrey, I have a proposition to put to you.'

Chapter Twenty-four

Mariah was stripping the beds, preparing to send the sheets to the Daffodil Laundry when Aubrey came looking for her.

'Can you stop that for a minute? I want to talk to you.'

'Why, what's up?'

'If you pay attention to me, I'll tell you.'

With a faint sigh of exasperation she perched on the end of their bed, removing the case from her pillow as she did so.

'Harry has just offered me the job of estate manager,' he began. 'Apparently Chad had that role until he was killed, and he's never actually been replaced.'

'I know that, Aubrey. In the beginning Harry didn't want to hire a replacement because he thought it would distress Meredith, and then later it was impossible to find anyone with the right qualifications because of the war. He's been carrying on himself, with the help of the under-manager.'

It suddenly dawned on Mariah what this offer meant to the pair of them. 'Aubrey! That's wonderful! Absolutely wonderful! This solves all our problems, doesn't it! Oh, I must go and let Mam know. She'll be so pleased!'

'Do sit down, old girl! I'm not sure I should accept this post, you know.'

Her face fell. 'Why ever not?'

'Because I don't want charity, Mariah. I want to get a job on my own merits. I wouldn't have been offered this job if I hadn't been married to you.'

'That's rot! Ever since Harry had that stroke he's been wanting to slow down a bit. I'm sure he's been planning to hire someone to fill the gap.'

'And what's worse,' Aubrey went on, 'I'm a stranger here. An Englishman. People aren't going to like it if I'm parachuted into the job just because of my family connections. You know what they'll say – jobs for the boys!'

'Come on, Aubrey. This is hardly the Mafia! Chad was in the same boat as you; an English chap who married the daughter of the house!'

'It was hardly the same. He was all set to inherit the place in his own right.'

Mariah could tell that it was useless to argue. 'Please, Aubrey, will you wait a day or two before making a final decision? Do it for me?' She kissed him lightly on the cheek and he returned the compliment with a quick hug.

'All right, I'll sleep on it, but don't expect me to change my mind.'

Mariah dashed off to find her mother, desperate to hear what she had to say about all this. Ellen took one look at her daughter's face and knew what had taken place.

'I gather he's told you, then.'

'You already knew about it, Mam? You should have said something. Then I'd have been prepared!'

'Of course I knew; Harry is my husband. We don't keep things from each other. And he did mention that Aubrey didn't seem too keen to accept.'

'But surely he won't accept a refusal, if that's what it comes down to?'

Ellen shrugged. 'It has to be Aubrey's decision, Mariah. He can't be forced into it.'

Mariah clenched her fists. 'It would be perfect, Mam! We could stay here and everything could go on as before. The last thing I want is to move up to London. Can't you talk to him? He might listen to you.'

Ellen looked doubtful. 'I suppose I could have a go, but I don't know what I can say that you haven't brought up already.'

'Will you do it now, Mam? Please?'

Ellen glared at her daughter, but nevertheless she went in search of her son-in-law. She found him in the greenhouse, moodily dragging dead tomato plants free of their moorings.

'I suppose Mariah sent you! Well, say what you have to, and let's get it over with, shall we?'

'I say, Aubrey, that's a bit strong, isn't it?'

'Sorry, Ellen. I didn't mean to be so rude.'

'I know, dear. You're just worried and upset. As a matter of fact, I am, too.'

'Again, I can only say I'm sorry. Naturally you want to keep Mariah here as long as possible.'

'Oh, no, Aubrey; you're quite wrong there. I won't deny that I'd be glad if Mariah could continue to live not far away from us all, but I've always known, and accepted the fact, that when she married she'd have to leave. No, it's my husband I'm worried about.'

'What's up with Harry? Isn't he well?'

'Oh, he's as well as can be expected, but the doctors want him to slow down a bit. That means handing over the reins of the estate to someone younger. We haven't been married very long, Aubrey dear, and I've no wish to be widowed so soon. Surely you can see that?'

She waited to see how he would react to this piece of blatant emotional blackmail, and when he failed to respond she took up the thread again. 'He'll have to hire a new estate manager, Aubrey, whether it's you or somebody else. To my way of thinking, that person may as well be you, with the added advantage that it will keep the money in the family!'

'I suppose so,' he said slowly, 'but won't Meredith mind?'

'Meredith? Why on earth should she mind?'

'I don't know. It's just a feeling I have. She may be upset because I'm taking Chad's place.'

'You can hardly do that, my dear. Chad was to have inherited Harry's estate in due course; you'll merely be a paid administrator, even if you stay on until Henry comes of age. If anything, she'll be grateful that his inheritance is being safeguarded in a proper manner.'

For every objection that Aubrey was able to put forward, Ellen was able to counter it with a sensible rejoinder. By the time he had run out of steam, promising to give the matter his careful consideration, she was exhausted.

'Honestly, I feel as if I've just run a marathon!' she moaned to her husband, who shrugged helplessly.

'I'm beginning to think he doesn't really want to stay here after all. Is he just giving lip-service to our proposal because he doesn't want to upset Mariah? I made him the offer in good faith and I assumed that he'd accept it in the same spirit.'

'If that's his game he's going the right way about it – upsetting the girl, I mean. She's torn both ways, Harry! She wants to support him as a good wife should, but if there's a chance of persuading him to stay in Cwmbran she'll be all for it.'

Feeling wretched, Aubrey phoned his mother's next-door neighbour that evening. She was the district nurse who had to have a telephone for professional reasons, while Mrs Mortimer, like most people in the avenue where she lived, was not on the phone.

'Of course I'll go and fetch your mum,' Nurse Rivers agreed cheerfully. 'Call back in um – what shall we say, ten minutes? – and I'll have her waiting to speak to you.'

Nurse Rivers's phone was picked up after the first ring and, as he knew she would say, his mother's first words after he'd identified himself were 'is something wrong?' She belonged to the generation of

113

those who made trunk calls only when there was bad news to impart. The fact that the country had just come through six years of war had done nothing to reassure her otherwise.

'Everything is fine, Mum,' he told her, when he could manage to get a word in after assuring her that he was well, his wife was well, and all their assorted relations were also alive and kicking.

'Then why are you. . . .'

'I just wanted a word, Mum.'

'What about, dear? You've had a job offer, is that it? You're not going back to that horrid Germany, I hope!'

'It's right here in Cwmbran,' he told her, going on to explain his dilemma.

'Don't be silly, Aubrey. Of course you must take it!'

'But don't you think I'll be sponging off Mariah's people!'

'Stuff and nonsense! You'd give value for money, wouldn't you?'

'Yes, of course.'

'And you'd put in more hours than the job requires, if I know you. For goodness sake, boy, snap it up before Mr Morgan changes his mind!'

'But wouldn't you prefer it if we lived nearer to you, Mum?'

'Certainly not!' she retorted, crossing her fingers. 'We both have our own lives to lead, and now that the beastly war is over we'll all be able to travel about quite easily. I can come to you for holidays. I've always wanted to see more of South Wales.'

'Then perhaps I will accept.'

'Of course you should, dear. I have to go now. Give my love to Mariah! Goodbye!' She wiped away a tear. Nurse Rivers looked at her with a professional eye.

'Bad news, dear?"

'Oh, no, the best! My son has just found a good job, and I'm so pleased for him.'

Chapter Twenty-five

Cwmbran was fortunate enough to possess a cinema, which was well patronized by the local people. New titles, featuring film stars from both Hollywood and Britain, were slow to appear in rural Wales, but when they did finally arrive they were much appreciated.

The Saturday matinées attracted large numbers of children, including the Swansea Six. If you didn't have the price of a ticket you could gain admission by handing over an empty jam jar, the collection of which had been part of the war effort. Ellen became rather tired of finding Dafydd going through her store cupboards, hoping to find such treasures.

'You know we make our own jam here, boyo!' She told him. 'I need all the pots I can get. Do I make myself clear?' In the end she found herself subsidizing their visits to the cinema, where they certainly received their money's worth. Usually there were cartoons, as well as perhaps a Charlie Chaplin movie, or a fast-moving western epic.

'I do wish they'd bring back *Gone With the Wind*,' Ellen enthused, a sentiment that was echoed by the female members of staff.

' "Frankly, my dear, I don't give a damn!" ' Aubrey quoted. '*In Which We Serve*. Now that's what I call entertainment! John Mills and Michael Wilding did a good job of that one. Don't you agree, Harry?'

'Or *Broadway Melody of 1940*,' Ellen added. 'That Fred Astaire may be no oil painting, but he can certainly sing and dance. I don't know where he finds his energy.'

On this January night, Aubrey and Mariah were planning to see Bing Crosby and Bob Hope in *Road to Utopia*, the latest in their series of Road films.

'I hope Dorothy Lamour is in this one,' Aubrey remarked, smacking his lips. His wife hit him with her handbag. 'Ouch! What was that for?'

'Think yourself lucky I wasn't carrying my good leather one,' she reproved him. 'Then you really would have something to complain about!'

They were standing in the front hall, almost ready to leave, when Mariah put her hand to her mouth.

'I've forgotten the Maltesers! I must dash up and fetch them. Wait there, Aubrey!'

'I could go.' Dafydd had been hanging over the bannisters, hoping in vain that they'd invite him to go with them at the last moment.

'No, thanks. I've got them hidden in my sewing basket. You'd never be able to find them.'

Before she could climb the stairs there was a sudden crash, and the sound of shattering glass. This was followed by a succession of loud screams, coming from the kitchen.

'That's Bessie!' Aubrey shouted. 'Go and make sure she's not hurt.'

He wrenched the front door open and disappeared into the night. With her heart thumping, Mariah ran to the kitchen, with Dafydd hot on her heels. Moments later Ellen appeared at the top of the stairs, brandishing a poker.

'Do stop that racket, Bessie!' Mariah ordered. 'Can you tell me what happened here?'

Gulping, Bessie pointed to a brick that lay on the floor near the table. 'Job!' was all she could manage to say before going off into another bout of hysteria.

Harry now entered the room, pushing his way past Rosie and Wyn, who had gathered in the doorway. 'Run up to my study and fetch the bottle of brandy, Rosie, there's a good girl,' he ordered. 'Bessie could do with a nip after this excitement.'

'I'll have you know I signed the pledge!' Bessie snapped, indignation overcoming her distress.

'You'll do as you're told, Mrs Prosser,' Harry insisted. 'This is for medicinal purposes. After the shock you've had you need something to steady your nerves.'

'Yes, sir.'

The slamming of the front door heralded Aubrey's return.

'Did you see anything, my boy?'

'I caught a glimpse of someone running away from the house, Harry. A man wearing a working-man's cap, I thought, although it was too dark to see properly. I gave chase but I tripped over a tussock of grass, and by the time I got to my feet the fellow had disappeared.'

'It could be anybody, then.'

'Oh, no, Mr Morgan!' The brandy had done its work and Bessie, who had imbibed rather too freely, was suddenly feeling quite cheerful. 'It was my Job. I know it was.'

'Did you actually see him in the act of throwing the brick, Mrs Prosser?'

'Course not. I was on the inside, wasn't I? There was this bang and I was too flustered to know what was going on.'

'We thought it was a bomb,' Wyn contributed. 'One of the unexploded ones, left over from the war.'

'We know it was nothing of the sort,' Harry retorted. 'It was a brick, and we have the evidence of our own eyes for that. However, there is no evidence to prove that it was, in fact, your husband, Mrs Prosser. You mustn't be so quick to accuse a possibly innocent man. We must leave the investigation to the police, and that reminds me, I'd better go and give them a ring. In the meantime, nobody must touch anything here. The constable will want to see for himself what has been done.'

'I suppose this puts paid to our night out at the pictures,' Mariah said. 'Dorothy Lamour will have to do her stuff without you there to see her, Aubrey. I can't help thinking that all this is more exciting than anything we'd have seen at the cinema, though. Could the man you saw have been Job, do you think?'

Aubrey shrugged. 'You forget that I've never met the man. All I know is that the chap I saw running away was of medium height, and all muffled up in dark clothing.'

'A description which could apply to half the men in Cwmbran on a dark night in January,' Mariah concluded.

A police constable arrived almost at once, introducing himself as Benjamin Probert. There was very little crime in Cwmbran, added to which the local constabulary knew better than to keep Harry Morgan waiting. He was the most important man in the area and a former magistrate to boot.

After taking a good look at the scene of the crime, and confessing that it didn't give him much to go on, Probert asked to speak to those who might have anything useful to pass on. Bessie, who by this time was in a happy daze, announced once again that the culprit was her estranged husband.

'But do you know that for a fact, Mrs Prosser?'

'Thash a fac!' she agreed, swaying slightly.

'Bessie Prosser, have you been drinking?' Probert asked sternly. 'As I recall you signed the pledge the same time I did. Not been backsliding, have you?'

'That's my fault,' Harry admitted. 'I forced her to take a drop, purely for medicinal purposes, you understand.'

'It seems to me, sir, that this woman has taken more than a drop! Are you sure you didn't smash the window yourself, Bessie, while you were under the influence?'

'Thash a lie!'

Mariah felt she had to interrupt, before their cook was placed under arrest.

'As you can see, Constable, the brick was thrown from the outside, and I can confirm that Mrs Prosser was indoors at the time. My husband and I were in the hall, preparing to go out, when we heard the sound of breaking glass, followed by her screams.'

'And I can confirm that,' Aubrey added. 'I dashed outside at once, just in time to see a man running away.' He went on to answer the constable's questions but had little more to add.

'Now, sir. Mrs Prosser has alleged that the perpetrator is her husband, Job Prosser. Would you say that the man you saw could have been him?'

Aubrey scratched his forehead thoughtfully. 'I don't know the man at all. I've only recently been demobbed and, as you probably know, I'm not a local man at all. I first met my wife when I came to the wedding of Mr Morgan's daughter, to serve as best man. I've come here on leave from the RAF occasionally but those visits were brief and I've seldom met any of the local people. I know Mr Prosser's daughter, Myfanwy, of course, because she's employed in this house, but I don't know much about her family.'

'Myfanwy, yes. I'd better have a word with her.'

'She won't be able to tell you anything,' Ellen said. 'She's in the nursery with the little boys, up on the top floor. I doubt if she's even aware that something has been going on.'

'She may be able to tell us something about her da's frame of mind, Mrs Morgan. Can she be sent for, please?'

'I'll go!' Dafydd offered, thrilled to be part of the excitement.

'And if you've finished questioning Mrs Prosser, I shall see her to her room,' Ellen said. 'She obviously needs to lie down.'

'I'll be back to see you when you're sober,' Constable Probert threatened, gazing at Bessie with a beady eye. Poor Bessie quailed. She had no doubt that she was already the subject of much gossip among the chapel crowd. If the old cats got to hear that she had taken to drink she would never be able to hold her head up again.

'I'm quite shober now, if you want to know,' she told him, with as much dignity as she could muster, but the effect was spoiled when she tried to stand up, wobbled, and sat down again. When Ellen took her by the arm she allowed herself to be led away.

Chapter Twenty-six

Myfanwy entered the morning-room with a frightened expression in her eyes. By this time Constable Probert was perched on a high-backed chair and she was standing on the other side of the table, with her hands clasped behind her back. Ellen was reminded of that famous old painting, *When Did You Last See Your Father?*, copies of which had graced many homes years ago. In that, several grim-faced Puritans

119

were interrogating a small Cavalier boy, while his younger sister wept in the background.

'What's happened, Mr Probert? Dafydd said you wanted to talk to me about Dada. He's not hurt, is he?'

'Na, na. Your stepmother has had a bad shock, though. Somebody threw a brick through the kitchen window, see, and I'm trying to find out who did it.'

Myfanwy's lip curled. 'And you want to blame it on my father, is that it? There's silly you are, Mr Probert! He'd never do a thing like that, not Dada. That's vandalism, that is!'

'I have to ask you some questions, *bach*. If your father is innocent, the sooner that comes to light the better, all right?'

'I suppose so.'

'I suggest we let Miss Prosser sit down,' Harry interrupted. 'I can see that this may take some time.'

Mariah patted the love seat on which she was sitting and, doing her best to hold back the tears, the little nursery maid sank down beside her.

'As we all know,' the constable began, while Myfanwy winced at the thought of her family's disgrace, 'your parents have recently, er, separated.'

'Excuse me, but they are not my parents. I mean, Dada is, but Bessie is my stepmother. They were only married three years ago.'

'Yes, yes, I know all that. I went to school with your poor mam, you know, although she was in Standard Six when I was in the Infants. Just a figure of speech, that was, when I spoke of your parents. I should like to know how your father took it when his wife left home to come to work here.'

'A bit upset he was, at first. Only natural, wasn't it?'

'And did he make any threats at all?'

'What kind of threats?'

'Like saying he would come up to the house here and make trouble?'

Myfanwy thought carefully before replying. Would she make it worse for her father if she had admitted that he'd bellowed like a bull when she'd gone home at Christmas, or was it better to pretend that Bessie's defection hadn't bothered him unduly?

'He did say she needed a clip round the ear,' she said at last, 'but isn't that something that any deserted husband might come out with? I'm sure he didn't mean it. Dada can be difficult at times – well, most of the time, really – but he's never been violent, see.'

'So he's never laid a finger on any of you children?'

'Well, only if we deserved it, I suppose.'

'And your stepmother deserved punishment for letting him down, isn't that it?'

'You're twisting my words, Mr Probert! What I'm talking about is things like the walloping our Micah got when he went scrumping apples, or when our Samuel cheeked the teacher at school and had to go to the Meistr. Any father would do that. It's like the Bible says: train up a child the way he should go.'

'And there's nothing in the Scriptures about giving your wife a thick ear, is there?'

'That's what I'm trying to tell you! If a brick came through that kitchen window it was somebody else that did it, not our Da! And that's all I've got to say, Mr Probert!'

'What will you do now, Harry?' The constable had left and the members of the household had gone their separate ways. Ellen was puzzled and upset by the unprecedented attack on their home.

'Do? Leave it to the police, of course. It's out of my hands now.'

'But if it turns out to be Job Prosser, will you prosecute?'

'He'll be taken to court, *cariad*. People can't go about chucking bricks through windows without punishment.'

'That's not what I meant. Will he be dismissed from his job? I hope you realize that if he is, this whole family will be affected. I can't see Bessie and Myfanwy staying on with us then, which will leave us with neither a cook nor a nursery maid.'

Harry sighed heavily. 'I hope you're not suggesting that the fellow be let off because of your staffing problems, Ellen. Goodness only knows what he might do next if he thought he could get away with it. In any case, Bessie should be pleased if the man has to go to court. I see no reason why she should side with him now.'

121

'Of course he shouldn't get off, but you haven't answered my question. Will you dismiss Job if he's found guilty of this?'

'This is the twentieth century, Ellen. All right, in my grandfather's day the whole Prosser family would have lost their jobs and their home and would probably have had to leave the district and go out to the colonies! But just imagine the hullabaloo if I tried that on now! No, he'll probably get a stiff fine and a warning, and we'll have to be content with   that.'

'You don't suppose it happened because of something different altogether, nothing to do with Bessie leaving Job? Something to do with the colliery?'

'Dissatisfaction among the miners, do you mean? If they were planning to strike I'd have heard about it from Roberts. They take their grievances to him, first. That's what I pay the man for. Now, can we drop the subject? After all the fuss I could do with a little drink; that's if Bessie has left us anything!'

'I had to laugh when I watched her swigging down your brandy! And it didn't take her long to get squiffy, either! She'll have a head like a bucket in the morning.'

'That's because she's not used to drinking, having signed the pledge. Do you suppose they'll drum her out of the chapel when the news gets out?'

'I daresay she's been drummed out already, as you put it,' Ellen replied, 'having broken up a happy home. I wonder what the gossips would say about me if I left Cwmbran?'

'They'd say you didn't know which side your bread was buttered, *cariad*. Now, am I getting that drink, or do I have to fetch it myself?'

'I'm coming! I'm coming! Keep your hair on!' Job Prosser shuffled to the door, pulling on his shirt as he went.

'Ben Probert! What brings you here?'

'Let me come in, man, and I'll tell you.'

Job removed a pile of newspapers from the nearest chair and gestured to the constable to sit down.

'There's been a bit of trouble, man. Up the House, see.'

'And what does that have to do with me, then? Our Bessie burned the supper, has she, and they expect her old man to pay for it?' He laughed grimly.

'This is not funny, Job. Somebody heaved a brick through the kitchen window and Mr Morgan called me in to investigate.'

'Wait a minute! You're not suggesting that I was responsible?'

'That's what your Bessie thinks. Revenge, see, because she left you and went to work for them up there.'

'That's her guilty conscience talking.'

'You know and I know you wouldn't do a thing like that, but I'm bound to look into this. Where were you this evening, man?'

'At home here. Been dozing in my chair by the fire, see, feeling a bit under the weather.'

'And you can prove that, can you? Have any of your boys been here with you?'

'Na, na,' Job admitted. 'Off to the pictures, the older ones, and the young ones went to the library. Something to do with homework, they said.'

'So we can't prove that you were here alone all evening.'

'And you can't prove that I wasn't, either, Ben Probert, except I give you my solemn word I had nothing to do with any of this!'

'All right, we'll leave it at that for now, then. I'll have to come back, mind you, if I find any evidence to place you at the scene.'

They both knew that this wasn't likely to happen. Unless any more witnesses came forward, who could positively identify the culprit who had been chased off by Aubrey, the case was at a dead end.

And this was how Probert described it when he reported back to his sergeant.

'Of course it could be the younger boys, up to mischief, see,' that worthy mused. 'Well aware of the disgrace their stepmother has brought on the house and wanting to teach her a lesson.'

'This was a grown man,' Probert reminded him. 'He was seen by Miss Mariah's husband.'

'So it was. Well, you've done your duty, man. I'll make a note of all this and we'll see if anything interesting crops up in the near future. That's all we can do, I'm afraid.'

Chapter Twenty-seven

'Who was that on the phone?' Ellen came into Harry's study just as he hung up after his call.

'A welfare officer. She wants to come and see us about the Swansea Six.'

'Oh, no! She's not coming to take them away, is she?'

'I hardly think she'd swoop down without warning and carry them off, especially in the middle of a school day, *cariad*.'

'But this is a warning, isn't it! Oh, Harry, I can't bear it. They've been here so long I feel as if they're my own children. You can't let her take them, Harry! Promise me you'll try to do something!'

'I certainly intend to discuss the situation thoroughly, but I make no promises. You always knew that this day had to come, Ellen.'

'But not so soon!' she moaned.

'There is no point in your getting excited until we know what this social worker woman has in mind, you know.'

'I want to be here when she comes,' Ellen insisted, her mouth set in a stubborn line. Harry looked at her over the top of his spectacles, but she refused to be intimidated. 'May I remind you that I've been the foster mother of those boys all these years, and I have a right to know what is going to happen to them.'

'We'll see,' he told her.

'We certainly will!' was her sharp rejoinder. As the wife of Harry Morgan, Esquire, she was no longer the meek little person she'd been during all those years when she'd been nothing more than his paid housekeeper. It wasn't often that she asserted herself, mainly for the sake of keeping the peace in the house, but she was jolly well going to have her way now!

So by the time that the loud rapping came at the main entrance to the house, there was a state of armed truce between husband and wife. Wyn, halfway down the stairs, went to answer the door.

'Can I help you?'

'I've come to see Mr Morgan, my girl. Is he at home?'

Wyn hesitated. The staff had been told to expect a welfare officer, who was to be shown into the morning-room, but surely that was a woman? This was a man, and a working man at that, judging by his appearance.

'Who shall I say called?'

'He knows who I am, *merch*! Job Prosser is my name.'

'O, *Duw*!' Wyn knew who this was, all right! What was she supposed to do with him now? 'If you'd like to follow me,' she squeaked, 'I'll let them know upstairs.'

She left him in the morning-room, looking around him in disbelief. He had been shown into this very room when he'd come courting Ellen Richards, her that was the boss's wife now. She had turned him down flat, and then he'd had to make do with second best, that hussy in the kitchen. Well, he'd show these Morgans what was what!

Wyn returned. 'Please to come with me,' she ordered, not waiting to see if he was prepared to follow.

'Shouldn't you go down there to see what he wants?' Ellen was saying, as Harry straightened his tie and ran a hand over his hair. 'I mean, letting the chap come up to our private quarters is a bit much, isn't it?'

'I'm not at his beck and call, Ellen. If he's not prepared to climb a few stairs to see me he can go back where he came from. He'll be lucky if I don't call the police. I have nothing to say to the man.'

'Perhaps he's come to apologize,' Ellen suggested, but before her husband could snap at her again Wyn appeared in the doorway.

'Mr Job Prosser!' she announced, in ringing tones.

'Thank you, Wyn, that will do,' Ellen told her, seeing that the girl appeared to have turned to stone. Job stepped forward, head held high.

'I have come to say that I have been falsely accused!' he announced.

'That's a matter for the court to decide, Prosser.'

'No, sir, it is not. I knew nothing about this until Ben Probert came knocking at my door, for I had not been out of my house all evening.'

'That brick didn't sail through the kitchen window all by itself, Prosser!'

'No, sir, but mine was not the hand that threw it.'

Ellen had to admire the man's poetic turn of phrase. Land of song, people called Wales, and that music was evident in the speech of her people.

'Can you deny that you have a grudge against your wife for leaving you? When you appear in court the magistrate will suggest that you became angry when she entered our employ, and in an unguarded moment you decided to make a statement by smashing the window of a room where she was most likely to be.'

'He can say what he likes, sir. That don't make me guilty. I shall say under oath what I have said to you now. I did not throw that brick through your window!'

Wyn now appeared at the study door again. 'Please, sir, there's a person downstairs. I put her in the morning-room, like Mrs Morgan told me. Shall I show her up here?'

'Certainly not. You may tell her that I shall be down directly. As for you, Prosser, you have made your point. If you have nothing more to say, you can go.'

Job hesitated for a moment but then he nodded to Ellen, replaced his cap on his head, and marched out of the room.

A short while later, while the welfare officer, a Miss Eileen Barton, was sipping a cup of tea, Ellen swooped in for the attack. Ignoring the furious glances sent her way by Harry, she leaned forward, smiling brightly.

'You've come to see our boys, have you, Miss Barton? I'm afraid they're not here at the moment. It is a school day, you know.'

'I'm aware of that, Mrs Morgan, and that's why I've come at this time, so we can discuss their placement without them overhearing.'

Placement! Ellen's heart sank. 'Oh, yes?'

'The thing is, you see, we're in a bit of a dilemma. At present we're not sure what to do with orphans of their age. I believe that the government means to address the problem eventually, but that will take time. There is so much to do, bringing the country back to normal, of course.'

'Of course!'

'For a good many years now orphaned or abandoned children have been sent overseas, to Canada or Australia, to start a new life which it was hoped would benefit them in years to come. The authorities are beginning to have second thoughts about these schemes, and I must say I've always had grave doubts about that sort of thing. Children as young as four years of age have sometimes been sent out there on their own. It hurts me to think about it. However, nobody has ever asked my opinion on the subject, and I don't imagine that will change now!'

'Shocking!' Ellen cried.

'Now there has been some talk about building cottage homes, where children can live in small groups, family style, with a married couple who will act as parents. That idea, too, will take time to implement, if indeed it comes to be.'

This was beginning to sound more promising. 'So what are you trying to tell us, Miss Barton?'

'Well, I know it's an awful cheek, but we were wondering if the Swansea boys could stay on here? You've plenty of room, I can see, and a staff to help you. . . .'

In her imagination Miss Barton saw the tiny flat over the ironmonger's shop in her native village, where she eked out an existence with her elderly mother. What wouldn't she give for a place with just one extra bedroom, so that she could get a good night's rest without poor Mam's snores to keep her awake.

Ellen looked at Harry, as if in doubt. If she fell on Miss Barton with cries of jubilation the gods might stick their oars in and they would lose the Swansea Six after all.

'I suppose it won't hurt to let them stay here for the moment,' Harry agreed. 'This has been their home for so long, it would be a shame to uproot them unnecessarily. Then, too, one of the boys is coming up to school-leaving age, and I've half promised to find him a job here in the district. Another of the children will be sitting the eleven-plus in a few weeks' time, and it would be a shame to deprive him of that. A good education will always come in handy, especially for a boy who has had such a bad start.'

Miss Barton's cheeks grew quite pink with excitement. 'This is good news indeed, Mr Morgan! A real act of Christian charity. I shall let my superiors know of your decision, and you'll be receiving confirmation in the form of a letter in due course.'

'And what is the good Christian man planning to do about old Prosser, now he's had time to think about it,' Ellen teased, when Miss Barton had trundled off in her ancient car.

'He seemed genuine. In the absence of any proof against him it seems foolish to waste the court's time. Perhaps he should be given the benefit of the doubt.' Harry grunted as Ellen flung her arms around his neck. 'No need for all this, *cariad*!'

Chapter Twenty-eight

As the weeks went by, and winter gave way to spring, life went on smoothly at Cwmbran House. For the children there were the high-lights of the school year to look forward to: St David's Day, when they were given a half holiday, and Easter, when they received a whole two weeks off. This compensated in some way for the longer hours they had to put in at their lessons, for during the war the school day had started at half past nine, but now it began at nine o'clock.

Aubrey had established a regular routine for himself, and Harry told Ellen that he was pleased with the way her son-in-law was shaping up.

'I'm glad now that I put off advertising for someone to take on the job,' he remarked. 'Aubrey is ideal for the post, I must say. Willing to listen to people's complaints, but firm when he thinks they're trying to pull a fast one.'

'I'm glad, too, of course. Not just that he's fitting in so well, but that Mariah is still here with us. It couldn't have worked out better, could it?'

Humming happily under her breath, Ellen made her way to the suite of rooms which had been allocated to the young couple. Unfortunately, it hadn't been possible to make a self-contained flat for them – building materials were still in short supply and qualified workmen were nowhere to be found – but they had the next best thing. Mariah's old bedroom now possessed a double bed, filched from another part of the house, and the room next door had been converted into a cosy sitting-room. Luckily, it possessed a fireplace, and Ellen could envision happy winter evenings with the two sweethearts cuddled up together on the sofa, looking into the flames and planning their future together.

Today, however, Mariah was feeling far from happy.

'What on earth is the matter?' Ellen cried, on finding her daughter dabbing her eyes with a damp hankie. 'You and Aubrey haven't had a falling-out, I hope?'

'No, Mam.'

'Then what is it?'

'I've just found out that there isn't going to be a baby,' Mariah sniffed. 'I was late this month and I was so hoping. . . .'

'There, there!' Ellen comforted, wondering as she said it why people mouthed such a useless expression. She rubbed Mariah's back. 'There's plenty of time, *cariad*.'

'That's what Aubrey keeps saying, and it doesn't help a bit. Men don't understand.'

'I expect you've got the winter blues, *cariad*. Why don't you go for a nice walk?'

'I don't want a nice walk!' Mariah groused, turning away. Ellen sighed. Should she have a quiet word with Aubrey, perhaps hint that he was being a bit insensitive? No, better not. That could be construed as interfering. Mariah's longing for a baby was all very well but she had no idea that motherhood was for life. You never stopped worrying about your children, even when they were married people!

She sighed again, but this time it was for herself. It was Bessie's afternoon off and somebody had to fill in for her. There was a cold pork pie in the larder, but somebody still had to cook vegetables to go with it, and Mariah was in no fit state to tackle the job, poor girl. Rosie couldn't even boil an egg, or at least, that is what she frequently asserted. Ellen suspected that this was a fib, to get out of doing the extra work.

Bessie was sitting in the old conservatory with her daughter, Gwyneth. A watery sun shone through the glass panes, taking the chill off the day. Nobody would find them here; if they stayed in the kitchen she might be asked to do something, and she was determined to make the most of the few hours she had to herself.

When the maids had time off they usually rushed out to savour the delights of downtown Cwmbran, where they gazed into the windows of the High Street shops or sat drinking tea in the Copper Kettle. Bessie kept herself to herself. She had no wish to flaunt herself in public, where she would have to endure the scornful looks of the self-righteous chapel matrons.

'What you doing, coming up here in the middle of the week, our Gwyn?'

'Early closing, Mam.'

'So it is. But still. . . .'

'I've got something to tell you, Mam. Something awful!'

Bessie's heart gave an uncomfortable lurch. 'Not in trouble, are you?'

'Na, na! You know me better than that, Mam. No, it's Llew, see.'

'Oh, yes? That's not news, my girl. You already told me he broke off your engagement. All I can say is, good riddance! It's a good thing you found out in time. Any chap who lets his father dictate to him about who he can marry isn't much of a man. And knowing what Job is like

I wouldn't want to see you taking my place in that house. Nothing but a slave I was, and no appreciation. That's why I had to leave.'

'I know, Mam, you've said.'

'Then what's going on now?'

Gwyneth looked over her shoulder and then, in a low voice, she said, 'It was Llew, Mam. It was Llew who put the brick through your window.'

'What! Llew bust the Morgans' kitchen window! I can't believe it!'

'Keep your voice down! Don't let the whole world know!'

'But why, our Gwyn?'

'I don't think he knows why. I understand they had a right set-to, with Llew saying he wanted to marry me and his da has no right to stop him, and the old man saying you and I are tarred with the same brush and I'd come into that house over his dead body. It was horrible, Mam. I wasn't there of course but Llew told me all about it later.'

'But the brick, girl! Tell me about the brick!'

Gwyneth shrugged. 'He told me later he was so angry he had to do something to relieve his feelings. That was all he could think of.'

'So he had to take it out on me. Typical, that is. His father is the cause of all this trouble, so why couldn't your Llew have smashed one of their windows instead of coming all the way up here and making a mess of my kitchen, eh? So what are you going to do about this, then?'

'I don't know what you mean. I've told you because I thought you ought to know, but I won't turn Llew in!'

'That's all very well, but are we going to let Job take the rap? There's no love lost between us, but still I don't want to see the man wrongly accused and punished on that account.'

'Will he lose his place, Mam?'

"That I don't know, but even being taken to court and standing up in front of the magistrate is bad enough. How will he ever be able to face them in the chapel after a disgrace like that? You must speak to Llew and tell him he has to come clean, our Gwyn.'

'If he loses his job he'll have to leave Cwmbran, and I'll never see

131

him again,' Gwyneth bleated.

'If he's the man you think he is, let him marry you and take you with him, my girl, but my advice to you is to let him go. There's better fish in the sea.'

Gwyneth set off home, scowling. There was something in what Mam had said. She would talk to Llew, but not about turning himself in to the police. No, she'd pretend that she'd been up to see her mother and had heard that Harry Morgan was bent on revenge, and was talking in terms of a prison sentence whenever the culprit was found. Therefore it was best if Llew left the area while the going was good, taking her with him, of course.

It did not occur to her that breaking a window was unlikely to result in a prison sentence. Knowing nothing about the law she believed that anything was possible when people like the Morgans held all the power. In Cwmbran they still told the story of how, in Harry's great-grandfather's time, two men were transported to Australia for stealing a sheep, even though their families were close to starvation at the time. The wife of one of the convicts had gone to old Rufus Morgan and appealed to him on her knees to pardon her man because of the circumstances, but he told her she was lucky that the fellow was getting off with a sentence of fourteen years' labour. At an earlier date he would have been hanged.

Staring out of the window, chewing on her finger nails, Bessie wondered if she should say something to Mr Morgan. She had a sneaking admiration for her husband, who had marched up to Cwmbran House to declare his innocence. A Daniel in the lion's den! Gwyneth would be furious, of course, and might never speak to her again, but that was something she'd have to face. What kind of man was Llew Prosser if he was willing to let his father take the punishment for his own misdeeds? Certainly not one she'd like to see her daughter married to.

Should she, perhaps, pay a visit to Job, and tell him what she had learned? Then he could deal with Llew, and the matter would be off her conscience. But how would Job react to the news that his own son was the culprit? She was likely to get the rough side of his tongue, if not something worse.

An anonymous letter, then? That was more like it. She would give it to one of the boys to post on his way to school and nobody could suspect her then.

Chapter Twenty-nine

'Who owns the flying biscuit box parked out at the front?'

'Biscuit box? What do you mean, Harry?' Ellen frowned at her husband.

'The Austin Seven, silly!'

'Oh, that! Some friends of Aubrey's. Apparently they were passing through the area and dropped in to say hello. I've invited them to stay; I hope that's all right.'

'Of course, of course. This is the boy's home now. He's welcome to have his chums here whenever he wishes.'

The visitors had driven up just as Aubrey had been walking round the side of the house, wondering if he had time to call at one of the outlying farms that morning.

'Frank Riley! This is a surprise! What are you doing here, of all places?'

Riley swung his legs out of the driver's seat and stood up, stretching. 'This is James Boyer, old boy. Jimbo, Aubrey Mortimer.'

The two men shook hands. Boyer got out of the car, slamming the door shut.

'But you haven't said what you're doing here! Never mind that now; come inside and get a hot drink.'

'This is quite a place you have here,' Boyer remarked, as they crossed the hall. 'Frank didn't tell me you had a pile like this!'

'Oh, it's not mine.' Aubrey laughed at the very idea. 'It belongs to my mother-in-law's husband, Harry Morgan.'

'Nice work if you can get it! You do live here, though, I gather?'

'Oh, yes. My wife and I have a sort of grace and favour apartment upstairs. I'm the estate manager here. And speaking of mothers-in-law, here comes mine now.'

Ellen was duly introduced, making noises of welcome.

'We shan't be bothering you for long,' Frank explained. 'We'll put up at the Red Dragon if they have rooms, but if you could join us for drinks later we could have a reunion of sorts.'

Ellen intercepted Aubrey's questioning glance. 'You'd be most welcome to stay here for a day or two, Frank, and of course you as well, Mr Boyer.'

'Call me Jimbo.'

She nodded, and bustled off to notify Bessie that there would be two extra people at lunch, and to round up the maids to make up the beds in two rooms. When they were all seated around the lunch table, she learned more about the two men.

'Frank was in the RAF with me,' Aubrey explained.

'Demobbed now, of course,' Frank added. 'Like a lot of other chaps I'm looking for a job. I'm hoping to land one at Cardiff. I was called for interview there, at County Hall. That's where I met Jimbo. He's on the short list too. It's a long way back to Norwich – that's where I hail from – and we felt like a bit of a holiday before heading home. That's why we thought of you, Aubrey.'

'Glad you did.'

'And what about you, Mr Boyer? I suppose you were in the RAF as well?'

'I was a civil servant all through the war, Mrs Morgan.'

'You weren't called up, then.' Ellen immediately felt embarrassed. Not only was this none of her business, but she'd didn't want to leave the impression that she thought he'd shirked his duty. 'I'm so sorry. I shouldn't have asked that.'

'That's quite all right. I worked at Whitehall, actually, in a reserved occupation.'

'That sounds interesting. What did your job involve?'

He grinned, tapping the side of his nose. 'I'm afraid I can't tell you that, Mrs Morgan. Hush-hush. The Official Secrets Act, you know.'

'I see,' she murmured, not seeing at all. Presently, she stood up and excused herself. The men half-rose politely before settling down again to linger over their pudding.

'Is it just you and your wife and in-laws living here?' Jimbo asked.

'Oh, far from it. Harry's daughter lives here, with her little boy, and then we have half a dozen orphans, all boys, who've been with the family for most of the war.'

'Then who gets this place when your father-in-law passes on? The daughter, I suppose.'

Annoyed, Aubrey murmured something to the effect that he knew very little about such matters, having only recently come on the scene.

'I don't know why the blighter thought he had the right to ask such personal questions,' he told Mariah later, when they were preparing for bed. 'What's it to him, anyway? None of his business!'

'I expect he was just making conversation, Aubrey. You know what the trouble is, we spent so long guarding our tongues during the war that we expected to see a spy behind every tree. Remember all the posters? "Careless Talk Costs Lives" and all that. Well, that's all over now, so you can put it out of your mind.'

'I don't think I should,' he argued. 'We don't know a thing about him or his background. He's just some chap who Frank chummed up with when he went for a job interview. That's old Frank all over, little friend to all the world, like Kipling's Kim. For all we know this Boyer may be hatching plans to make off with the family silver.'

'Now you're being silly. Do come to bed, Aubrey. It's been a long day, and I need my beauty sleep.'

Aubrey lay awake for some time, worrying. Boyer certainly hadn't been very forthcoming when Ellen had innocently asked what he'd done in the war. It was a natural enough question to ask, when every-body had been involved in one way or another. Many people had been involved in hush-hush work, of course, and Boyer could well have been one of them. But why be so cagey now? Aubrey didn't know a great deal about the Official Secrets Act and it was possible that certain wartime activities had to remain hidden, even now, but it was almost as if Boyer wanted them to know he'd been up to something important. He could so easily have said that he worked for the Ministry of Food, or something, and left it at that.

Aubrey turned over to his other side, pulling the bedclothes with him. Mariah complained sleepily and he arranged the blanket over her bare shoulders.

The following evening the family, with the exception of the boys, were gathered in the main drawing-room with their guests. Aubrey and Frank were reminiscing about their days in the service, oblivious to the others in the room.

'I say, old boy! Remember when old Barnes tried to smuggle that popsie into the Nissen hut—'

'And Hopkins appeared out of nowhere and wanted to know what was going on? I thought I'd die laughing!'

They grinned at the memory. Jimbo, who hadn't been present at the time, had no idea what the joke was, so he turned his attention to Meredith, laying on the charm. Watching them, Harry was pleased to see her expression coming to life as she chattered away. It was good of the chap to show an interest. The poor girl didn't have much of a life, stuck here in the country, surrounded by women and children.

'Excuse me, sir!' He looked up to see Rosie, hovering in the doorway. 'Can you come, sir? You're wanted on the phone. It's a trunk call, the operator said. I told her we'd accept it. I hope I did right, sir.'

'Yes, yes. Run along now, girl. I'll take it in the hall.'

'Yes, sir,' Rosie disappeared as Harry lumbered to his feet.

'Hello? Hello? Is that Mr Morgan?'

Harry held the receiver away from his ear. The female at the other end of the line was evidently unused to telephones.

'Can I help you?'

'This is Mrs Crossley; Mrs Meredith's cook.'

'Is there something wrong? Is Mrs Meredith ill?'

'Not to say ill, exactly, but she's going a bit funny. She's had me sleeping at the house for a week or so, afraid that people are going to break in and burgle the place, but I can't keep that up. My hubby don't like me being away from home like that. What if people broke in and you got hurt, he says.'

'Have you seen any strangers near the place, watching the house and so on? Perhaps you should ring the police.'

'I think it's all in her mind, really. Now she's taken to hiding all the cutlery. That way the burglars can't find it, she says. Trouble is, I can't find it either, and how am I supposed to lay the table with that going on all the time? I can't be doing with this any more, and that's a fact. It's my belief she should be in a home, Mr Morgan. Somebody is going to have to come here and sort it out, or I'll have to give in my notice!'

'All right, Mrs Crossley. I'm glad you called, and you can leave this in my hands.'

'Who was that on the phone, Harry?' Ellen asked.

'Henrietta's cook. Apparently the old girl is getting a bit muddled – Henrietta, not the cook – and she wants somebody to go to Hereford and see what can be done. I have meetings all week so I can't get away at the moment. I think you should go, Meredith. Will that be all right?'

His daughter nodded. She had always been fond of her grandmother. 'I'll start off in the morning, Dad. I'd better go and pack now.'

Chapter Thirty.

Jimbo Boyer spoke up at once. 'We could run you to Hereford, Mrs Fletcher, couldn't we, Riley?'

Frank looked taken aback for a moment but he recovered himself quickly.

'Yes, of course we could. Be glad to be of service.'

'That's very kind, but I couldn't possibly,' Meredith protested.

'Of course you could. We'd be glad of some feminine company. You can do the driving, Riley, and I'll squeeze in at the back. Keep Mrs Fletcher entertained.'

Mariah could see that Meredith was wavering. 'But it's so far out of your way, Mr Riley, that is, if you're heading back to Norwich.'

'I thought you said you were going on to Pembroke, Frank?' Aubrey interrupted, eager to give Meredith an out if she needed it. He was still suspicious about Boyer, who seemed rather too interested in the girl.

'That was just an idea. It would have been nice to explore some new country, but then I don't know Herefordshire, either, so that would be just as good.'

Aubrey tried to persist. 'Don't you have to call in at Cardiff to find out if you've got the job?'

'Oh, no,' Boyer told him. 'We're to be notified by letter, or so they said. All the more reason to push on home, in case something is waiting for us on the doormat.' He rushed away, saying he'd go and fetch the book of road maps from the car, so they could plan their route.

'Funny, that,' Aubrey remarked. 'I thought you said you'd met Boyer when you went for interview.'

'That's right.'

'Then he's not from Norwich?'

'How should I know? I've never asked the fellow. It's a big place. I don't know half the people there.'

'It's a bit of a coincidence, though, isn't it? Two of you from the same place, turning up in Wales, going after the same job?'

'I don't see that it matters, old chap.' Frank was a steady, unimaginative sort of man, not given to flights of fancy. Despite having come through a war where he had witnessed all sorts of horrors, he still believed in the basic honesty and goodness of his fellow man. 'As Boyer says, having Mrs Fletcher's company will make it a pleasant journey for us, and by taking her directly to her grandmother's house it will save her a beast of a train journey with all that stopping and starting.'

'Can you do it all in one day? I bet that wreck of yours can't do more than thirty!'

Frank looked at him strangely. 'What's the matter with you, Mortimer? You're behaving very oddly, I must say! The girl already has one father, without you putting your oar in! We're not planning to ravish her along the way, if that's what you're worried about!'

'Sorry! I'm being overprotective, I suppose. Meredith has been through a bad time, Frank. Her husband was killed at Dunkirk, and I feel responsible because I was the one who talked him into going over there with me to help with the rescue effort.'

'I know. I heard her telling Boyer all about it when you were out of the room!'

'What!'

'Oh, she didn't imply that you were to blame, old man. She did give him the pathetic little widow act, though. Laid it on a bit too thick, I thought. Still, you can hardly blame her, can you? Only married a short time and then left all alone with a kiddie to bring up.'

Bring on the violins! Hardly alone, Aubrey thought, surrounded by family, servants and everything that money could buy, but who then was he to criticize his wife's half-sister? He, too, could have been killed during the war, and then Mariah would have been left alone as well. He would not have grudged her the support of her family, or have expected her to stay at home for the rest of her life, grieving for him.

Meredith was a grown woman. Surely she could take care of herself? Why deprive her of a mild flirtation with the too-charming Boyer? Frank would see that she came to no harm; he would deposit her at her grandmother's house, and the two men would continue on. It was highly unlikely that any of them would come across Jimbo Boyer again.

The next morning the trio set off in style, with the boys running after the car, shouting and cheering. Waving from the nursery window, Henry was furious when his mother failed to look up and he had to be pulled off the sill, kicking and screaming.

'No need to worry,' Myfanwy told him, as she deposited him on the hearth rug, rubbing her shin where he'd landed an unlucky blow. 'Your mam is coming back. She's just going away for a few days, see?'

'I wanted to go too!' he roared. 'She should have taken me!'

'You have school to go to, *bach*.'

'Don't want to go to school. I hate school. I hate Miss Adams. And I hate you!'

Biting back a cross retort, Myfanwy walked away. She had learned long ago that when Henry was in this sort of mood it was wise to leave him alone to simmer down; just so long as he didn't start throwing things.

'She'll bring me a present when she comes home,' he said after a while. 'Do you think she will, Vanny?'

'We'll have to wait and see, won't we?'

'She will. I know she will. She won't give you a present, though,' he sneered, turning to Lucas. 'She's not your mummy.'

'Henry! That's unkind.' Myfanwy said it automatically, well used to his nasty streak.

'It's true, though! Isn't it true, Lucas?'

Lucas, pushing a toy car along the linoleum, kept his head down and said nothing. He, too, knew what to expect from Henry Morgan.

'Thank goodness you've come, Miss! Mrs Fletcher, I mean. She's having one of her bad days. I can't do nothing with her. One minute she's all right, and the next she's talking about having to get home or her parents will start worrying about her, and her over eighty! You'll have to get the doctor to her, dear, you will really!'

'All in good time, Mrs Crossley. Do you think she'll know me?'

'I can't say, I'm sure. Perhaps if you say who you are? Introduce yourself, like?'

But Meredith need not have worried. Looking up from the tapestry cushion cover she was working on, Henrietta greeted her with a pleasant smile.

'There you are, dear! I was beginning to think you were lost!'

'You were expecting me, then? Mrs Crossley let you know I was coming?'

'Of course I was expecting you. I may be old, my dear, but I'm not senile.'

Having seen that all was well, Mrs Crossley excused herself, saying that she had to put the potatoes on. Henrietta beckoned Meredith to her side. 'Open the door and make sure that woman doesn't have her ear to the keyhole. She listens at doors, you know. Always has to know what's going on.'

'It's all right, Grandmamma! She's gone to the kitchen.'

'Just do as I say, there's a good girl.'

For the sake of peace, Meredith glanced outside the door.

'There you are, you see. There's nobody there.'

'It's that woman, Meredith. She steals things.'

'Surely not, Grandmamma. What sort of things?'

'My engagement ring, for one thing.'

'But you're wearing it, Grandmamma. See? Here it is, on your finger. You've put it on the wrong hand.'

'Ah, but that's where I've been clever, you see? When the woman stole it she hid it in my face powder box, until she could get it out of the house without my noticing. I found it hidden under the powder puff. Now I wear it on my right hand where she can't recognize it.'

That evening, when Henrietta was sleeping, Meredith phoned Cwmbran.

'Is everything all right, *cariad*? How is Henrietta?'

'Mrs Crossley was quite right, Dad. Grandmamma seems quite well physically, but mentally she's – well – I don't like to say round the bend, but she's certainly not her old self. She's not fit to be left on her own. Should I be looking into nursing homes for her?'

'First things first. Get her doctor to come out and take a look at her. See what he advises. For all we know she could be having some sort of reaction to her medications. Most people of her age have something or other prescribed for them.'

'She says she doesn't want the doctor. She was quite cross when I suggested it.'

'That can't be helped. Phone his surgery in the morning and explain the situation. If you have to, pretend to be surprised when he arrives.'

'All right, Dad. Look, I must go. I'm in my dressing gown, and it's draughty here in the hall. I had to wait until she was asleep before I dared to come down.'

'Good night, then, *cariad*. Sleep well.'

'Good night, Dad. I'll call again tomorrow.'

Chapter Thirty-one

One fine September morning a small boy stepped off the train at Cwmbran and looked around him as if bewildered.

'Is somebody meeting you, boyo?' the station master asked, but the boy shook his head and walked off down the platform. Since the child seemed to know where he was going the man shrugged and went into the waiting-room, checking that there was nobody there who should be boarding the train.

The boy trudged up the road to Cwmbran House, changing his cardboard suitcase from one hand to the other as it dragged on his thin shoulders. He took a short cut through the shrubbery, but there was nobody about to see him there. On reaching a side door he let himself in, and stood looking about him, expecting a servant to appear to ask him what he thought he was doing, but nobody came.

He climbed the stairs like a toddler, lifting one foot to the step above, then pulling the other up to meet it, before repeating the process. Finally he reached the top and waited for a moment, leaning on the banister, before limping down the passage and disappearing inside the door leading to the boys' dormitory.

Later, Ellen was to say that they really had to do something about security in the house; if the war had still been on, a spy or an assassin could have come sneaking in, and none of them the wiser. Harry scoffed at that until she reminded him that a brick had already been thrown through a window, and not only had the culprit got clean away but there was no telling what else he might be planning to do.

On that autumn morning, all the inhabitants of the house were about their business. Harry and Aubrey were making their monthly tour of the farms, and the boys were all at school. Ellen and Mariah were going over the boys' clothing, trying to decide which of the garments could be mended, and which were only fit for the ragbag.

Myfanwy was there too, frowning over some shirts belonging to Henry. 'He is growing so fast it's unbelievable. He can't even do up the buttons on this one. I'd pass it down to Lucas, but he's almost the same size.'

'Plenty of people would be glad of it,' Ellen told her. 'Leave it here and I'll package it up for the Salvation Army.' She knew better than to suggest the grey Viyella shirt that Ceri Davies had outgrown. No second-hand goods for the heir to Cwmbran House, even though clothing was strictly rationed!

Mariah held up a pair of pyjama trousers which had both knees ripped out. 'What on earth do they do with them, Mam? How can things get torn to shreds when the boys are supposed to be asleep when they have them on?'

'I suppose the material has worn thin after repeated washings, *cariad*. I'm only thankful that boys in this country wear shorts in the daytime. Just think of the state they'd be in if they wore long trousers!'

Mariah now held up a wool jersey, pushing her hand through a massive hole in the elbow. 'I can see I'll have to get busy with the darning needle,' she sighed, wiggling her fingers in the air. 'Will you give me a hand, Myfanwy.'

'I suppose so, but let's make sure we've gathered everything up before we get started. If there's one thing I hate it's finishing up a basket of mending, only to find there's more to come!'

'I'll have a look in the boy's dorm,' Ellen murmured, getting to her feet. 'Then I'm going for a walk. It's too nice a day to waste sitting inside. Why don't you take the deckchairs out and work in the fresh air? Take advantage of the sunshine while you can. Winter will be here soon enough.'

Humming under her breath, Ellen went on her way. When she

entered the dormitory she stopped short in surprise. A huddled form was visible under the eiderdown on the end bed, which had never been used since Evan Phillips's departure for Canada. What on earth? She had waved the boys off to school that morning; had one of them sneaked back in without her noticing? She ripped back the covers in one swift movement and her mouth dropped open.

'Evan? Is that you? What are you doing here? Is your mam downstairs?'

The child opened his eyes, muttered something, and then rolled over with a low moan. She pulled up the covers again and slowly left the room. It was obvious that the child was too far gone to talk, so explanations would have to wait until later.

She hurried down to the kitchen, where she found Bessie rolling out pastry on the marble slab.

'Is Mrs Phillips here, Bessie?' In the heat of the moment she'd forgotten the woman's new surname. Doherty; that was it.

'Mrs who?' Bessie pushed back the hair on her forehead with a sweep of her arm.

'She's the mother of one of our evacuees. They went to Canada but I've just discovered the boy upstairs, so obviously they didn't stay there. I want to know what's going on.'

'Nobody's been here but me, madam. Have you spoken to Wyn, or Rosie? If that person has called, they probably put her in the morning-room, same as always when visitors come. Have you thought of looking there?'

But the only person in the morning-room was Wyn, who was dusting the furniture with a damp cloth. She gave Ellen a blank look when asked about visitors from Canada. Rosie, run to earth in the nursery, where she was gossiping with Myfanwy, was equally puzzled. She was even more put out when Ellen spoke to her quite sharply, telling her to get on with her work and to leave Myfanwy to do hers.

Ellen hurried off to tell Mariah, who was just setting up chairs on what was left of the lawn. Most of it had been turned over to vegetables during the war, and would continue to be used for that purpose until rationing was over.

'You can't be serious!' Mariah said, starting to laugh. 'Is this some kind of joke?'

'Go and see for yourself if you don't believe me!'

'Are you sure, Mam? It must be one of the other boys.' Mariah was sceptical.

'Of course I'm sure, girl! Do you suppose I can't recognize the boy after looking after him for so long? He's been gone from us for a year now but he hasn't changed much.'

'But what is he doing here? And where is Mrs whatshername, his mother?'

'I've searched the house from top to bottom and she isn't here. I've spoken to Bessie and the girls, and they haven't seen her either. He's simply appeared out of the blue.'

'This is ridiculous,' Mariah said, lowering herself into her deck chair. 'Unless, of course, she's brought him here and done a Dulcie!'

There was silence as they digested this. Dulcie Saunders had foisted her son on them and run off. Could Mavis Phillips – or Doherty as she was calling herself now – have done the same?

'But why would she have done that?' Ellen wondered at last.

'Isn't it obvious? She knows that Harry is a wealthy man and she thinks she can take advantage. The boy has probably told her all about Lucas, or at least that his mother dumped him here, and that has given her ideas.'

'Be reasonable,' Ellen remarked. 'It costs money to travel abroad. Is it likely that she'd come all the way from Canada just to leave him here, only to turn around and go straight back? If your theory is right, surely she wouldn't have collected him from us in the first place?'

'Well, if you have a better idea. . . .'

'This is getting us nowhere! We'll just have to wait until the boy wakes up, and then, no doubt, we can get the story from him.'

Ellen was too rattled to settle down to any useful work, so she set off on the walk she had promised herself earlier. On her way she met Evans the Post wobbling his way up the drive on his ancient bicycle.

'*Bore da*, Mrs Morgan!'

'*Bore da*, Mr Evans! Do you have something for us? If it's not too heavy I can take it now, and save you a few yards.'

'*Diolch yn fawr*, Mrs Morgan.' He reached into his bag and handed her several envelopes, which she glanced at before pushing them into her coat pocket. All were addressed to her husband. Two were probably bills; the third was a cheap envelope, with the address written in a childish hand. Squinting in the sun, Ellen noted that the postmark was Cwmbran.

Still restless, she was relieved to see Harry's car approaching in the distance. Normally she would have waved and walked on, but now she flagged him down and climbed into the passenger seat beside him.

'I'm happy to see you getting some fresh air,' he remarked. 'You don't get out enough, *cariad*. Everything all right up above, is it?'

'Oh, Harry!'

'What's the matter, something wrong? Is it Mariah? Not one of the boys, is it?'

'No. I mean, yes. Oh, dear!'

He smiled. 'The house doesn't seem to be on fire, and I don't see the doctor's car, so I assume it's nothing much!'

'It's Evan, Harry. He's back from Canada. He's in bed asleep, this very minute!'

Chapter Thirty-two

'Nanny! Nanny! You've got to come and see! It's Evan! He's in his own bed!' Ceri Davies had come flying into Harry's study, without bothering to knock, the rest of his room-mates hard on his heels. For once Harry forebore to scold them; the situation was highly unusual. Who could blame the child for forgetting his manners?

'We know,' Ellen said. 'I found him while you were at school.'

'But he's supposed to be in Canada!'

'Obviously he's not there now. And before you ask, we have no idea why he's come back or where his mother is, or indeed, how he came here.'

'Have any of you heard from him recently?' Harry asked. 'A letter, perhaps, mentioning that he and his mother might be returning to Wales?'

'We had a picture postcard with a picture of a beaver on it,' Dai volunteered, 'but that was ages ago. All it said was, "How are you? I am well. Wish you were here".'

'Typical of a boy of his age,' Harry told Ellen.

'I tried to talk to him just now,' Dafydd said, looking concerned, 'but he wouldn't wake up. He feels pretty hot to me. Shall I take his temperature?'

'No, I'd better come and take a look at him.' She bustled off, but moments later she was back again.

'The child is burning up. I do think we should call the doctor. Ask him to take a look at him.'

It turned out that Cwmbran's newly qualified doctor was away at a hill farm, assisting the district nurse with a difficult maternity case. 'And it could be ages before he gets back,' the doctor's young wife told Harry, 'because it's Mrs Patten's first, and you know what first babies are like.'

Harry didn't, but he told her not to worry, he'd make other arrangements, after which he rang off.

'I'm going to call James Lawson,' he told Ellen. 'I know he's supposed to be retired, but he'll come for me, I know. After he's done his stuff we can have a drink and a bit of a chinwag. We haven't seen each other for a while.'

Dr Lawson was even older than Harry, and had been both friend and family doctor since what Harry referred to as the year dot. Sure enough he was glad to get out of the house and was soon bending over Evan's bed, watched by an anxious Ellen.

'Is he unconscious, Doctor?'

'No, just dead to the world, Ellen, and feverish, too. What on earth has the child been doing to get himself in this state?'

147

'That's the worst of it; we have no idea. He went to Canada last year with his mother, and we didn't expect to see him again. Then I found him here in his old bed, with no idea how he came here.'

'I hope he didn't travel in his pajamas, then.'

Ellen returned his smile. 'No, I undressed him, of course, and replaced his damp bedding with what he has on now, but he didn't come to for a moment. Will he have to go into hospital, Doctor?'

'I'm of the opinion that we should wait and see. It may be just a sore throat and overexertion. I'll write out a prescription that should help. I daresay someone will pop down to the chemist's to collect it?'

'Of course, but I do wish he'd wake up. Then perhaps we'd know what's going on.'

'I wouldn't push him too far, Ellen. The sleep will do him good, and if he does have anything to say for himself when he wakes up, fair enough. Meanwhile, I'm afraid you'll have to possess your soul in patience!'

Ellen resolved to sit by Evan's bed until there was a change in his condition. Thus she was there when he finally opened his eyes, looking around in fright and bewilderment. She half expected him to say 'where am I' as in the classic melodramas, but instead he said 'Nanny!' which was what the Swansea Six had always called her.

'Yes, Evan, I'm here.'

'Thirsty!' he croaked.

'I'll fetch you a drink of water.'

When he had emptied the glass she settled him back on his pillows and pulled the eiderdown up over his chest. Mindful of Dr Lawson's advice, she wondered how much she dared ask the child, while knowing that it was important to get to the bottom of all this. His mother could be searching frantically for him at this very moment.

It was like those fairy tales involving a genie in a bottle. You were offered three wishes, but no more. You had to consider very carefully what you would ask for, because if you didn't get it right there were no more chances.

'Where is your mam, Evan? Do you know where she is right now?'

'She's in Canada, Nanny. Don't you remember?'

'Well, yes, of course, but so were you, at least, we all thought you were. I had quite shock when you turned up in your old bed, like Goldilocks in the bears' house.'

'Goldilocks was a girl,' he said scornfully. This was getting them nowhere.

'Evan, I really must know what this is all about!' she told him, trying to remain calm.

'It's in the letter, Nanny.'

'Letter? Your Mam wrote me a letter?' He nodded. Ellen then recalled the letter that Evans the Post had handed to her on the road. She'd thrust it into her coat pocket and then forgotten all about it in the excitement of finding the boy.

'Thank you, Evan. I'll go and read it immediately. I want you to tuck down now and go back to sleep. Mariah has gone to the chemist to get you a bottle of jollop. It will help you get better in no time.'

'Will it taste horrible?'

'It will be cherry-flavoured, I expect. Now then, you do as you're told, please.'

The boy rolled over obediently.

Ellen pulled the letter from her pocket. She remembered now; it was a plain white envelope with a local postmark. It seemed odd that this should be the case. Letters from Canada usually came in a thin blue airmail envelope, with a five cent stamp. She forced her thumb under the flap and ripped the thing open. There was a single sheet of lined paper inside, which must have come from one of those three-penny pads they sold in the newsagent's shop. She stared in disbelief at the few words written there.

Job Prosser didn't do it.
Somebody else did it.
Signed: One Who Knows.

'Where did this come from?' Harry asked, turning it over in his hand. She had raced to his study at once, eager to learn what he had to say about it.

149

'It came in the post. I forgot to give it to you earlier. What do you reckon?'

'About this? Nothing much. It doesn't prove a thing. Prosser could have written it himself, come to that. If anyone really had information, they should have gone to the police station. Why waste a stamp sending this up here?'

Ellen was disappointed with his response. 'Perhaps it's come from somebody who is concerned about him and wants to throw us off the scent. One of his younger children, for instance.'

'The handwriting is rather childish, I'll grant you that. Throw it on the fire, Ellen. It's nothing but a red herring.'

But Ellen was in detective mode. She went looking for Dai Jones, who was playing a game of Ludo with Huw and Ceri.

'You're in school with one of the Prosser boys, aren't you, Dai?'

'Yes, their Micah.'

'Have you heard him say anything about his father?'

'Like what?'

'Well, I'm sure he's upset that Mr Prosser is in trouble because of our broken window.'

'Dunno. He hasn't said.'

'Why do you want to know, Nanny?' Huw asked.

'Because somebody in Cwmbran has written me a letter, saying that Mr Prosser didn't do it. Micah, or one of his brothers, may have been trying to help.'

She showed them the letter, holding that in one hand and the envelope in the other. 'Oh, I know who sent that!' Ceri piped up.

'Are you sure? Think carefully, Ceri. This is important.'

'It was Mrs Prosser. Her in the kitchen.'

'Oh, I don't know about that, Ceri.'

'It was her, honest! She gave it me to post on the way to school yesterday. I put it in that pillar box down by the chapel, didn't I, you lot?' Dai and How nodded solemnly.

'I see. That's all right, then. Enjoy your game.'

How very strange. What could Bessie be up to? Why should she wish to defend her husband, when his difficult behaviour had driven her away from her home and her marriage? Was it guilt? And if she did know something, why go to the length of smuggling a letter out of the house and letting it return there by way of His Majesty's postal service? Why not drop a word in Myfanwy's ear, or mention it to Ellen herself?

She marched down to the kitchen, where she found Bessie enjoying a cup of tea. She waved the paper under the woman's nose.

'I hardly expect you to admit it, Bessie Prosser, but I have reason to believe that you know something about this! Would you care to explain yourself?'

Bessie gulped and put her half empty cup down on the table.

Chapter Thirty-three

'You did send this, didn't you?'

Bessie nodded.

'Would you care to tell me why? I should have thought you'd be the last person to come to Job's defence, after what he's put you through. And not only that; sending an anonymous letter is a despicable thing to do. Why not come straight to me if you had something to say?'

'I didn't want anybody to know what I'd done, madam! That it was me passing on the information, that is. Our Gwyneth would kill me if she found out!'

'Gwyneth? Your daughter, do you mean?'

'That's right. She was engaged to Llew Prosser until Job put his foot down and said like mother, like daughter. He ranted on and on until Llew broke off the engagement and nothing our Gwyn could say would make him change his mind. Then Llew got mad and started blaming it all on me, and the next thing she knew he was up here with a brick in his hand. It was him that Mr Aubrey saw running away. He might have known that Job wasn't that limber.'

Ellen realized now what had been bothering her about Aubrey's tale. After years of working below ground in damp conditions Job was probably plagued by rheumatism. You could tell his age by the way he plodded along rather than striding out as a younger man would do. Running would have been beyond him.

'Our Gwyn made me promise not to tell,' Bessie went on, 'but that wasn't right, see, Llew letting his father take the rap for what he done. What will happen to him now, madam?'

'That will be up to Mr Morgan. Breaking a window may not be the worst of crimes, but laying the blame on an innocent person makes it worse. We'll have to wait and see.'

The whole business seemed silly now. Ellen had better things to worry about, the foremost of which was Evan Phillips and the events which had led up to his return to Cwmbran. The housemaids, too, had other things to worry about.

'What's that suitcase doing stuck in the corridor like that?' Wyn demanded. 'Barked my shin on it twice this morning, I have.'

Rosie shrugged. 'I expect Mrs Fletcher left it behind by mistake, or else they couldn't cram any more luggage into that little car she went off in.'

'What'll I do with it, then? Put it in the cupboard under the stairs?'

'Better not. Lug it up to Mrs Fletcher's room and leave it there, why don't you.'

Meanwhile, Gwyneth Harries, serving in the greengrocer's shop, had troubles of her own. Putting her numb hands in her arm pits she stared at Llew Prosser as he hovered in the doorway.

'Don't stand there like a lump, boyo! Shut the door, do. You're letting all the cold air in. It's like a tomb in here this morning. That'll be two and six, Mrs Barnes, please.'

The customer handed the money over reluctantly. She sensed a drama here and didn't want to miss anything. Disappointed, she turned away. The door pinged shut behind her. Gwyneth looked up hopefully.

'Come to make it up with me, have you? Kept me waiting long enough, and that's a fact.'

'Na, na.' Llew shuffled his feet. 'Come to say goodbye, see. Couldn't leave without letting you know, never mind what Dada says.'

'Goodbye!' Gwyneth shrieked. 'Where d'you think you're off to, then?'

'Canada, probably, if they'll have me. They're looking for people with skills, and they've coal mines there, see. No problem finding a job when I get there.'

'You can't just walk into Canada,' Gwyneth frowned. 'I'm sure you have to fill out forms and that. It might take weeks.'

'Then I'll go down to Cardiff and sign on as ship's crew. That shouldn't be so hard.'

'But why, Llew? What's brought this on?'

He kicked at the counter, causing a tin of peas to fall down to the floor, where it rolled into the corner. 'It's everything, Gwyn. Dada, this place, you and me, and now I'll be in trouble when they find out it wasn't him who broke that window. I'm fed up to the back teeth and I want a new start, see?'

'But what about me, Llew? I can't sign on to work on some tramp steamer. I'll have to wait till you get settled before I can come out there to wherever you land up. You haven't even asked me if I want to live abroad.'

'I'm not expecting you to come with me, Gwyn. That's all over between us now. I told you that before. I only come here because I didn't want you to hear it from somebody else.'

For a moment there was a buzzing in her ears which seemed to drown out all sound. 'Then get out!' she shrieked. 'Just get lost, Llew Prosser, and good riddance!' Despite her fury she didn't expect him to do as she said, but he turned on his heel and left, and once again the door pinged as it closed behind him.

Gwyneth realized that she had taken another tin of peas off the display and had been about to hurl it after him. And a fine thing that would have been, if she had managed to knock the glass out of the door. One smashed window was enough.

153

Poking her head round the door which led to her employer's living quarters, she called through to him.

'Sorry, Mr Williams. Been taken bad, I have. I'll have to go home, I'm afraid.'

'You were all right first thing,' he complained.

'It's that time of the month, see,' she told him, knowing that he'd be too squeamish to question her further.

'You can spare me the gory details, miss! This is what I get for hiring a woman. If you're not off sick you're holding the counter up gossiping to everyone who comes in. You keep this up, Miss Harries, and I shall have to think seriously about replacing you.'

His criticism was untrue and quite unfair, but at that moment she could not have cared less. Pulling her green overall over her head she thrust her arms into her swagger coat, gathered up her handbag and walked out, leaving him muttering imprecations. At times like this a girl needed her mother.

'Not you again!' Bessie yelped, sniffing.

'Charming! Should I turn round and go right back the way I came?'

'Na, na. Sit down and I'll make you a cuppa. Sorry if I was a bit abrupt, but I've already had Madam Morgan down here last night, giving me an earful. I don't want her on my back again.'

'What about? Something up with your cooking?'

Bessie thought it as well not to mention her letter writing activities. 'What brings you here at this time of day, anyhow? Shouldn't you be at work?'

'I told old Williams I had cramps. He didn't like it but I couldn't stay behind that counter another minute, Mam! Llew dropped in this morning to say he was leaving the country, if you please.'

'At least he let you know what was up, instead of leaving you to wonder.'

'I might have known I'd get no sympathy from you!' Gwyneth put her head down and began to sob.

'Here, none of that, my girl. I've told you before, Llew isn't good enough for you, so don't waste good tears on him! And get your arms off my table. They'll be all over flour before you know it, and you with that nice coat on.'

'But what am I going to do, Mam?' Gwyneth wailed.

'Do? I don't know what you mean. Go on as usual, I suppose. Hold your head high and don't let on to anyone that you've been jilted.'

This brought a fresh outburst of tears, and Bessie patted her daughter on the back, having run out of suggestions.

'I wanted to be married, Mam! Not just plain Gwyneth Harries any more, but Mrs Llew Prosser, see.'

'Not so much of the plain, my girl! Nothing wrong with being a Harries, and I wish I'd stayed one, believe you me! Marriage isn't all it's cracked up to be. Look what happened to me.'

'Dada was a good man, Mam.'

'He was that, until he up and died, leaving me alone to struggle on bringing up a family. Nobody will ever know how lonely I felt, all those years. I prayed and prayed that I'd find somebody new one day. You never knew that, did you? I was like you, our Gwyn, thinking Job Prosser could supply what I lacked. Instead, what did I get? I sold myself into slavery, that's what I did, and now look at me. Back working for a living, and all the chapel cats looking down their noses.'

'Oh, Mam!'

Bessie wiped away a tear. 'Don't mind me, *cariad*. Feeling a bit low this morning, that's all. Drink your tea, and tell me what you mean to do next. I know it's not much fun, living in one room and working in that cold old shop. Why don't you come and work here? I've heard that Mrs Morgan is still looking for another maid. It wouldn't cost you anything, living in like I do, and you could save for a rainy day. How about it?'

'I'll think about it, Mam,' Gwyneth muttered, looking glum.

Chapter Thirty-four

With the resilience of youth, Evan had bounced back to health after a few days of doing little but eating and sleeping. Dr Lawson pronounced him fit to get up.

'He seems fighting fit to me. It was probably just exhaustion.'

'Is it all right if we question him now, Doctor?' Ellen wanted to know. 'We have no idea what he's doing here, or where his mother is. She must be out of her mind with worry.'

'Yes, let him talk as much as he likes, but don't press him if he seems unable or unwilling to say too much. The mind is a wonderful thing, Ellen. At times it can protect us from recalling experiences we'd rather not remember!'

As she got him dressed, she ventured a few questions, ending up none the wiser. 'Where is your mam now, Evan? Do you know?'

'Course I know!' he said, his facial expression showing his scorn. 'She's in Canada, isn't she?'

'On the ranch?'

'It's not a ranch. It's a farm.'

'The farm, then. Is she there?'

' 'Spect so.'

'Evan, I would really like to know where your mother is at this moment! If she is where you say she is, how did you get here? You couldn't have come all by yourself.'

'It was the Methodist lady, Nanny. Can I go to the bathroom? I think I'm going to be sick!'

'And that's all I could get out of him!' Ellen reported to her husband. When she had left, the child was sitting at the table with a jigsaw puzzle in front of him.

'He'll talk when he's ready. I tell you what, we'll get the Swansea Six together this evening and let the boy say his piece to them. They've been dying to hear all about Canada and he's more likely to open up to people his own age.'

So that evening the Morgans, together with Mariah and Aubrey, were seated beside the fire, with the boys sprawled out on the carpet at their feet. Without prompting, Huw set the ball rolling.

'Tell us about the ranch, boyo! Were there a lot of cowboys? Did you see any Indians?'

'Na. It wasn't a ranch at all, see. That Jimmy was fibbing when he told Mam that. I didn't like it much, and that Jimmy was horrible. Sometimes he made me stay home from school to help him with the work, and then he got cross because I couldn't do it right.'

'Did you like the school?' Mariah asked, wanting to change the subject.

'It was OK. It was out in the middle of nowhere and I had to walk a couple of miles to get there. It was just one big room, with all the classes sitting together, and only one teacher. Grades, they call them over there, instead of standards. There's a big stove in the middle of it to keep the place warm in winter, but they never use coal, like here. They have wood, see.'

Ellen couldn't hold back any longer. 'Evan, what about the letter you mentioned, the one from your mother. It hasn't come yet. I hope it hasn't been lost in the post.'

'It's in my suitcase, Nanny. Didn't you see it?'

'Suitcase? What suitcase?' Of course the boy must have brought luggage with him; he could hardly have spent a week on board ship without a change of clothes!

'The rest of you carry on without me. I must see if I can find that case.'

She made her way down to the kitchen, where she found the staff relaxing.

'Don't get up, please. I'm looking for the suitcase that Evan brought with him. Have you seen anything of it?'

'Not me!' Wyn said, looking blank.

'Yes, you have,' Rosie reminded her. 'Remember, it was standing in the corridor and you kept tripping over it.'

'Na, na, that was the one Mrs Fletcher left behind. I took it upstairs and put it in her room.'

Ellen raised her eyes to the ceiling. She was even more put out when she entered Meredith's room and saw the battered cardboard case which Wyn had left on the bed. How on earth could the maid have believed that such an object could belong to Harry Morgan's daughter? Not for the first time, she suspected that Wyn was not quite sixteen ounces, as the people of Cwmbran liked to express it.

Ah, success! The bulky envelope was hidden in a jumble of dirty washing. She slit it open, using her thumb. Scanning it swiftly she digested the contents, outraged by what she was reading.

'Did you find it, *cariad?*' Harry whispered. Evan didn't hear what was said. He was telling a long-winded story about life on board ship, to which his friends were listening with rapt attention.

'Yes, I did.'

'Let's have a dekko, then.'

'Later. When they're all in bed the four of us can come back here and I'll read it out to everyone at the same time.'

'I don't see why I can't have a look now,' he grumbled, but Ellen had made up her mind. This was drama of the highest order, and she wasn't about to relinquish her hold on it. She smiled and tucked the letter away in her cardigan pocket.

As promised, she read the letter aloud, later that evening, when Mariah could be present. That seemed to be only fair, since Mariah had had the most to do with Evan since he had come to Cwmbran. Mavis had begun:

I must begin by telling you that the situation here is not what I was led to believe. While I intend to hang on as long as possible in the hope that it will improve, I feel that I must send Evan away, for his own protection. Jimmy, my new husband, expects too much of an eight-year-old when it comes to working on the farm and on several occasions has knocked him down when things went wrong.

I have met the wife of the Methodist minister here, who tells me that she, and others, will shortly be making a trip to Britain with a group of children who were evacuated to Canada at the start of the war, and who are now going home. She sympathizes with my plight here and has offered to take him with them. Fortunately I have some savings which Jimmy doesn't know about, and I can pay Evan's passage. I don't have enough to cover the cost of a ticket for myself or I should certainly be leaving with him. Mrs Dawson will be travelling as far as Cardiff, where she promises to put Evan on the train for Cwmbran.'

'Poor little scrap! Mariah remarked, dabbing at her eyes. 'And as luck would have it they put him on the milk train, which stops at every station between here and the moon! No wonder he collapsed when he got here.'

Harry was furious. 'Why didn't the woman phone us? The minister's wife, I mean, not Evan's mother. We could at least have met him at the station instead of leaving the child to drag himself all the way up here on foot.'

'It hardly matters now, Harry! Do you want to hear the rest of this, or not? Ellen took up the tale again.

I know it's a lot to ask, but because my future is so uncertain I'm hoping that you will take him in once again, since he knows you all in Cwmbran.'

'Cheek!' Aubrey muttered. Mariah pulled a face at him.

If that isn't possible, perhaps you can find out where the other Swansea boys have been sent and find him a place there. I am sorry to put you to all this trouble, but I'm at my wits' end to know what to do.'

'The woman must be mad!' Aubrey snapped. 'Even supposing what she says is true, don't they have any orphanages in Canada? It's a bit much to expect us to deal with this, you know. It's not as if we can send him back if it's an inconvenience, is it?'

'Aubrey Mortimer! How can you be so callous? I'll have you know that Evan has been a member of this family for a lot longer than you have. Furthermore, he's just a little boy! Of course we'll look after him. Any decent human being would do the same!'

'I only said—'

'I know what you said, and I couldn't believe my ears!'

'Steady on, old girl!'

Harry held up his hand. 'That will do, the pair of you! I don't want this to degenerate into a family row. All this shouting won't help the child, and I wouldn't want him to overhear what is being said. As far as he's concerned it will be the last straw if he thinks he's not wanted here, after all that's happened to him. Let's all calm down, shall we?'

They had the grace to look shamefaced. Ellen put the letter back in its envelope and turned to Mariah. 'I'll fill you in on the rest later. The men know the basic facts, and I doubt they'll be interested to hear any more of Mavis's woes.'

At that moment Dafydd burst into the room. 'You'd better come, Nanny. Evan just wet the bed!'

'No problem. I'll come with you and dig out some clean sheets,' Mariah told him.

Chapter Thirty-five

'Here, you'd better read this for yourself.' Ellen held out the letter to Mariah. 'I've done too much talking. My throat feels quite sore.'

'I've noticed!' Mariah's eyes twinkled.

'Now, now! No need for sarcasm! I can't help feeling all wound up. It's not every day that we get unexpected visitors from abroad, especially one the size of young Evan Phillips!'

Mariah turned to page two of the missive.

"I must admit that Canada was a bit of a shock at first,' Mavis had written, 'especially when I found that Jimmy had lied to me about his circumstances. On the boat coming over somebody I'd got to know told me that all the big ranches are out West, but how was I to know the difference? I'd seen a map of Canada when I was in school, of course, but just looking at a page in the atlas doesn't give you much idea, does it? I've found out since that Canada is more than three thousand miles wide but just hearing that doesn't mean much, either.

Jimmy does own a one–hundred-acre farm, which is pretty standard in this part of Ontario, but it's nothing like the farms back home. It's covered in snow for five or six months of the year, and you can't go anywhere without a horse-drawn sleigh. Country people take the wheels off their cars and put the vehicle up on blocks for the winter. Did you ever hear anything like it? We're ten miles from town, so we seldom get there, but do our shopping at a little store at the crossroads, which also houses the post office.

'As for the house, well! No electricity, just kerosene lamps, and the privy is yards away from the house. At times the temperature drops to thirty or forty below zero in winter, so a trip outside involves a lot of dressing up!

'I thought that Canada was quite civilized,' Mariah remarked, looking up from her reading. 'This sounds awfully primitive to me. I wonder if she's telling the truth, Mam?'

'Oh, I'm sure it's quite different in the towns. Anyway, we can't talk! There are plenty of outside privies right here in Cwmbran, although we have indoor plumbing here, thank goodness! Go on, see what she says next.'

'All that wouldn't be so bad if things were better between me and Jimmy. His mother and two sisters live with us (they kept the farm ticking over while Jimmy was serving overseas) and they seem to resent me very much, particularly his mother, whom I'm expected to address

161

as "Mother Doherty". She doesn't like the fact that I've been married before, or that I have a son. She keeps telling me that she hopes I'm young enough to have more children because Jimmy needs a son to inherit the place, which has been in the family for generations. Poor little Evan doesn't count. He's "not of the blood" as the old girl says. Honestly, you'd think they owned a stately home, not a hundred acres of rock.

'I must sound like a real moaning Minnie, but it's Jimmy's unkindness to Evan I can't stand. I can't bear to see the sadness in the child's eyes, or the way he flinches when anyone makes a sudden movement. That's why I've decided to send him back to Wales, Mrs Morgan. I do hope you'll understand.'

'Dear, oh, dear,' Mariah said. 'What a story! She's landed herself in a real old muddle, hasn't she?'

'And Aubrey was quite right in saying she's got a nerve, expecting us to pick up the pieces. Still, he's here now, and we'll take care of him, poor little chap.'

'If you ask me she's lucky to be so far away, or she might find herself in even more trouble. Fancy sending a child of that age across the Atlantic by himself! I've never heard anything like it. All sorts of things could have happened to him.'

'Come, now, that's a bit steep. She did put him in the care of that minister's wife, and when it boils down to it there's not much difference between that and evacuating all the kiddies during the war. You must remember how the Swansea Six arrived here with labels attached to them, like parcels!'

'If I'd had children I should never have let them be sent away!' Mariah sounded quite fierce.

'You don't know what you might have done under those circumstances, *cariad*. If you'd been up in London with bombs raining down every night, wouldn't you have wanted your child to get away from that? And they did evacuate some mothers, as well as babies, so everything was done for the best.'

Mariah was not convinced, but Ellen was well aware of what lay behind her vehemence.

'No sign of a baby coming yet, then?' she asked.

'Oh, Mam! I'm beginning to think that I can't have children. Aubrey wants children too, of course, but he seems to think there's no hurry. "Let's enjoy being together for a bit before we get involved in bottles and nappies", he says, but he's a man. He can't understand how a women feels about motherhood.'

'Never mind. A little stranger may turn up when you least expect it,' Ellen murmured.

Mariah burst out laughing. 'That's already happened, Mam, but his name is Phillips, not Mortimer!'

Ellen chuckled too. 'What I had in mind was something much smaller, and a good few pounds lighter!'

Mariah stopped laughing and studied her hands. 'Do you think I ought to go and see somebody, Mam?'

'A doctor, you mean?'

'Well, some sort of specialist. A gynaecologist, perhaps.'

Ellen considered this. 'Possibly, but I wouldn't go that far yet. You and Aubrey haven't been back together for all that long, and there are adjustments to be made. I'm sure that the war caused you a lot of stress, just like everyone else. It's bound to have had an affect on your body.'

'I don't see why it should,' Mariah grumbled. 'I was reading something in the newspaper the other day about all the babies that were born to single mothers during the war. If that's true, how come all those women were more fertile than me?'

Ellen was out of her depth now. She could only repeat what she had already said, that Mariah should be patient and let nature take its course. 'Meanwhile, I must write to Evan's mother and let her know that all is well. I'm sure the minister's wife will have said something but she can't know what has become of him since she put him on the train at Cardiff. Why on earth the stupid woman didn't phone me here, or at least give Evan details of where I might reach her, heaven only knows. This is just not good enough, Mariah!'

'You ought to be careful what you say in your letter, Mam.'

'I don't know what you mean.'

'Well, don't say anything bad about Evan's stepfather. If these people are as awful as Mavis says, I wouldn't put it past the old mother-in-law to read your letter. If she knew that Mavis had been complaining about her son, it could cause a lot of trouble.'

Ellen considered this. 'I'd give a lot to know what her precious Jimmy had to say when he learned that Evan has been sent away. Is he angry because Mavis has stood up to him, or is he relieved to have the little cuckoo gone from the nest?'

'I should think he'd be more angry to find out that Mavis had some secret savings that she didn't want to hand over to him. Don't you feel that she must have had some inkling that things might not work out over there?'

'Who knows? This war has made us all wary. Take Harry, for instance. All the while it was on he kept an attaché case beside his bed filled with important documents in case he had to leave in a hurry. "What's the point of that?" I asked him. This part of Wales has yet to see a bomb, and if one did come this way, it probably wouldn't hit when he was in bed. What good would it do if he was out visiting one of the farms, for instance, and the case was at home? Far better to lock things up in the safe, I told him, but would he listen? No.'

'I expect it gave him some comfort, knowing he was doing something to safeguard his valuables, Mam. There were times when simply working in the potato patch made me feel I was doing something to control the situation. I'd have felt so helpless otherwise, with the war raging on for so long.'

With that Mariah left the room, leaving her mother to get on with her letter. As she passed Harry's study she heard the telephone ring, followed by his deep voice as he picked up the receiver.

'Meredith! Here you are at last! I was about to ring you myself. No, no, everything is as usual here. Nothing new to report at this end. I've been concerned about you, though. How are you getting on with Henrietta? Is she as far gone as Mrs Crossley makes out?'

Mariah tiptoed on. No doubt she'd hear all Meredith's news in due course, but she wondered how he could possibly suggest that everything at Cwmbran House had been smooth sailing since his daughter left for Hereford. Perhaps he hadn't mentioned Evan's arrival in case it worried her? Knowing Meredith and her distraught reaction when poor little Lucas had been foisted on them, it was possible that she'd fly off the handle when she heard that Evan, too, had been returned to them here.

Chapter Thirty-six

Meredith opened the door, to find a tall, good-looking young man waiting on the doorstep. He had brown eyes and sandy, not quite red, straight hair which flopped over his left eye. Quite easy on the eyes, she decided, chiding herself for noticing.

'Can I help you?'

'I'm Ambrose Bevan. Dr Bevan, that is. I've called to see Mrs Meredith, if she's at home?'

'Oh, I'm so sorry! Do come in, please. I was expecting Dr Wainwright.'

'Actually, I'm his new partner. I've only recently joined the practice, which is why we haven't met before. Dr Wainwright has been cutting back on his house calls, so he asked me to make this one.'

'I see. Well, my grandmother is at home, but I'm afraid you may find her a bit difficult, Dr Bevan. She insists that there is nothing wrong with her, and I don't suppose there is, physically, but as I explained to your receptionist when I phoned, I'm afraid that she's not quite right in her mind.'

'*Anno domini,*' he said, nodding.

'What's that? Oh, you mean she's getting on a bit! But I was worried because I know of several eighty-year-olds who are perfectly normal, you see. Grandmamma is quite different.'

'Who was that at the door, Meredith?' Henrietta called. 'Come in and shut it at once! We don't want strangers getting in, looking for things to steal!'

'That's my grandmother now. I'll take you in, but please do remember that she doesn't know why you've come!'

Henrietta inclined her head in a graceful gesture when they entered the room.

'Good morning! You must be Meredith's husband. Why haven't you brought him to meet me before now, you naughty girl?'

Meredith's cheeks turned crimson, but their visitor seemed not at all put out.

'I'm Ambrose Bevan, Mrs Meredith. I'm new to the district so I thought I'd call to introduce myself.'

'How kind! Although etiquette demands that it is I who should call on you. Where are my cards, Meredith? Perhaps I shall call on your wife after a decent interval.'

Meredith's blush deepened. If her grandmother followed this up with a spiel involving having to look into their credentials before deciding if they were worth knowing, she would die on the spot! Henrietta was well known for her snobbery, and although under normal circumstances she would have died before making such remarks to a stranger, she could no longer be depended on to keep such thoughts to herself. Her good breeding seemed to be disappearing, along with her memory.

Fortunately the doctor seemed to take all this in his stride. 'This is a very pleasant house. Have you lived here long, Mrs Meredith?'

'Oh, for many years. My husband brought me here when we were first married, and our daughter, Antonia, was born here.'

Meredith waited for her grandmother to say that her husband had just nipped out to buy a newspaper, and would be back shortly – a remark which she had made to Mrs Crossley earlier in the day. However, she now went on to explain that Paul had died earlier in the war, and that their only daughter had died in childbirth when Meredith was born.

'Won't you stay for morning coffee?' she asked, but the doctor declined, smiling, saying that he must get on. Meredith saw him to the door.

'I'm so sorry, I feel a bit of a fool, calling you in for nothing. She seems quite normal at the moment, but when our cook went to turn the oven on this morning she found a box full of trinkets inside. My grandmother must have hidden it there.'

'This is quite typical of patients suffering from dementia, Mrs–er. . . .'

'Fletcher. My name is Mrs Fletcher. So that is what is wrong with her, then?'

'It would seem so, although she appears to be in the early stages.'

'But what can be done for her?'

'Probably nothing at the moment, although if her condition worsens you must contact Dr Wainwright who can refer her to a specialist. For the present you must make sure that she isn't left alone, in case she causes harm to herself.'

Meredith's eyes opened wide. 'You don't mean that she might do something silly!'

'I'm so sorry! I didn't intend to give that impression! No, not at all. Some elderly persons tend to wander off, and then have no idea how to find their way home. Others may leave a saucepan to boil dry on the stove. That sort of thing.'

'Oh, I see.'

'I gather from what Mrs Meredith says that her Mrs Crossley doesn't live in. What about you, Mrs Fletcher? I suppose you have to return to your husband soon. Is there anyone else who can stay here?'

'My husband!' Meredith was taken aback for a moment. 'I'm a widow, Doctor. My husband was killed at Dunkirk. I live in my father's house in Wales, and I can quite well be spared to stay on here for as long as necessary. I do have a little boy, but he has a nursemaid, and in any case he's in school now so he's away from the house for much of the time.'

Dr Bevan removed his hat from the stand in the hall and prepared to leave. 'I can leave Mrs Meredith in good hands, then,' he concluded, and was gone, striding out to his car without a backward glance.

'I wonder if he's married?' Meredith said, unaware that she'd spoken aloud.

'What was that, dear?'

'That doctor. Dr Wainwright's new partner. I just wondered if—' She broke off as the doorbell peeled. Had Dr Bevan forgotten something? She was sure he'd had his medical bag with him when he left.

'Oh, my goodness! What are you doing here?' she blurted, when she saw Jimbo Boyer standing in front of her, his forefinger poised to make another assault on the bell.

'I've come to see you, of course!' he grinned. 'That's all right, isn't it? Mind if I come inside?'

Not knowing what else to do she stood aside, standing well back to let him pass. Without being asked he peeled off his overcoat and hung it on the stand from which Dr Bevan's hat had just been removed.

Henrietta appeared in the doorway of her sitting room. She frowned. 'Are you collecting for something, young man? I don't see your tray of flags and collection tin.'

Meredith hoped that her grandmother was about to send this unwelcome visitor on his way, but it was not to be. He bounded forward, hand outstretched.

'You must be Meredith's grandmother! I'm James Boyer. Pleased to meet you!'

'How do you do?' Looking bewildered, Henrietta went back into the room, with Jimbo in her wake. There was nothing that Meredith could do, other than follow them in. What was the man doing here, and what did he want? He knew where she was staying, of course, because he and Frank had kindly driven her here, but the pair of them were supposed to be miles away by now.

'Aren't you meant to be in Cardiff now?' She had to say something to break the silence.

'What? Oh, that fell through. I didn't really want the job, actually, but I had to go through the motions. I mean, one does, doesn't one?'

168

'So what comes next, then? Are you after a job in this area, perhaps?'

'I happened to be in the district, so I thought I'd call on you. Perhaps you'd like to have dinner with me this evening? I'm sure we can find a nice quiet restaurant where we can get to know each other better.'

'That's very kind, but I don't think—'

'You must go, Meredith,' Henrietta interrupted. 'You should have some outings while you are here, and I'm sure that Mr Boynton will take good care of you!' She turned to him, simpering.

'Boyer,' he told her. 'And yes, Mrs Fletcher will come to no harm in my company. That's settled then, Meredith. I'll call back for you this evening, then. Shall we say seven o'clock?'

Meredith thought fast. 'I wouldn't dream of going out for a delicious meal while my grandmother is left sitting at home with a sandwich! You'd like to come too, wouldn't you, Grandmamma?'

'Why yes, I should like to, very much! How kind of you to invite me, Mr Barnham! It's not often that a handsome young man invites a lonely old woman out to dine!'

Anger flared in Jimbo's eyes for a second, but he quickly recovered his aplomb. When Meredith had closed the door behind him she found herself shaking, and she wondered why she should be upset. After all, there was no harm in going out for a meal with the man, although she hardly knew him, and she would be safe enough with Henrietta as chaperone. She was pretty sure, though, that he hadn't been in the district on any kind of business, but had come here specifically to see her. What could be his motive for doing such a thing? Should she be flattered? She felt no attraction for this Jimbo Boyer, and knew that it would be best to nip this association in the bud.

Chapter Thirty-seven

Ellen happened to be outside when the boys came home from school. Henry rushed past her, scowling, but Lucas stopped to show her a painting he had done, of a tall, scarecrow woman, standing next to a much smaller man.

'This is you, Nanny, and that's Uncle Harry,' he explained.

'Very nice, dear. Did you have a good day at school?'

He looked up at her, his little face wearing a sly expression. 'Henry got the stick!'

'Henry got the stick! Whatever did he do?' But the child broke away from her and ran to meet the older boys, who were approaching at a more leisurely pace.

Now what had that child been up to? He and Lucas were in Standard One now, where poor behaviour was likely to be rewarded with a stripe on the hand, but even so the teachers seldom used this form of punishment unless it was absolutely necessary.

'Do any of you know why Henry had the cane today?' she asked, as the boys reached her side. Evan nodded.

'I heard Miss Williams telling my teacher about it. They were having music, and Henry was supposed to play the triangle, but he wanted the ring of bells. He took it away from Angharad Rees and she started to cry. Then her friend hit him over the head with her tammerlean.'

'I think you mean tambourine, don't you?'

'That's what I said, Nanny. After that Henry hit her back and Miss got cross. She gave him two cracks with the cane, one for taking something which didn't belong to him and the other for hitting a girl.'

'Are you sure you heard all this, Evan?'

'Oh, yes, Nanny, honestly! My teacher said she dreads the day when she gets Henry in her class.'

'I can well believe it,' Ellen told Harry later. 'She probably won't have to teach him in Standard Four, though, if he goes away to prep school as planned. But really, Harry, this has to stop. It isn't the first time he's caused trouble in the music class, and you've seen what he's like at home. He's turning into a real little bully.'

Harry yanked on the bell pull. When Rosie arrived he asked her to send Myfanwy to him immediately.

'You're not going to give her a hard time, are you?' Ellen asked. 'You know her hands are tied. She has to choose between obeying Meredith's instructions or losing her job.'

'Meredith isn't here.' Harry's expression was grim.

'I suppose you've heard what happened at school today?' he asked, when Myfanwy stood facing him, with her arms folded.

'Yes, Mr Morgan. His poor little hand, all red and swollen! It's not fair, sir. It was Ceridwen Beynon who should have been punished, not him. She hit him with her tambourine.'

'Is that what he told you! You may be interested to know that she did that in defence of a smaller child, whose instrument Henry wanted for himself.'

'I believe that the two little girls are cousins,' Ellen put in.

'So he's fibbing, on top of all the rest,' Myfanwy concluded. In her book this was far worse than the actual physical assault, for children did indulge in horseplay until they were trained out of it, but telling lies was a sin.

'I'd like you to bring Henry to me, please,' Harry told her. 'This nonsense has to stop. It won't look well on his prep school application if he's expelled from Cwmbran Primary!'

Henry stood in front of his grandfather, scowling. Ellen noticed that the two of them looked very much alike at this moment, despite the many years between their ages. She hid a smile.

'What's this I hear about you being in trouble at school again, Henry?'

'I didn't do anything, Grandpa!'

'I heard that you took Angharad's bells away from her.'

'She's a silly cry baby. I was going to give her my triangle instead.'

'That is not the point, young man. When Miss Williams gives out

171

the instruments she expects her pupils to use them as she directs.'

Henry was still mutinous. 'Ceridwen hit me first!'

Ellen felt it was time for her to say something. 'Henry, dear, you're old enough to know right from wrong. You must try to do as the teacher tells you.'

He faced her, hands on hips. Sticking out his lower lip he yelled. 'You're only a servant! You can't tell me what to do!'

Before he had time to realize what was happening, he found himself bent over his grandfather's knee, receiving the first of three heavy smacks on his well-padded bottom. Roaring with indignation and hurt pride he slid down to the floor where he sat hunched over, rubbing his eyes with his knuckles.

'Now you listen to me, Henry Morgan Fletcher, and listen well! How dare you speak to my wife like that! She is also your grandmother. And, come to that, everyone in this house, servant or not, is worthy of respect, and I'll thank you to remember that.'

'She's not my grandmother,' Henry gulped. 'That's Granny Fletcher and Granny Meredith!'

'Granny Meredith is your great-grandmother, Henry. When Ellen married me, she became your grandmother, too, or step-grandmother, which amounts to the same thing. Now, I want you to apologize to Ellen.'

'Sorry,' he muttered.

'I'm very sorry I was rude,' Harry prompted. 'I won't do it again.'

Sullenly, the boy repeated his grandfather's words.

'Take him away, Myfanwy,' Harry snapped. 'No, wait. On second thoughts I have something to say to you. Cut along, Henry.'

When the child had bolted out of the room, Harry turned his attention back to the girl.

'Now, then, Myfanwy! What is all this talk of my wife being "only a servant"? I am seriously displeased. The boy would hardly have come up with that by himself. He must have overheard other people gossiping, and I want to get to to the bottom of this. If I find that you have been running my wife down behind her back, I shall have to think twice about keeping you on my staff.'

It was good of Harry to defend her, of course, Ellen reflected, but there was no getting away from it. She had been a servant in this house for many years until she'd married Harry, and she was proud of having given value for money during all the time she'd been his housekeeper. As for where the child had heard such talk, Harry must know that he wouldn't have far to look. His daughter, Meredith, had always been disparaging of Ellen. However, she was surprised by Myfanwy's answer.

'Oh, no, sir, I would never speak in that way against Madam, who has always been so good to me!' She looked pleadingly at Ellen, who gave her an encouraging smile in return. 'It was Wyn, sir!'

'Wyn! What does she know about it?'

Myfanwy hung her head. 'She's a bit nosy, sir, wanting to find out about all of us, and I think she talks to Bessie, see. One day she came up to the nursery with the clean laundry and she was asking questions of me in the children's hearing. I've been here longer than Bessie so I suppose she thinks I know more than she does. We didn't say nothing bad, sir.'

Harry grunted. 'Off you go, then. I shall speak to the pair of them and make my decision later as to whether you go or stay.'

'Oh, Harry, can't we just let this drop?' Ellen sighed, when Myfanwy had gone away, sniffing into her handkerchief. 'Henry's had a good smacking for being rude. Let that be an end to it.'

'Ellen, I will not have dissension and insolence in my home. Servants should not gossip about their employers, nor should they pry into their private affairs. If women like Wyn and Bessie had chattered in front of a son of the house in my mother's day, they would have been dismissed without a character before nightfall.'

'Servants have always gossiped about their employers, Harry. You forget that I've been on both sides of the fence!'

'This has gone beyond that, and if I don't put my foot down now there will be no end to it all. I'll give Wyn a severe dressing-down and let her stay on for the moment, but Bessie Prosser is a different matter. First the broken window, then an anonymous letter, and now this! I knew it was a mistake to hire a woman who had left her husband, but

I let you talk me into it.'

'That's hardly fair, Harry! It was Meredith who wanted to take the woman on trial, and against my better judgement, I may add!'

He glowered at her. 'Then you should have told her no!'

It was hardly the right moment to point out that he would brook no criticism of his daughter, nor would it ever be. Ellen was well aware of that, so she simply smiled and excused herself, saying that she had things to do.

Chapter Thirty-eight

Meredith woke up to find the sun streaming in at her window. Yawning, she sat bolt upright when she noticed the time; past nine o'clock! What on earth had made her oversleep like this? Then she remembered that she'd sat up late listening to a thriller on the wireless and after that had not been able to get to sleep. The room had seemed full of menacing shadows, and although she had told herself not to be so silly, she had not been able to shake off the fear that something, or somebody, might be waiting to pounce. She longed for a night light, like the stubby little candles standing in a saucer of water she'd had as a child.

Mrs Crossley was in the kitchen, chopping onions. A small dish of mince, two large carrots and a packet of Bisto awaited her ministrations. She looked up and smiled.

'Like me to make you a cup of coffee, Mrs Fletcher? It's only Camp, mind, but there's fresh milk.'

'Yes, please, that would be lovely. Have you seen my grandmother?'

'Oh, she went out, half an hour since.'

'Have you any idea where she went?' Meredith felt faintly alarmed.

'She didn't say, miss. I just saw her putting on her hat and coat, and off she went. I don't suppose she'll be long. She never is. Even if she meets up with friends she's always back by lunchtime, and she knows it's shepherd's pie today. She enjoys that.'

Sipping her coffee, Meredith wondered if the old lady should be out and about unaccompanied. But then, why shouldn't she? She had lived here for most of her life and knew the district well. She had probably established a little routine over the years, and keeping to it after her husband died was most likely a comfort to her.

As Mrs Crossley had said, she wouldn't be out for long. As if reading her thoughts, the woman remarked that it wasn't as if Mrs Meredith had to queue for foodstuffs.

'I tell her what we've run out of and she makes up a list for me to drop in at the Home and Colonial on my way home. That's where we're registered, see. If it's a big order they deliver, or if it's just a few bits and pieces I pick them up on my way to work the next time.'

Ten o'clock came, and eleven. Meredith found herself pacing up and down, giving numerous glances out of the window which overlooked the street. When noon struck with no sign of her grandmother she went out to the gate, looking up and down.

'Good day!' a man tipped his hat as he strode by, with a large retriever on a lead.

'Good morning!' she responded, although she had no idea who he was. Should she ask him if he'd seen Henrietta? But no, he might be a complete stranger, simply being polite.

'Shall I put this in the oven, or not?' Mrs Crossley asked, indicating her handiwork as she piped rosettes of mashed potato on top.

'I think we'd better wait and see. I can't think where she's got to.'

'I'll leave it on the marble slab in the larder, then. She won't want it all dried up, and it's a crime to waste good food with this rationing still on.'

'I'm a bit worried, Mrs Crossley. If she's not back by two, I think I'd better go and look for her.'

'You do that, miss. Now, what about your own lunch, then? If we're not going to have this pie, I can make you a nice meat paste sandwich. There's anchovy and tomato. Or there's lettuce,' she remarked doubtfully. 'I never thought to see the day when I'd serve a sandwich with nothing but lettuce in it; no meat or egg or anything. That Herr Hitler has a lot to answer for!'

'I don't think I could manage a thing just now, thanks all the same.'

'How about a nice cup of tea and a Marie biscuit, then? You need something to keep your strength up. You're thin as a lath already, if you don't mind me saying so.'

'Where do you think she might have gone, Mrs Crossley? In a town this size I've no idea where to start looking.'

'There's the library, of course. She could have gone there to change her book; but no, she can't have got through that so quickly. I picked up the new Ngaio Marsh for her just a couple of days back.'

Meredith doubted whether Henrietta really took in the content of her books these days. Just yesterday she had looked over her grandmother's shoulder and noticed that the book was being held upside down, while Henrietta looked at it with every appearance of enjoyment.

'Does she have any particular friends whom she might have visited, do you know?'

'There's Mrs Simpkins in Cherry Tree Close. Number 10, I believe it is. They used to walk in the park together. Or she used to be in thick with some of them in the Mothers' Union. You could call on the vicar and ask, I suppose.'

That gave Meredith a new idea. Her grandfather was buried in the churchyard. No doubt his widow went there often to make sure that his grave was being kept in good order.

'I'm off, then, Mrs Crossley. I'll be back as soon as I can.'

'Have you got a key, miss? Better borrow mine then, in case you don't get back before I'm off home.'

The head librarian knew Henrietta well, but when Meredith asked if her grandmother had called in that morning, the woman shook her head.

'I haven't seen her for ages, actually. Her Mrs Crossley usually comes in to return the books, and I pick out something I think she'd enjoy. How is she getting on with the new Ngaio Marsh I sent her? I read it myself and it's jolly good. That's one of the perks of being a librarian. I get first dibs at all the new arrivals!' She laughed, patting her glossy hair, which was done up in sausage curls. Meredith thanked her and left.

She tried the park next, but it was empty apart from an elderly man, sitting on a bench and engrossed in the *Daily Mirror*. She popped into a nearby florist's shop, on the off chance that Henrietta might have purchased flowers to put on Paul's grave, but the assistant shook her head.

'It's been a very slow morning, madam. Hardly a customer since we opened. I don't know the lady you refer to, but I'd remember if an elderly person had come in. We do have another branch near the church, though. Why don't you try there?'

'That's a good idea. Thank you.'

But when she entered the shop she drew a blank there as well. 'Of course I know Mrs Meredith,' the woman in charge told her, 'but I haven't seen her for ages. She's getting on a bit, isn't she, so the walk is probably too much for now. You're her daughter, are you?'

'Granddaughter. I'm staying with her for a bit.'

'That's nice. Some old folks never get a visitor from one year to the next. Criminal, that is. You give birth to children, spend half your life bringing them up, and then they never bother coming to see you.'

When she was able to stem the flow, Meredith purchased a small posy to place on her grandfather's grave. The graveyard was deserted when she arrived. She placed the flowers in front of his headstone, murmured a short prayer, and left. She then entered the beautiful old church, hoping to find Henrietta in one of the pews there, but it, too, was deserted. There appeared to be nobody home at the rectory, when she tried the broken bell without success and then rapped several times on the door. It was as if everyone had died or been spirited away and she had been left alone, like the haunted woman in last night's play.

After an hour of aimless wandering in the side streets she decided to go back to the house, hoping that her grandmother had arrived there before her. Her heart sank when Mrs Crossley called out to her.

'Is that you, Mrs Fletcher? Did you find your gran?'

'No, I didn't! I've been everywhere I can think of. Do you suppose she's lost?'

'Not very likely when she knows the place like the back of her hand, is it? Perhaps something's happened to her. Got herself knocked down by bus, say, or fainted dead away in the Blue Lady Caff.'

'Really, Mrs Crossley!'

'Well, these things happen, don't they! And she won't have been kidnapped by white slavers, not at her age. You did go to Mr Meredith's grave, I suppose, and made sure she wasn't there?'

'Yes, I did, and I put flowers on it. I also went into the church but there was nobody there, and there was nobody home at the rectory, so I had to come away.'

Mrs Crossley's eyes brightened. 'That's funny. There should be somebody there this time of day, if only the woman what does for them. What if he found your gran stretched out on the grave, overcome by grief? He'd have dashed off to call the ambulance, of course, and then he'd have gone with her, in case she pegged out on the way to the Infirmary.'

Meredith had had as much of this ghoulish talk as she could stand. 'That does it!' she snapped. 'I'm going to ring the police!'

Mrs Crossley had the last word. 'Better ring round the hospitals while you're at it. She might be in Casualty, waiting for someone to identify her!'

Chapter Thirty-nine

Bessie approached Harry Morgan's study with a sinking heart. As she climbed the stairs she met Wyn coming down. The girl's face was tear-stained.

'Don't know what he was going on about, silly old buffer,' she muttered. 'All I said was that his wife used to be a servant here, and what's wrong with that? It's true, isn't it? That fool of a Rosie thinks it so romantic, them getting married after knowing each other for years, but I can't see it myself. The old boy's got money and she was just a skivvy in his house, so why wouldn't she jump at the chance to marry him?'

'Ssh! If anybody hears you we'll be in more trouble than we are now. Did you get the boot?'

'Na. I'm to be given another chance. I'm not sure if I want it, though. It's not much fun working here. A bit of a dead and alive hole is this, if you ask me!'

'Nobody is asking you,' Bessie told her as she pushed past her on the stairs.

'Come in, Mrs Prosser.' Harry's voice was cold. She sidled in and stood waiting, while he pretended to be studying some papers on his desk. At last he looked up.

'Mrs Prosser, I'm sorry to have to say this, but your being here has not worked out for the best. I shall have to terminate your employment forthwith.'

Despite the stilted language she gathered that she was getting the sack. She resolved to go down fighting. 'Hasn't my cooking given satisfaction, then?'

'Your work has been quite acceptable, Mrs Prosser. It is your attitude I deplore. Writing anonymous letters is a despicable thing to do. I am surprised that you, as a member of the chapel, would not have known that! As for talking about my wife in derogatory terms, that I will not have!'

'It wasn't me as spoke up in front of the boy,' she muttered, for her stepdaughter had come down to the kitchen to warn her of what was afoot, and had let her in on the whole sorry tale. 'I happened to mention something to that Wyn, seeing as she asked me, and she had to go asking more questions of our Myfanwy. It wasn't my fault she blabbed in front of the boy.'

'That will do, Mrs Prosser. I'll pay you a week's wage in lieu of notice, and you can leave as soon as you've cleared away after the evening meal. Mrs Morgan will hand you the money after the work is completed to her satisfaction. That will be all, thank you.'

Bessie trudged back to the kitchen, fuming. For two pins she'd walk out the door right now, she thought, except that she'd lose the extra pay if she did. The cunning old devil must have read her mind when he told her she wouldn't get her money until the washing-up was done!

Now what was she going to do? Her first problem would be to find a bed for the night. Should she go to Gwyneth and see if the landlady would allow her to share her daughter's room for the night? Or perhaps she could get the girl to smuggle her in while the woman's back was turned.

Unfortunately the landlady was at home when Bessie arrived.

'You're not coming into my house,' she snapped, when she noticed Bessie's suitcase. 'No decent woman in Cwmbran would let you in, Bessie Prosser.'

'I've only come to have a word with my daughter,' Bessie lied. 'I didn't want to stop.'

'Huh! I know your sort! Think you can pull the wool over a poor widow's eyes. Once you get in I'd never get you out. For your information your Gwyn isn't here. She gone up the chapel, I think. It's choir practice tonight. Not that you'd know anything about that, after living up there with that church lot.'

Now what? There was only one thing left to do. Digging in her handbag she found the key to Number 17, Jubilee Terrace, which she had never relinquished. Praying that Job hadn't had the locks changed when she left, she trudged along to her former home.

Job didn't look up when he heard the key turning in the lock.

'That you, our Griff? You're home early, boyo!'

Bessie felt her heart beating wildly as she sidled into the kitchen where she had once held sway. 'It's me, Job. I've come home.'

Without looking up from his paper he growled something at her.

'What was that you said? I didn't quite catch.'

'Then you can catch this, woman! You can't come back here because I don't want you, see? I suppose your fancy job has fallen through, but

180

that's your problem. You clear off and take some other poor chap for a ride, cos you're not wanted here.'

'I got the sack because I stuck up for you, Job Prosser.'

'What do you mean?'

'Our Gwyn told me it was Llew who broke that window, not you. I told Mr Morgan that, and that's why they dropped the charges against you.'

'And I'm supposed to be grateful, is that it? You turn informer on my eldest son and you think I can overlook that? And now our Llew has gone abroad, or so he says, and I may never see him again. This is all down to you, Bessie Harries, and any man would find that hard to forgive.'

'Prosser,' she said automatically. 'Bessie Prosser is my name. I'm still your wife, Job. And as for this being all my fault, your precious son only smashed the window in the first place because you made him break off his engagement to the girl he loves. He did it so you'd get the blame, Job. What do you say to that, hey?'

'I say that if you'd been a proper wife to me you'd have stayed home where you belonged. Since you failed to do so, you're not coming back here.'

Bessie took a deep breath. 'I have news for you. Here I am, and here I'll stay!'

She prepared for flight, half expecting him to leap up and fetch her a clout, as he'd so often threatened to do. She didn't know whether to believe it when he simply shook his paper before turning to another page. She waited a few moments before she announced that she was going to put the kettle on.

'Please yourself!' he snapped, and to her relief said no more.

Whereas Job Prosser had come off worse in his battle with his wife, Harry Morgan remained very much the master in his own house. Ellen had pleaded with him in Bessie's cause, not so much because she was in sympathy with the woman as because she herself would now be stuck with cooking for sixteen people. Her husband, who of course had never boiled an egg in his life, was unimpressed.

'You can phone the Labour Exchange in the morning and get them to send somebody up for interview.'

'We've been through all this before, Harry. Times have changed since the war. Nobody wants to go into service nowadays. This was why Meredith took Bessie on in the first place. We were in desperate straits.'

'I'm sure that's an exaggeration, *cariad*.'

'And since you were kind enough to come to my aid when you thought I was shown disrespect, I'm surprised that you don't mind leaving your wife with all that washing-up. What we need is a kitchen maid and we haven't been able to find one for love nor money since the last one left to go and do war work.'

'Then you must tell that scatterbrained Wyn to help you in the kitchen. That'll teach her to watch her p's and q's.'

'She'll probably give in her notice,' Ellen warned, but Harry wasn't interested. In his own way he was as much of a stubborn male as Job Prosser. Household affairs were the province of women. He paid the bills, and in return he expected his home life to run smoothly.

'I'm sure you'll think of something,' he said dismissively.

Ellen went to see Myfanwy. The girl eyed her warily. Her stepmother had left an hour before and, looking out of the window, Myfanwy had seen Bessie shaking her fist up at the house. Was she to be next? She was amazed by Ellen's first words.

'Can you cook?'

'Um, I suppose I can.'

'I know you looked after your father and brothers after your mother died. That meant doing the cooking, I take it?'

'Yes, Mrs Morgan.'

'Then how would you like to take on the job of cook here? It would mean more money, of course.'

'But what about the boys?'

'They are in school now. They don't really need a nanny. Mariah and I look after the Swansea Six now, so what's two more?'

'I don't think Mrs Fletcher will like it much when she comes back and sees what has happened. She is my employer after all. I wouldn't want to upset her. I might lose my job as well as our Bessie.'

'Her father is the one who pays your wages, Myfanwy. And as for losing your job, you'll be working for me now, not Mrs Fletcher. So, what do you say?'

Myfanwy grinned. 'I say yes, please, Mrs Morgan, if you think it's all right!'

'That's settled, then. Sit down, and we'll work out the details.'

Chapter Forty

'I'd like to report a missing person,' Meredith said firmly.

'Yes, madam. And what is the name, please?'

'Fletcher. Mrs Fletcher.'

'And how long has Mrs Fletcher been missing?'

Meredith felt stupid. 'No, no. I'm Mrs Fletcher. It's my grandmother who has disappeared. Mrs Henrietta Meredith, her name is.'

'Address, please?'

Meredith supplied it. 'She went out early this morning and she hasn't been heard from since. I've looked everywhere I can think of, and she's nowhere to be seen.'

'So let me get this straight,' the disembodied voice said. 'This lady left home a few hours ago and hasn't yet returned. Have you any reason to suppose that she has met with an accident?'

Meredith felt like shouting into the telephone. She forced herself to remain calm. 'That's the whole point, Constable! I've no idea what has become of her. I've called the hospital, I've canvassed the neighbours, I've been to all the places she normally frequents, and she seems to have disappeared off the face of the earth!'

'I'm sure there's nothing to worry about, madam. I expect she's simply lost track of time and will turn up in due course, properly apologetic for having caused distress. And in the unlikely event that she has gone away without notifying you, she's over twenty–one and has a perfect right to make that choice. I'm afraid there's nothing we can do.'

'My grandmother is an elderly woman,' Meredith said, through gritted teeth. 'She's been a bit muddled lately and anything might have happened to her. Can't you just send someone out to make enquiries or something?'

'I'm sure everything will be all right,' the maddening voice said. 'We cannot file a missing persons report until twenty-four hours has elapsed. If Mrs Meredith hasn't returned by then, do call again and we'll take it from there.'

'Thanks for nothing!' Meredith retorted. 'Honestly, what do we pay your salaries for? This is not a lost dog we're talking about. It's an elderly person, not in the best of health! Surely you can do better than this!' But the line had gone dead and she was left holding the earpiece in her trembling hand.

Mrs Crossley had long since removed her overall and gone home, secure in the knowledge that her employer's disappearance was not her problem. The granddaughter was there, thank goodness; let her deal with it. It would soon be getting dark and she didn't like being out and about at night, even though the ban against street lighting had been rescinded since the end of the war.

The telephone rang, making Meredith jump. She raced to answer it, hoping for good news.

'Hello? Is this the Meredith residence?'

'Yes, it is,' she panted.

'The Hoxley police station here. We have a lady with us who says she is a Mrs Henrietta Meredith of that address. Is that correct?'

'Thank goodness! Yes, she's my grandmother. I've been half out of my mind with worry!'

The man at the other end hesitated for a moment. 'If you don't mind my saying so, the lady seems a little confused. She was found wandering the streets near here, and when asked for her name and address she at first told us that she was a Miss Henrietta Wentworth of

St Briavel's. It wasn't until she permitted us to look inside her handbag that we found an identity card showing her as Mrs Paul Meredith of your address.'

'Is she free to leave?'

'Absolutely. She's done nothing wrong. The couple who found her brought her along for her own protection. All we want is to hand her safely back to her family.'

'I can't tell you how relieved I am,' Meredith murmured. 'What happens next?'

'We could see her on to a bus travelling in your direction, if you could be there to meet her when she arrives. How would that do?'

Meredith wasn't sure. 'I'm just visiting Hereford; I'm not a local person. I'd be afraid of missing her somehow. And what do we do if she decides to get off the bus, somewhere along the way? Those people were kind enough to help her, as you said; we might not be lucky enough a second time.'

'That's true enough. Well, then, madam, you'll have to send someone to pick her up here. We'll provide her with a nice cup of tea and keep an eye on her until he comes.'

'I don't know of anyone I could send, so I'd better come myself,' Meredith said. She felt she really couldn't impose on the vicar, although if asked, the man would probably feel it his Christian duty to help.

'Right-ho!' The sergeant sounded cheerful enough. She supposed it was all in a day's work for him.

Buses going out to Hoxley came every half-hour. Meredith had stopped a respectable looking woman to enquire about this, but she was unable to recall the exact time of arrival.

'I have an idea that it's on the hour and the half-hour, dear, but I could be wrong. Still, you'll find out in due course, I expect.'

Unfortunately, when Meredith arrived at the bus stop it began to rain, and she had come out without an umbrella. There was nowhere to shelter, and she knew she'd be looking like a drowned rat before she arrived to spring Grandmamma from the police station. Once they left the place Henrietta would soon be in a similar condition and Meredith could only hope and pray that this little expedition didn't end in both of them being laid up with pneumonia.

'Can I offer you a lift somewhere?' Meredith was all ready to put her nose in the air and ignore the strange man, when she realized that his voice sounded familiar.

'It's me, Ambrose Bevan! Do get in, Mrs Fletcher. You're soaked to the skin!'

Meredith scrambled into the passenger seat, gasping.

'Where can I take you? Shall I deliver you to your grandmother's house?'

'I'm afraid they've got her at Hoxley police station. I'm going there to pick her up.'

He threw back his head and roared. 'Don't tell me she was caught shoplifting!'

The look she gave him would have frozen hot embers.

'That was a joke, Mrs Fletcher.'

She gave him a weak smile. 'I'm afraid I'm not in a laughing mood, Doctor. My grandmother slipped out of the house before I woke up this morning, and I've been hunting for her all day long. I phoned the local police station but they didn't want to know. She's over twenty-one and therefore has the right to come and go as she pleases. If it wasn't for the fact that some kind people found her in distress in Hoxley and took her to the police station there, anything could have happened.'

Suddenly overcome by the strain of the long day, Meredith began to weep. He handed her a spotless white handkerchief.

'Fear not, your knight in shining armour is here! I'll take you to Hoxley and then bring the pair of you home again.'

'You're so kind,' she whispered. As the car purred along she began to wonder what she would have done if he hadn't appeared when he did. Getting herself to Hoxley was one thing. Bringing Henrietta home if she declined to come, would be quite another problem, one she might not be able to handle.

'I'm sure you won't thank me for telling you this,' he said suddenly, 'but, speaking as a doctor, I have to point out that this can't go on.

She's been lucky this time, but what about the next time? And it will happen again, believe me.'

'I'll stay with her all the time,' Meredith promised.

'You were there when she left this morning, but she still got away. What do you mean to do, stay awake twenty-four hours a day? Tie a string from her toe to yours so you'll know when she's on the move?'

Despite herself, Meredith began to laugh.

'That's better! But while we're on the subject, I must say that the time is fast approaching when she'll need more care than you are able to give her. She needs to be in a secure environment, watched over by qualified staff.'

'You don't mean a lunatic asylum! She's not mad. Just a bit muddled.'

'Steady on! Nobody said anything like that. I was thinking more of a nice nursing home in the country, with other elderly patients. I know of a very pleasant private establishment, called The Firs. I could dig up a brochure for you if you like.'

'It won't do any good. I've heard her say that she'd never go into a home. Wild horses couldn't drag her there.'

He smiled, and Meredith decided that he really was a very nice man. 'Your grandmother was born in 1865, I believe. In those days people greatly feared going into the workhouse and they had good reason for that. Queen Victoria's dead, you know, and things are vastly changing in the field of medicine. Mrs Meredith would be well cared for, living among other people of her own sort. There's plenty of time. You don't have to decide anything tonight, but it will be good to have a plan up your sleeve in case matters come to a head sooner than we think. All right?'

Chapter Forty-one

Apart from Ellen and Myfanwy, nobody in the house was pleased with the change of plan.

'This is a daft idea, Ellen!' Harry said.

'You said it was up to me!' she retorted.

'Maybe I did, but I thought you'd find some experienced woman, not a young nursemaid. What does she know about cooking?'

'Quite a bit, apparently. Good, plain cooking, anyway. She may not be able to produce cordon bleu stuff at present, but she can learn. I'll find someone to teach her.'

'And another thing,' Harry went on, his face set in stubborn lines, 'what about Henry and Lucas?'

'What about them?'

'They can hardly stay up in the nursery by themselves, *cariad*, especially with winter coming when we'll have to keep the fires in. Anything could happen to those two little imps.'

'I've thought of that. I'm having their beds brought down to that big empty bedroom next to the Swansea boys' dorm. They'll be happy enough there.'

'I don't know, I'm sure!'

'Harry, this is the best plan all round. The boys are at school all day and there isn't much for Myfanwy to do. She told me she's been feeling restless lately and thinking about moving on. We don't want that, do we?'

'My nanny stayed here until I went away to school,' Harry insisted.

'So you've said, and you had a tutor in the house as well. You didn't go to the local school, as the boys do now. Times have changed, and we have to change with them.'

'Meredith won't like it,' was his parting shot, but Ellen was halfway down the hall and took no notice.

'Meredith will have to lump it,' she muttered under her breath.

Myfanwy was in the kitchen, singing as she worked. This was the life! A job she enjoyed, a raise in pay, and, best of all, no more Henry! He had come down to the kitchen yesterday, demanding that she clean his shoes, and she had told him off in no uncertain terms.

'You're a big boy now, Henry, old enough to see to your own shoes.'

'I don't know how,' he whined.

'Then it's time you learned. Get one of the Swansea Six to show you, and mind you don't get them to do the job.'

'I don't like you, Vanny!'

'So you've said before. You keep this up and you won't get any pudding. Now run along. I've no time to talk to rude little boys.'

He kicked the table leg before sauntering out of the room.

'And pick your feet up!' she shouted after him. 'You'll have the soles off your shoes in no time!'

Dealing with Henry was one thing; Wyn was quite another.

'This is exploration!' she grumbled, up to her elbows in soapy water.

'Exploitation,' Myfanwy said automatically.

'That's what I said. This isn't right nor proper. I'm a house parlour-maid, not a blinkin' skivvy!'

'Madam is paying you extra, isn't she?'

'A few blinkin' bob!'

'You should be thankful, then. Before I came here I was doing worse than this for eight people, and not a penny to show for it. My mother died when I was young and I had to step into her shoes, see, being the only girl. If you had to tackle dirty pit clothes like I did you'd have something to moan about, I can tell you that!'

'Your da sounds like a right old slave driver,' Wyn said, pushing the hair out of her eyes with her forearm.

'He's a good father and a good provider,' Myfanwy said primly, well aware that Bessie would say different, and frequently did, to anyone who would listen. 'Never mind him. I happen to know that Mrs Morgan has a plan, so you won't have to do double duty much longer.'

'I'd better not!' Wyn growled, 'or she'll have my notice, quick sharp. I don't know whatever possessed me to go into service. I'd be better off working in a shop. I fancy a nice dress shop with lovely clothes, or p'raps a flower shop, making up bokeys.'

'The money is better here, and we have our board and lodging thrown in. At least we get a chance to save a few shillings. I hope to have a bit put by before I marry.'

'Marry! That's a laugh! No chance of meeting any nice young chaps in this house! The only men around here are Mr Morgan and all them young boys. Oh, and that old dodderer working in the garden. When I went into service I thought there'd be a few footmen at least, or a handsome butler I could get to know.'

'They used to have some here at one time, but the war put paid to all that. Plenty of nice young miners in Cwmbran, though. You could have your pick of those.'

'Fat chance, working up here! How am I supposed to meet any of them? They don't even have a dance hall in this mouldy place.'

'Come to chapel and get to know them there,' Myfanwy told her. Wyn curled her lip. That wasn't her idea of a good time. Perhaps this dishwashing lark wasn't such a bad idea after all. She'd wait until she had a few pounds put away in the post office and then she'd be off, seeking the bright lights.

After much thought, Ellen went to see Myfanwy.

'I'm sure you'll agree that this can't go on much longer,' she began, having almost been knocked down by a truculent Wyn who was rushing out of the kitchen.

'No, madam. It is rather difficult, I must admit, being so short-handed. Not that I'm complaining, you understand,' she added, in case Ellen thought she was being difficult.

'I've been on to the Labour Exchange yet again, and the answer is still the same. Nobody wants a live-in job these days. So we'll have to see if we can get some part-time workers, perhaps some married women who'd like to earn some pin money.'

'What did you have in mind, madam?'

'Perhaps one or two who could come up in the morning, after they've seen their children off to school, do a couple of hours' work and then get off home again. It would mean putting the dishes in to soak overnight but I'd ask the gardener to bring in one of the tubs from the old wash house, and set it up in the scullery. And that's where you come in, Myfanwy.'

'Me, madam?'

'Yes. You must know everyone in Cwmbran. I'll give you an extra afternoon this week and you can go and call on one or two women and try to talk them into taking on the work.'

Myfanwy hesitated. Ellen noticed this and misunderstood the reason.

'You'll be paid a finder's fee, of course.' What was wrong with a little bribery if it led to a solution to their problem?

Myfanwy blushed. 'Oh, it's not that, madam. I'd be only too glad to help. It's well – you know what my father was like when Bessie came here to work, and before that when I started here – very upset, he was, and other husbands will be the same. Men don't like their wives going out to work, see.'

Ellen sighed. 'I know. It's an insult to their pride. They believe it reflects badly on their ability to provide for their families. You'll just have to try your best, that's all. And while you're at it, do you know of anyone who has a reputation as a good cook and baker?'

Myfanwy's face fell. Ellen was quick to reassure her. 'Oh, I don't want to replace you, my dear. Your work is quite satisfactory. More than satisfactory, in fact, but how would you like to take cookery lessons from someone who is really experienced? Perhaps you could go to this person's house one evening a week and pick up a few hints.'

Myfanwy was delighted with this idea. The first person she thought of was her stepmother, but Bessie turned her down flat.

'What, me help them out after being sacked? Not on your life! Anyway, old Morgan would never allow it.'

'You wouldn't have to go out to the House, Bessie. I'd come here to learn, Madam said. She'll pay you well.'

'And I know what would happen next! Your da would dock my housekeeping! What about your friend, Bronwen Evans, her you went to school with?'

'Bron? She can't boil an egg!'

191

'Na, na, her mam, silly!'

The wife of Evans the Post jumped at the opportunity to share her skills. 'The times I've offered to teach our Bron, and she can't be bothered. You'll be sorry one of these days, my girl, I said, when you get yourself a husband and can't feed him proper!'

Mrs Evans also knew of two neighbours who were having trouble making ends meet, so Myfanwy was able to return to Cwmbran House with good news for Ellen.

Chapter Forty-two

Relations were strained between Meredith and her grandmother over the next few days. Henrietta studiously avoided Meredith's eye, apparently realizing that she'd done something silly, but not wishing to acknowledge it.

After careful questioning Meredith managed to get part of the story out of her. She had decided to go to the town centre, to indulge in a little harmless window-shopping, and had set out to catch a bus to take her there. Unfortunately, she had boarded the wrong one. Anxiously looking out of the window in search of landmarks she recognized, and finding none, she had stayed on the bus until it reached the end of the route and then had been asked by the driver, kindly enough, to get off.

By now she knew she'd made a mistake, so she decided, quite sensibly, that she would remain on the bus for the return journey. Unluckily, that wasn't on the schedule and the driver explained that he had to carry on in a different direction, in order to deliver the vehicle to a garage where it was due for an inspection. Another bus would arrive in two hours' time, and Madam could take that. Meanwhile, why didn't she find somewhere to have a refreshing cup of tea?

'It's a good job she didn't lose her bag while she was at it,' Mrs Crossley remarked, when she heard this sorry tale. 'Imagine her telling them she lived at St Briavel's, like when she was a young girl, and her a married woman all these years! That's one good thing about them identity cards they made us get in the war, at least the coppers knew where to find you.'

'I'll have to find someone to live in permanently,' Meredith told her.' My grandmother obviously isn't fit to stay on her own any longer.'

'I hope you're not thinking of me! I've got a home and a husband to see to. It was all right when the war was on, and him away in the army, but it won't work now.'

'I know that, Mrs Crossley, and I'm grateful for all you do. I was hoping to find her a companion, perhaps an elderly person who'd be glad of a nice home in return for a bit of light housework and looking after my grandmother. A paid person, of course.'

'She won't like that.'

'She won't object if I put it in the right way. People of her generation did have companions, you know. My mother did, for one.'

Surprisingly, Henrietta agreed. 'My daughter, Antonia, had such a person. Lavinia somebody. I wonder what happened to her? Perhaps she would agree to come here.'

'I expect she's dead by now,' Meredith said, diplomatically. 'I didn't know her, of course, but I believe she was years older than Mother.' For all she knew the companion and Grandmamma were contemporaries, but it wouldn't do to point that out. Henrietta was rather vain about her age. Besides, some energetic, middle-aged person was what she was looking for, someone capable of running in pursuit of Henrietta if she took it into her head to play truant again. Meanwhile, that left Meredith herself to play nursemaid.

'Grandmamma, I have to ask you something.'

'Yes, dear, what is it?'

'I want you to promise me that you won't leave the house again without telling me.'

Henrietta's eyebrows shot up. 'Why should I do that, dear? I'm not

193

senile, you know. I'm used to coming and going as I please, and I shall continue to do so.'

Oh, dear! 'It's just that I worry about you, Grandmamma. You did end up at Hoxley by mistake, and you'd been missing for hours before I finally found out where you were. I can't let that happen again.'

'Is that so!' Henrietta was very much on her dignity now. 'When I want a chit of a girl to tell me what I can do, I shall let you know! Now, if you'll excuse me, I'm going upstairs for a nap!'

Meredith was greatly relieved when Dr Bevan called in to see how his patient was feeling after her ordeal.

'Grandmamma seems perfectly well, Doctor! I'm the one who's a nervous wreck!'

He grinned. 'Giving you a hard time, is she?'

'That's the understatement of the year! She refuses to listen to me and she makes me feel as if I'm back in the schoolroom, causing trouble for my governess!'

'You'll have to develop a thicker skin, Mrs Fletcher. There's no reasoning with a patient in this state. Look, I've brought you a brochure for The Firs, as promised.'

'Thank you very much, but I'm sure it won't be any good. She'll simply refuse to countenance the idea of moving to a home, and I can't very well tie her up and drag her there, can I?'

'Even if you could, it wouldn't be feasible now. I've made enquiries and there's a long waiting list for The Firs, and it's the same at any similar facilities. It could be months, even a year or more, before a vacancy comes up.'

'There isn't much of a turnover, then?'

The doctor's expression grew serious. 'I'm afraid that a vacancy only crops up when a resident dies. Unless someone's relations have a change of heart and remove that person from the home, people who go into these places don't come out again.'

'That sounds so final, Doctor!'

'Oh, don't mind me! I've had a difficult morning. The Firs is a pleasant place, and the people there quite enjoy life, in company with others in their age group. The alternative is for them to struggle on in their own homes, which can pose problems, such as you've experienced with your grandmother.'

Meredith blinked back her tears. 'What are we going to do, Doctor? I don't know what to do for the best.'

'First of all, I'd advise Mrs Meredith to grant power of attorney to someone she trusts.'

'I don't understand. What does that mean?'

'It means that she authorizes that person to deal with any necessary matters if she should become incapacitated in the future, whether it has to do with health, or finances, for example. Whereas everything is ticking over relatively smoothly at present, we must be prepared for some sudden change in her condition.'

'You mean if she becomes even more confused?'

'Perhaps, or say she had a stroke, or fell and broke a hip. Anything like that, where she was no longer able to manage for herself.'

Meredith was sceptical. 'I can't see her giving me that power of whatever it is.'

'Perhaps not, but isn't there some reliable male relative whom she trusts? Women of her generation, who have been sheltered all their lives, often have the notion that a man should be in charge. Misguided, but there it is!' He laughed heartily, and Meredith wasn't sure whether he agreed with the idea or not!

'There's my father, of course. She's always gone to him for advice. He's a former magistrate and he knows how things should be done. I'll give him a ring later and ask his opinion.'

'That's settled, then. Now, what about you?'

'Me?'

'Yes. Is it possible to stay on here indefinitely, or can your grand-mother afford to pay nurses to stay in the house after you leave? She really shouldn't be left on her own, you know.'

'I do understand that. I was thinking of advertising for a compan-ion. Meanwhile I can stay on.'

'Surely you have to get back to your little boy?'

'There's no rush, Doctor. He has a nanny, and there are plenty of other people in the house. My father is there, and his wife, and the servants, of course, and our evacuees. But if I'm going to be here for a while I should register with a practice in case I need a doctor for myself. Can I sign on with you?'

Dr Bevan looked at her with an enigmatic smile before replying. 'No, Mrs Fletcher, I don't think that would do at all!'

Quite taken aback by this refusal she stared at him in return. 'Why on earth not?' she blurted.

'Because I'd like to invite you out to dinner, and it's quite unethical for a doctor to socialize with his patients in that way. If I asked you, would you come?'

Blushing, she said she'd be delighted. After he'd gone she pondered this new turn of events. It had been years since any man had shown an interest in her – apart from the awful Jimbo – and she'd become used to thinking of herself as a widow, more or less on the scrap heap. But she wasn't thirty yet, and, fingers crossed, she had years left to live. Surely it was time she came out of her shell. She could marry again, have brothers or sisters for Henry, perhaps leave Cwmbran and see something more of the world.

Laughing, she pulled herself together. 'Idiot!' she told herself. 'The man has simply asked you out for a meal, and here you are, planning a future with him. You don't even know each other!'

Then it hit her. How could she possibly go out for the evening, leaving Henrietta alone? She had visions of her grandmother perhaps putting the kettle on, forgetting it, and leaving it to boil dry. She could burn the house down!

Chapter Forty-three

'Here you are at last!' Mariah greeted her husband with a kiss, but he could see that she had other things on her mind.

'What's the rush? I'm not late. Were we meant to be going somewhere and I've forgotten all about it?'

'No, no. It's your pal, Frank. He's phoned three times already today. Says it's urgent, but he won't let me take a message.'

'I'll call him back. Did he leave a number where he can be reached?'

'He said he was phoning from work, so he'll call back around five. It's gone that now; that's why I was afraid you wouldn't be home in time and he'd be out of luck again.'

'I'll just run up and change out of these damp clothes,' Aubrey told her. 'If the phone rings before I get back, just tell old Riley to hang on. And before you remind me, I know it'll be a trunk call. I'll be as quick as I can.'

Half an hour later he was waiting by the telephone when it rang, making him jump.

'Hello? Cwmbran House?'

'Is that you, old bean? Frank here. Glad I caught you at last.'

'What's up? Mariah is being very mysterious. I'm quite intrigued. Congratulations, by the way! I gather you got the job.'

'What? Oh, yes. I started last week. That why I didn't want you calling back. No personal calls, that's the rule here in the lower echelons. Look, you remember that chap Boyer I brought to visit you? I've been asking a few questions, Mortimer, and it seems he's a wrong 'un. The thing is, he seemed to have taken a fancy to Meredith, and I think she should be warned.'

'There was something about him that I didn't take to. Mariah thought I was making too much of it, but he was asking too many questions for my liking. I got the impression he fancies his chances there. When Harry goes, young Henry inherits the house and the estates but if he's still a minor when that happens I expect that the lawyers or their appointee will administer it all for him. Obviously Meredith will have a finger in the pie, and it may well be that she'll receive a sizeable inheritance of her own. If she remarries – and we all hope that she will, some day – I suppose her husband will share that.'

'I had an idea that something like that might be on the cards. That's why I wanted to warn you.'

'If she's unlucky enough to get involved with some unscrupulous devil she could lose the lot, but I don't believe there's much danger of her falling for Boyer. Even if he does turn up again, she's not here at present.'

'Haven't you forgotten something? We delivered her to the grand-mother's house. Boyer knows exactly where Meredith is staying, and none of you is there to protect her. You won't be so complacent when you hear what I have to tell you.'

When Aubrey had hung up the phone he found his wife at his elbow, all agog to know what was going on.

'Come on, Aubrey! Don't keep me in suspense! What's going on with Frank?'

Aubrey repeated what his friend had told him. Frank had landed the job at Cardiff, which meant of course that Boyer had not. He was just starting to get into the swing of things when a fellow clerk came up to him and whispered that there was a young woman to see him.

'I've left her in the foyer, though. If old Peters finds out you're entertaining girls during working hours he'd throw a fit!' They were all aware of the chief clerk's evil temper. Frank found the girl, sitting bolt upright on a wooden bench, clutching her handbag with both hands. She would have been pretty if she hadn't had such a worried look on her face.

'I'm Frank Riley. Can I help you?' The girl sprang to her feet. She barely came up to his shoulder and he found himself looking down at a mass of red curls, topped with a saucy little hat.

'I'm Brenda Deacon. I've come here to see Jim, but that other man told me he doesn't work here!'

'I'm afraid there was just the one job going, and I've got it,' Frank said apologetically.

'Jim told me about you. You went on holiday together while you were waiting to hear about the job, didn't you? That's how I know your name, you see.'

'Yes, well, I'm afraid I don't know where he is now. To tell you the truth I don't know where he's from at all, other than that he worked in London during the war. Whitehall. Something hush hush, that he's still not allowed to talk about.'

Brenda frowned. 'Oh, no, I'm afraid you've got that wrong. We're from Bedford, both of us. Jim worked in the council offices there. That's why we thought the Cardiff job would be a step up. We're going to be married, you see.'

'You mean to say he didn't do any war work? Wasn't he called up?'

'He had his call-up papers all right, but they wouldn't have him. He was born with a heart murmur, you see. He wasn't a shirker, if that's what you're thinking!'

'That didn't occur to me, Miss Deacon.' Just a liar and a chancer, Frank thought. 'I'm so sorry, I have no idea where Boyer is now. There is nothing I can do.'

One of the typists now walked by, casting a curious look at the new employee and the distressed-looking woman. She hoped they weren't married, because she rather fancied him herself.

'But I must find him!' Brenda insisted.

Frank tried to edge away. If he didn't get back to his desk soon he could be in trouble. 'I suggest you go home, Miss Deacon, and wait for him there. I bet he's gone after another job somewhere, and doesn't want to tell you until it's in the bag.'

'But I have to find him now!' she wailed. 'We have to bring the wedding forward! If we wait until next spring it'll be too late!'

Now he understood. She must be expecting a baby and she hoped it would be born in wedlock.

'I'm sorry,' he muttered again, and walked away, feeling like an utter heel.

'And that's where he left it,' Aubrey explained. 'He has a nasty idea that Boyer knows that the girl has a bun in the oven and she's about to be let down.'

'And what's worse, he's got his eye on poor Meredith instead!' Mariah groaned, upset by the sordid little tale. She didn't always care for Meredith's attitude, but they were half-sisters after all, and families have to look out for their own. 'You'll have to put Harry in the picture, so he can warn her. I know what'll happen if I say something. She'll be convinced that I'm just trying to spoil things for her. If Jimbo does turn up at Henrietta's she's likely to listen to what he has to say, just to spite me.'

'Women! You're all alike. Why can't you tackle things in a straight-forward manner, like men can?'

Sensibly, Mariah ignored this sally. 'Go on, why don't you speak to Harry right away? Mam says he means to phone Meredith this evening. I suggest you get to him first.'

So Aubrey made his way to Harry's study, and told his story for the second time.

'I'm glad you put me in the picture,' Harry told him. 'I should hope that my daughter would have more sense than to get involved with such a bounder, yet it wouldn't be the first time that a girl's head has been turned by a charming scoundrel.'

Harry was furious when he mentioned this to Meredith that evening and she told him that Boyer had already turned up in Hereford.

'Actually he took both of us out to dinner the other evening. Grandmamma was quite taken with him.'

'The nerve of the fellow! Who does he think he is! You can tell him from me that if he dares to show his face there again I shall take steps to ban him from coming within a mile of the place!'

'You can't do that, Dad. There's no law against a single man inviting a lady out for a meal. It was all very respectable, and I was well chap-eroned.' She conveniently ignored the fact that she hadn't taken to Jimbo and that her every instinct had warned her not to be left alone with him. She now put that down to the fact that she had led too shel-tered a life since her husband's death, living in the family home with her father and servants to look after her. She was no longer a giddy girl. If she ever hoped to lead a normal life she would have to get into the swim of things. Paddle her own canoe. Wasn't that what the Americans said? She decided to change the subject.

'Actually, Dad, someone else has asked me out!'

'Who might that be?'

'Grandmamma's doctor. He seems very nice.'

'A doctor, eh? That sounds better than an unemployed clerk who likes to lie about what he did in the war! Shall you go?'

'I'm thinking about it. The only trouble is, I can't leave Grandmamma on her own. Which reminds me, I have to discuss something with you.'

The talk then turned to Henrietta's health, and Jimbo Boyer was forgotten.

Chapter Forty-four

Matters came to a head when Meredith wanted to make a flying visit to Cwmbran. Harry's seventieth birthday was coming up, and although he insisted that he didn't want a fuss, the whole family felt that such an important milestone couldn't be allowed to pass uncelebrated.

'Bad enough that I've got this far,' he grumbled. 'I don't need reminding of how old I am. Makes me dwell on my own mortality.'

'Nonsense! You'll go on for years yet,' Ellen insisted. She knew she had to tread carefully. He was inclined to be sensitive about the more than twenty years' difference in their ages.

At last he agreed that there could be a family dinner, but no gifts. As for any feudal-type activity with his employees and tenants coming to the house to pay their respects, that was totally out of the question.

'That might have been all right in my grandfather's day, but it certainly won't do now!' he told Meredith, his disgust plainly evident over the phone. Nevertheless, there would be this family gathering – he could hardly prevent that when almost everyone was already living in the house – and she wanted to be present. That meant that somebody had to be with Henrietta while her granddaughter was away.

The agency had sent three women to the house for interview.

Henrietta had agreed to the idea of a companion; now that she was used to Meredith being in the house she didn't relish the idea of staying alone overnight. She visualized an obedient servant who would do her bidding, rather than the jailer whom Meredith had in mind.

'You'll talk to them, won't you, dear?' she asked, sounding plaintive. 'I can feel a headache coming on.'

'Yes, Grandmamma. You'd better go and lie down before it gets any worse.' Just as well to chat to them without Gran butting in, she thought.

'I've shown them into the morning-room,' Mrs Crossley announced, when Meredith came downstairs, tugging at the hem of her jumper, which seemed to have shrunk in the wash. She was badly in need of a replacement but had run out of those wretched clothing coupons.

'Thank you, Mrs Crossley. I'll see them individually in the sitting-room.'

The first candidate was a Miss Elinor Robinson. Tall, thin, slightly stooped, she wore a flannel skirt which drooped at the hem, and a grey wool twinset. She was inclined to twitter, and to Meredith's way of thinking she was the epitome of a distressed gentlewoman, as Harry would have said, could he have seen her. It turned out that she was one of that dying breed of spinster daughters who had given up a life of their own in order to minister to ageing parents, or, in this case, a widowed father.

'And of course I quite expected to have our home after his death,' she bleated, 'but when his solicitor read out the will after the funeral, I was left with nothing. The house went to my brother, who seldom came near the place when Father was alive. Father was old-fashioned, you see, Mrs Fletcher. He believed that property was best left in the hands of the men.'

'How awful for you!' Meredith was appalled. 'Perhaps he felt that your brother would provide for you.'

'Jeremy? Not he! He's gone back to Torquay, and the house is to be sold. He's made it quite clear that his wife has plans for the money it will bring, and no doubt it will fetch a good price, with so many people desperate for accommodation.'

Meredith longed to be able to do something for the poor soul, who was currently living in a bedsitter where she heated soup on a gas ring. However, she had to decide what was best for Henrietta, and Miss Robinson obviously wouldn't do. Henrietta would walk all over the poor soul. When the unhappy woman had stopped rabbiting on Meredith told her that she'd be in touch, and handed her a florin for bus fare, which the woman gratefully accepted.

The next candidate was a cheerful cockney, a middle-aged woman who introduced herself as Madge Harlow. 'Like Jean, only not as blonde and not as well off!' she roared, laughing at her own wit. Anyone less like the famous star of the silent screen was hard to imagine. The colour of Mrs Harlow's hair was such a flaming red that there was little doubt it had come out of a bottle, while rouge and lipstick had been applied to her wizened face with a heavy hand.

'Never had much to do with old people,' she explained, 'but I brought up six kids. and that ought to count for something. Where's the old girl I'm supposed to be looking after, then? Didn't peg out before I got here, did she? What a cheek!' She roared with laughter again.

'My grandmother is lying down,' Meredith said faintly. 'She's not feeling very well.' She went on to ask a few more questions, but her mind was made up. Henrietta would suffer this vulgar crone for no more than five minutes before showing her the door.

This left the third woman. 'She'll be here in a minute,' Mrs Crossley said, whispering behind her hand. 'Had to go to the lavvy.'

'And her name is?'

'Sabrina Cole, or so she says! What a name to go to bed with! Oops, here she comes now. Hope she didn't hear me!'

Miss Cole was streets ahead of the previous pair. Thirtyish, Meredith decided, summing her up. Neatly dressed, sitting with her hands folded, waiting for the interview to start before she began to speak.

'Do you have experience in looking after older people, Miss Cole?'

'Oh, yes. I worked for some years as an auxiliary in an old folks' home.'

'Where was that?'

'In Coventry, that was. It was bombed, though, flat as a pancake.'

There was no need for either of them to elaborate on that. Everyone knew how badly the beautiful town had suffered, with its medieval buildings destroyed, the cathedral shattered, and its terrible death toll. Hitler had ordered its destruction in retaliation for the bombing of Munich by the RAF, and his Luftwaffe had returned again and again to wreak havoc there.

'Can you provide references, Miss Cole?'

'No can do. The matron and the rest of the staff were killed outright. Lucky for me it was my days off and I'd gone to see my sister, in Reading. Nobody left to say whether I'd worked there or not.'

'But surely you've been in work since then?'

'I went to look after an old lady in Croydon. Bedridden, she was, after a stroke. She died in the end, but it was a merciful release, poor soul. After that I went to work in a fishmonger's, but I really want to get back to my real work. Looking after people is what you might call my vocation, Mrs Fletcher.'

Meredith was impressed. She knew she ought to check Miss Cole's references before coming to a decision, but she was desperate. She'd miss Harry's birthday if she couldn't find somebody to stay with her grandmother, and in any case, what could the fishmonger tell her? Chopping the heads off cod was hardly a recommendation for an old lady's companion.

'I'm willing to take you on trial,' she said. 'I have to go away for a few days, leaving almost immediately. When I return I shall see how you've got on, and I may be able to confirm your position then. Can you start tomorrow?'

'Yes, Mrs Fletcher. I'll pack my bits and pieces and report for duty in the morning.'

'Good. Shall we say nine o'clock, then?'

'I've done it, Mrs Crossley!' Meredith poked her head around the kitchen door, feeling very pleased with herself.

'Oh, yes? Which are we getting, then? Not that hussy with the dyed hair, I hope!'

'No, the last one, Miss Cole. She's worked with elderly people before, so she should know how to handle Grandmamma.'

Mrs Crossley sniffed. 'Best of a bad bunch, I suppose.'

'You didn't take to her?'

'Nothing wrong with her that I could see, but I was hoping for a more homely sort of body. A comfortable sort of person you could have a chat with.'

Meredith looked forward to reporting her success to Ambrose Bevan. She wanted to impress him as a capable woman who could take charge of any situation. Although he certainly hadn't chided her in any way, she had the feeling that he must think of her as a useless case, letting her grandmother wander off as she had done.

After spending several years in a sort of social wilderness she was rather pleased to find herself with two men on her string. Was that really true? She decided that it might well be. Jimbo Boyer was definitely interested, and although Ambrose hadn't exactly expressed undying love, they had spent an evening together on several occasions, whenever Mrs Crossley could be bribed to sit in.

That lady had expressed the opinion that the doctor was only interested because he was a newcomer who didn't know anybody in the town, but what did she know about it? It appeared to Meredith that he was genuinely interested in her, and he'd even asked questions about young Henry, which pleased her.

Chapter Forty-five

'Feeling a bit blue, love?' Aubrey rubbed Mariah's back by way of consolation. She leaned into his shoulder, seeking comfort.

'It's no go again, I'm afraid.'

'Plenty of time, love.'

'I'm starting to think we'll never have a family, Aubrey. Mam says it was stress and strain that stopped me conceiving, but the war's been over for more than a year, and still not a sign of a baby. What if we can't have children? I don't know if I can bear it. And don't start telling me I've got the Swansea Six! I want a child of our own!'

'I wasn't going to, Mariah. Maybe you should go along and have a word with the doctor. He might be able to suggest something.'

'Such as?'

'How should I know? If I had all the answers we wouldn't need to pay him!'

Mariah went to find her mother. 'Aubrey thinks it's time I saw a doctor, Mam. There must be something wrong with me if I can't conceive.'

'It could be him,' Ellen reminded her. Still, it did seem odd. She herself had conceived after only one encounter, while her daughter had been married for several years with, sadly, nothing to show for it.

So Mariah went to consult a young and newly qualified doctor who had recently taken over Dr Lawson's old practice. She came back looked thoroughly dissatisfied.

'That was a waste of time and money!' she grumbled to Aubrey. 'He wants to send me to a specialist.'

'That's all right; we can afford it.'

'That's not what I'm worried about. I don't want to be poked and prodded by some stranger with cold hands!'

He laughed. Mariah pulled a face at him. He was a man. How could he possibly understand? She was surprised by his next words.

'We could always adopt, you know.'

'Don't be silly. You've always said you wouldn't feel happy about bringing up a child who wasn't your own. Don't deny it. I heard you saying that to Meredith one day, when she was having one of her tantrums over Henry and Lucas having a spat.'

'I was only showing the woman a bit of sympathy. None of you seems to understand what she's been through. How would you like it if my love child suddenly turned up to haunt you?'

'You have a love child?'

'No, of course I don't! I was just using that as an example. You know how she idolized Chad – quite mistakenly, as it turned out – and she was shocked to the core when Dulcie arrived with Lucas on her hip.'

'I'm sure she was, but that doesn't excuse the way she's been behaving towards an innocent child.'

'We could do something to alleviate that situation, Mariah. Why don't we adopt Lucas?'

'Adopt Lucas!'

'Yes, why not? He's a nice little chap and he could do with some loving parents.'

'But would we be allowed to? I'm sure there's a lot of red tape to untangle before one can adopt a child.'

'It shouldn't be too hard. Lucas is already a blood relative.'

'How do you work that out?'

'Well, Chad was a distant cousin of Harry, who happens to be your father, so that must make you and Lucas some sort of cousins too.'

'I suppose it does. Let me think about this for a while, OK?'

Aubrey patted her arm, well pleased with his suggestion. He hated seeing his wife looking so drawn and pale, and if adopting the little boy would make her smile again he was more than willing to go along with it. Besides, he had heard of several cases where women who had believed themselves to be barren went on to have more children after adopting their first one. He had no idea how that could be, but possibly it had to do with them becoming more relaxed after they stopped fretting.

'I'm not sure, Mam. What do you think?' As always in times of inde-cision, Mariah had gone to her mother.

'I think it's a splendid idea. The poor little chap could do with a more settled home life. I'd consider adopting him myself if Harry and I were a few years younger. You don't sound too sure, though. You like him, don't you?'

'Of course I do. But I already have quite a lot to do with Lucas, more than ever now that Myfanwy has changed roles. To me he just feels like an addition to the Swansea Six. I can't see how things would be much different if we adopted him formally.'

Ellen nodded agreement. 'There's no need to rush into anything, of course. Think it over carefully. Mind you, if you do this you won't have to keep that appointment with the specialist that you're so worried about!'

'I won't have to do that in any case, if I decide to cancel!' Mariah declared, but she smiled as she said it.

Meanwhile, Aubrey was not about to let the matter rest. When he and Harry were out doing a tour of the farms he brought the subject up.

'What would you say if I told you that Mariah and I are thinking of adopting Lucas?' he began. Harry raised his eyebrows.

'I'm glad to hear it, my boy! And you won't be the loser for it. I'll settle something on him to help provide for his future. I'll see my solicitor at once.'

'Whoa! Wait a minute. I only said we're considering it. Mariah hasn't made up her mind yet and I don't know what she'll decide in the end.'

'I'd say it was a foregone conclusion, wouldn't you? I've seen her with the little chap. Quite the little mother.'

'Still, we mustn't try to force her into anything, Harry. She has a stubborn streak, you know. It might tip the scales in the other direc-tion.'

'She gets that from her mother. She'll come round in the end. Ellen always does.'

'We mustn't let Lucas get wind of this until it's all cut and dried,'

Aubrey cautioned.

'Of course not, but there's no harm in planning ahead! I say, why don't I put his name down for my old prep school? He can go there when Henry starts. Up to you, of course, old boy.'

'I don't think that Mariah would approve of that, Harry.'

'That school gave me a good start in life, and it can do the same for our boys. I can't think what she could possibly have against it.'

Aubrey certainly could, but he didn't dare voice his opinion to Harry. Young Henry made Lucas's life a misery now; what would it be like when the pair of them were far away from home, trying to fit into the group? He wouldn't put it past Henry to spill the beans about his half-brother's parentage. As far as he was aware, Henry didn't yet know the whole story, but that didn't mean he wouldn't find out in due course, and blurt it out to all and sundry. No, if Lucas did go away to school when the time came, it would have to be to a totally different establishment.

When Mariah finally came to terms with the idea of adopting Lucas, Aubrey was delighted. 'I knew you'd come round to my way of thinking,' he told her.

'Is that so!' She looked so stern that for a moment he believed he'd put a foot wrong and she was going to change her mind, but then she burst out laughing.

'Got you there, Aubrey Mortimer!'

'So where do we go from here?'

'I think the next step is to sound Lucas out, don't you? He's six years old and should have a say in the matter. He can't be handed over like a parcel.'

So they took Lucas out for a walk, turning down Ceri's plea to accompany them.

'We've got something to ask you,' Aubrey began, leaning against the chestnut tree.

'Yes, Uncle Aubrey?'

Aubrey took a deep breath. 'How would you like a mummy and daddy of your own?'

The boy looked up at him, not understanding. 'I've already got a mummy and a daddy. They're in heaven, and I don't think they're coming back. I want them to, but God won't let them. Why is that, Auntie?'

Mariah swallowed the lump in her throat. How was she supposed to answer that?

'It's a mystery,' she said at last. 'The thing is, Lucas, Uncle Aubrey and I, we'd like to be your parents now. How would that suit you?'

He thought for a moment. 'Do we have to have Henry as well? Because if we do, I don't think I want it.'

'No, no, dear. Henry has his own mummy. She's only gone away for a little while, to help her grandmother, but she's coming back for Uncle Harry's birthday.'

'Oh. All right, then. You can be my mummy if you want to.' He looked up at Aubrey. 'And you can be my daddy.'

'Thank you, Lucas.' Aubrey suddenly felt very emotional. He bent down and gathered the child into his arms before walking on. They were going to be a family.

Chapter Forty-six

Jimbo Boyer approached the house cautiously. The last time he had presented himself at the door Meredith had all but sent him away with a flea in his ear. She was too well bred to speak to him rudely, but she hadn't invited him in, saying that it wasn't a convenient time. That could have been true, because he'd caught a glimpse of the old grand-mother in her nightgown, trailing her dressing gown behind her. On the few occasions he'd been in her company she'd seemed sensible enough, but Meredith had hinted that she was apt to become confused, so that she couldn't be left alone.

Raising his hand to the bell push, he was surprised to see that the front door was ajar. Odd, that. Women alone in the house were always careful to lock up at night. Had Meredith slipped next door for some reason, intending to return within minutes?

He put his head round the door. 'Hello? Anyone home?' There was no answer. 'Meredith? Are you there? It's me, Jimbo.'

Still no reply. He tried again. By now he was becoming alarmed. Deciding it was time to investigate, he stepped into the hall, stopping to pick up a walking stick from the hall stand. It wasn't much of a weapon but it would do at a pinch if an intruder was in the house. It did not occur to him that he, himself, was an intruder.

All the downstairs rooms were unoccupied. There was a faint light upstairs. He went up, hearing his heart thumping. He pushed open the first door he came to, and saw Henrietta, lying on her bed. He tiptoed away and went to try the other doors. When he was sure that Meredith was nowhere in the house he stopped for a moment to consider this. She had been adamant that she would not leave the old lady alone in the house, so what could have happened? While he'd suspected that she might be trying to give him the brush off, he was sure she'd been sincere in telling him that.

He went back into Henrietta's room. She was lying so still that he feared the worst, but when he drew closer he realized that she was breathing noisily, not snoring, but a strange snuffling sound that seemed all wrong. He spoke her name, but she did not stir. He tentatively touched her shoulder, which had no effect.

Should he call an ambulance? That might not be the right thing to do. After all, he had no medical experience. For all he knew there could be no need for alarm. On the other hand. . . .

He made his way downstairs where, to his relief, he found a card by the telephone which listed emergency numbers. He took down the earpiece and asked the operator to be connected to Dr Bevan's surgery.

'Bevan!'

'Er, I'm calling from Mrs Meredith's home. She's all alone here and I can't rouse her. I'm no doctor but there seems to be something wrong with her breathing.'

'Stay where you are. I'll be there as soon as I can.'

Jimbo sat down on the stairs, relieved that the matter was now in professional hands. True to his word, the doctor arrived within minutes.

'Wait there, will you? I'll have a look and see what's going on, but I might need your help.'

'Right-ho!'

Dr Bevan returned moments later, his face grave. 'It looks to me as if Mrs Meredith has had a severe stroke. She'll have to be removed to hospital.'

When he had made his call and hung up the phone, he frowned at Jimbo.

'I've met you somewhere before, haven't I?'

'We met briefly when I came to see Meredith the other day – Mrs Fletcher, that is. I'm a friend of the family.'

'So we did. I remember you now. But what brings you here? Meredith has gone home to Carmarthenshire for her father's birthday celebration.'

'That explains why she's not here, then.'

'It does, but it doesn't explain what you are doing in the house. How did you get in, and where is Sabrina?'

'Sabrina? I've no idea what you're talking about. When I arrived I found the front door open. I called out and when nobody answered I was worried in case there had been some sort of break-in. I don't normally walk into people's homes uninvited but this had me worried. For all I knew Meredith and her grandmother could be lying somewhere, bound and gagged.'

Ambrose looked sceptical and Jimbo bristled. 'Look here, man, I'm telling you the truth. It all happened just as I've said.'

'All right, keep your hair on! Another time, call the police and let them do the searching. Still, it was just as well you found Mrs Meredith when you did. The sooner she starts receiving treatment the better.'

Jimbo calmed down. 'What about this Sabrina person, then? What's happened to her?'

'Miss Cole? Obviously she's not as reliable as we thought. If she's gone out this evening, leaving my patient alone, I shall see to it that she doesn't get a job in this district again. At least, not in this line of work.'

The ambulance arrived then, accompanied by the ringing of a loud bell. Jimbo stood to one side while the attendants rushed up the stairs, carrying a stretcher, and minutes later they returned at a slower pace, carrying Meredith's grandmother between them.

'What do we do now?' he asked, when Dr Bevan had seen his patient safely into the ambulance.

'We'll lock up and go on our way,' the doctor decided. 'You'd better let me have an address where you can be contacted, in case the police want a word with you.'

'I'm staying at a bed and breakfast place, Number 16, Restharrow Road, but why should the police want to speak to me?'

'They probably won't, but I'm going to report this to them as a matter of course. This may be nothing more than a case of an unreliable employee, but we won't know that until she turns up. When Meredith comes back she'll have to take a look around, to check if anything has gone missing.'

'I'll give the Morgans a call, to let her know what's happened.'

'I'd rather you didn't do that, Boyer. Why spoil her enjoyment of being home with her family? If she comes rushing back here she'll miss her father's birthday. I'll phone myself when I have a better idea of her grandmother's condition, and that may not be for a couple of days.'

When Ambrose arrived at the hospital the next afternoon, having had to see patients during his surgery hours beforehand, he was amazed by what the ward sister had to tell him.

'I don't believe that Mrs Meredith has had a stroke at all, Doctor!'

'What gives you that idea, Sister?' Ambrose had only become qualified a few years before this, and he was used to encountering experienced nursing sisters who thought they knew best, and frequently did!

'See for yourself, Dr Bevan!' She escorted him down the long ward, stopping at a bed where, marvellous to relate, Henrietta was sitting, propped up by pillows and drinking a cup of tea.

'You see, Doctor? Fully conscious and not a sign of paralysis!'

'And grumpy with it,' he noted, as Henrietta proceeded to give him what-for.

'Why am I here, Doctor? How did I get here? There's nothing wrong with me, and I want to go home!'

'You were taken ill last night, Mrs Meredith. A friend of your grand-daughter found you, and very properly contacted me.'

'I don't recall anything like that, Doctor!' Henrietta seemed very sure of herself, and not at all confused.

'And what exactly do you remember about last evening, Mrs Meredith?'

'There was nothing out of the ordinary. We listened to a play on the wireless—'

'Who do you mean by we?' Ambrose interrupted.

'Myself and Miss Cole, of course. I was doing my knitting and she was busy embroidering a pillowcase. When it was over I went up to get ready for bed, and she brought my Horlicks up to me when I was settled. Nothing else happened, I can assure you of that!'

This needed looking into, but there was no point in distressing his patient by telling her of his suspicions. Accompanied by the ward sister he walked back down the ward, puzzling this over in his mind.

'When is Meredith coming to take me home?' Henrietta called after him. 'I don't want to stay in this place any longer. It reeks of disinfectant and they don't know how to make a decent cup of tea!'

'I'm keeping her in for observation, sister. There's more to this than meets the eye.'

'I agree. Are there any special instructions?'

'Not unless her condition changes. But I want the nursing staff warned that she's taken to wandering off, all right?'

'Of course, Doctor. I understand.'

Ambrose left the hospital, deep in thought, planning to put Meredith in the picture.

Chapter Forty-seven

Harry and Meredith travelled to Hereford together. Since Henrietta had recovered so well Dr Bevan waited until after Harry's birthday to notify the pair of her unpleasant adventure. They were mystified and furious by turns.

'You'll come back with me, won't you, Dad?' Meredith pleaded. 'You'll simply have to talk Gran into giving you this power of attorney that Ambrose has in mind.'

'So it's Ambrose now, is it?' Harry teased. His daughter's face turned crimson and she did not reply. He hoped that something might come of their friendship. He wished with all his heart that she could find happiness with somebody new, and a caring doctor was just the ticket. Better than a fortune hunter like Jimbo Boyer in any event. At least Boyer had come along in time to save Henrietta, and that was worth a great deal.

When the father and daughter arrived at Henrietta's house, she was delighted to see them. Meredith, in turn, was pleased to see that her grandmother seemed none the worse for her nasty adventure. Henrietta listened quietly as Harry explained what was meant by a power of attorney, and why it was in her best interest to sign such a document.

'I hope you feel that you can trust me, Henrietta. Apart from authorizing me to act on your behalf if you should fall ill, it also protects you from any unscrupulous persons who might try to take advantage of you.'

She nodded. 'Of course I trust you, dear Harry. I'm sure you know best, as always.'

They were interrupted by Mrs Crossley, who burst into the room looking excited.

'There's a police inspector here to see you, sir. He says it's important.'

'Show him in, Mrs Crossley, please.' It wasn't Harry's place to give orders in the home of his former mother-in-law, but Henrietta didn't object. She sat with her hands folded in her lap, taking a mild interest in whatever might be going on.

The introductions over, the officer took the seat offered to him and cleared his throat. 'You'll be interested to know that we've caught up with Miss Cole.'

'Sabrina!' Meredith exclaimed.

'Alias Peggy Cole. She's been known to us for some time. She manages to gain access to people's homes in one way or another, usually by posing as a domestic servant, and then at an opportune moment she leaves, after helping herself to any property of value.'

'Where did you find her?'

'She had been staying at a boarding house a mile or so from here, but we caught her as she was boarding the London train. It appears that she kept her room on after she took up residence in this house, and when we searched it, a great number of valuables were found. It isn't clear whether she meant to return at a later date to retrieve them, or if she got the wind up and decided to make a break for it.'

Henrietta became indignant. 'Do you mean to tell me that woman has stolen some of my nice things?'

'I can't say at present, Mrs Meredith. I must ask you to have a look around your house, and if anything seems to be missing, you can let us know. Later we'll want you to come to the station to identify anything of yours which may be among the items we've recovered. There's a good chance that you'll get your possessions back. I'm afraid that's not likely to happen if any money was stolen, though. The woman may have spent that.'

Meredith grimaced. Things were always disappearing from view in this house, usually because Henrietta forgot where she'd left things or, occasionally, because she'd hidden her valuables in case of theft. Peggy, or whatever her name was, might not have got away with as much of a haul as she'd hoped for!

Ambrose arrived as the inspector was leaving. Mrs Crossley handed the police officer his hat and greeted the doctor with a nod.

'It's like Paddy's market here today!' she muttered. 'People coming and going all over the place!'

'Has Mrs Fletcher arrived back?'

'Yes, Doctor, and her father, too. He'll sort things out now. That dreadful Miss Cole! Did you know she's done this sort of thing before, stealing from her employers? It's disgraceful, preying on helpless people like that!'

'So I've been told. May I go in? I can find my own way, Mrs C.'

'Follow me!' She moved ahead of him, determined to wring the last ounce of drama from the situation. When she had announced him she left the door slightly ajar and hovered outside in the hall, her ears pricked for any juicy bits of scandal.

Harry took an instant liking to the young doctor, but he was wise enough to keep his thoughts to himself. He had always been sorry that he had encouraged the romance between Meredith and his cousin Chad, who had turned out to be a bounder. Ellen had told him a thing or two about that young man, part of it being that he had tried it on with her Mariah, while engaged, and then married, to Meredith. He had passed it off as exaggeration for a long time; that is until Dulcie Saunders had turned up, claiming that Chad had fathered her son, Lucas.

'How are you feeling this morning, Mrs Meredith?'

'I'm quite well, thank you, Doctor. I have no idea what all the fuss was about! There was no need to take me to the hospital. No need at all.'

Ambrose turned to Harry. 'It appears that Mrs Meredith was drugged by her minder. She was given some sort of sedative to knock her out, while Cole assembled some valuables and made her getaway. Sorry to sound like a penny dreadful, but that seems to be what happened. That is why she couldn't be roused last night, and why she presented every appearance of having suffered a stroke.'

Meredith gasped. 'That's awful! Anything could have happened.'

'It could, indeed. As far as we know Cole has no medical training and wouldn't have known the correct dosage, or even if the medication was suitable for the patient under normal circumstances, which it was not.'

'Then you know what the stuff was?' Harry asked.

'Not at this stage, although I can make a guess. What I'm saying is that Mrs Meredith has never been prescribed such pills, so her possible reaction to them could not have been known in advance. For all she knew, Cole could have found herself facing a charge of attempted murder to add to the accusations of fraud and theft.'

Henrietta sat placidly listening to this tale of horror, seemingly not connecting it with herself. Harry stirred in his seat.

'I've brought some documents with me for Henrietta to sign. I'll ask you to witness this, if you'll be so kind.' This was done, and Ambrose took his leave, promising to call in later.

'You'd better have a look around the house now, Henrietta' Harry remarked. 'I suggest you take Mrs Crossley with you. She's been here for years and she may have a better idea of what's missing than you do.' Behind the door, the cook-general hugged herself in glee. What a story to tell her cronies at the Mothers' Union!

'Mrs Meredith's fur coat has gone, for a start,' she announced,when the search was underway. 'Beaver lamb, that is, and cost a pretty penny. If it's gone for good she'll never be able to replace it. Think of the clothing coupons that would take, even if a coat like that could be found!'

Eventually the two women compiled a list which included a few trinkets and a pearl necklace. All Henrietta cared about was her wedding ring, a memento of her late husband, but that was still safely on her finger, much too tight to come off.

'It could have been worse,' Mrs Crossley concluded.

'Much worse!' Meredith replied. She was still feeling guilty because she had unwittingly exposed her grandmother to danger, although the Cole woman had seemed so plausible at the time.

'Next time I'll do the interviewing!' her father told her, but she was still too shaken and distressed to feel insulted by his taking charge.

'You must stop blaming yourself, my girl. From what the police had to say it's obvious that the woman is a professional con artist. You are not the first to be taken in by her and, sadly, you probably won't be the last. If she ever gets out of prison, that is!'

'I hope they lock the beastly woman up for a long time, Dad!'

Eventually, Harry returned to Cwmbran. A trained nurse had been found, a superior person who came with the highest references. Meredith announced that she would stay on until everyone was sure that Henrietta was quite settled with this Nurse Helferty. After all, they didn't want a repeat performance of what had just happened, references or no!

Harry hid a grin when he heard this. Probably she was quite sincere in this, and may even have believed it herself, but he was absolutely sure that the town held another attraction! As for the kindly young doctor, he seemed unusually devoted to making house calls.

With Nurse Helferty safely installed, Ambrose and Meredith were able to spend more time together, and when he finally worked up the nerve to propose, she was delighted to accept.

Chapter Forty-eight

Ellen studied the proofs with great delight. The photographer had submitted several for her consideration and it would be hard to choose between them. Although Harry had forbidden the family to give him gifts on his seventieth birthday, he had agreed to have a family photo taken. That was when Ellen had come up with her great idea.

On the wall of his study he kept a large framed photo which had been taken in his grandfather's day. The Morgans, evidently wearing their Sunday best, were standing in front of Cwmbran House, while their household staff were ranged on the lower steps. The thing which interested Ellen most was that the servants were all clutching the tools of their trade. The plump woman brandishing a wooden spoon was obviously the cook, a man in gaiters carried a spade, and each of the grooms held up a curry comb and a dandy brush. A housemaid displayed an old fashioned wicker carpet beater, shaped something like a tennis racquet, and the scullery maid, who faced the camera with a mad grin, held a saucepan aloft. At the foot of the steps there were several spaniels, but one of them was a blur because it had moved at the wrong moment.

The photographer whom Ellen had chosen was a man from Llanelly, who made a good living by touring the county taking pictures of wedding groups, and special anniversaries. At the outbreak of war he had done a wonderful trade, taking pictures of men and women who had been called up for service.

'That happened in the Great War, as well,' she remembered sadly. 'I have a photo of my brother in uniform. It's all I have left of him, for he was killed at Ypres.'

But these were happier times, and Ellen wanted a record of Cwmbran House as it was today. 'There were sixteen servants here when I first came,' she went on. 'Times have changed, of course. Luckily we have the Swansea Six to make up the group, so the ranks won't appear too sparse!'

It was too bad that a similar picture hadn't been taken while Harry's first wife, Antonia, was alive. What had become of all the servants who had kept the household running smoothly back in those days? The companion, Lavinia Phipps, must be dead by now, and the butler, who had still been with them at the time of Meredith's wedding, had also gone to his reward. Daisy, Antonia's lady's maid, had married a miner and was still in Cwmbran, now in her seventies. Several of the young footmen had gone away to war and paid the supreme sacrifice.

With an effort, Ellen wrenched her mind back to the present. All these new birthday photographs were very good. Harry was standing on the top step, looking very dapper in a smoking jacket and a paisley cravat. Ellen was standing beside him. Did she appear this peculiar to other people, she wondered? She hated being snapped!

On the next step were her daughter and husband. War had torn them apart, but, please God, they would be together from now on, going forward with their lives. Mariah's sadness at being unable to conceive a child had cast a shadow over their contentment for a time, but that would surely fade, now that their adoption of Lucas was going forward.

On their left stood Meredith, the daughter of the house. Her happiness had been blighted when her husband, Chad, was killed at Dunkirk. Aubrey had always felt responsible for that, because it was he who had persuaded Chad to accompany him in the flotilla of small craft which set out across the Channel, to rescue the troops stranded on the beaches under enemy fire.

Now it looked as if Meredith's life was about to take a turn for the better. She was still at Hereford with Henrietta and had been seeing a lot of the young doctor, Ambrose Bevan, who had eventually proposed. For a while it had seemed as if that wouldn't come off, because their relationship had hit a snag. The doctor had bought into old Doctor Wentworth's practice, where he looked forward to a long stay. Meredith, on the other hand, was not prepared to make a permanent move to Hereford. How could she? Her little boy was in Cwmbran and she didn't want to uproot him at this point; getting used to the idea of a stepfather would be difficult enough for him, even though he couldn't remember his own father.

In the end it was Harry who found a solution. 'If you don't mind a long engagement,' he said, 'why not wait until the boy goes away to prep school? That's less than two years down the road now. If you marry then, you'll have some time alone together at the start, as all couples should. During the holidays Henry can divide his time between the two places, your new home in Hereford, and here.'

Meredith was content to go back and forth between Cwmbran House and her grandmother's home, which gave her ample opportunity to see her fiancé.

Standing self-consciously on the next step were the staff, holding their utensils. Myfanwy, slim as she was, hardly presented the traditional picture of a cook in a large household. Bessie would have been more suited to the role, being pleasingly plump. Still, swathed in a voluminous starched apron and holding a soup ladle, the girl played her part to perfection. Rosie and Wyn, holding feather dusters aloft, appeared to have been consumed by a fit of the giggles.

The two daily women stood at the end of the row. They wore wrap-around aprons and carried small dish mops. Their hair was hidden in turbans, which they insisted on wearing as a tribute to the war just past. Turbans had been part of the civilian uniform worn by the many gallant women who had worked for the war effort in factories and shops.

The elderly gardener, Jones, had them all in stitches as they lined up, jostling for position. He had turned up for the photo session wearing a flowerpot on his head, as a sort of terracotta fez.

'Oh, Mr Jones!' Rosie spluttered. 'There's funny you look! If you stand on your head you'd look like a giant plant!'

'Not today, thank you!' he countered, removing the pot and producing a trowel from behind his back. 'Perhaps this will do instead!'

His helper, Dafydd, unable to decide between a rake and a hoe, chose to hold both. He had now left school and was in paid employment at Cwmbran House. Dai Jones was still at school, but he was determined to become a shepherd. He could think of nothing which would delight him more than spending his days up on the mountain, caring for a herd of sheep and sleeping in a *bwth*. Strictly speaking he wasn't yet entitled to display a tool of his trade, but knowing how much it meant to him, Ellen had allowed him to borrow a shepherd's crook for the occasion.

Huw had passed his eleven-plus and now sported a grammar school blazer. Each morning he raced down to the station to board a train for the next town. The Morgans had great hopes for his future. Perhaps he might even qualify to attend a university. However, that great day was seven years off; too early to worry about that now.

Ellen's gaze lingered on the earnest faces of the younger boys. There was Trevor, always on the go. Evan, who had ventured across the Atlantic and come back again. Little Ceri Davies, an affectionate little chap who was always coming out with some funny remark. She didn't care what it took, she was determined to keep those boys safely at her side until they were old enough to fly the nest. Just let anyone try to stop her!

Last, but not least, were the two smallest boys. Henry, Meredith's son, all dressed in his Sunday best, looked as if butter wouldn't melt in his mouth. Nobody looking at this photograph would guess that he had a catapult stuffed in the back pocket of his grey shorts. She'd had to remove that before any damage was done. She wouldn't have put it past the child to have shot the poor photographer while the man was crouched over his tripod with his head hidden in that black cloth he used.

Next to Henry, with his knee socks falling down, was Lucas Saunders, soon to become Lucas Mortimer. He was aware that he was an orphan but that didn't seem to bother him too much because he shared a home with the Swansea Six, who all appeared to be cheerful enough. Ellen wondered how Mariah would choose to explain his special circumstances when he was old enough to understand.

Harry believed that he should be told now that Chad was his birth father, and that Henry was therefore his half-brother, but Meredith flatly refused to allow that and, as Chad's widow, she did have some right to make that decision. Ellen only hoped that the revelation wouldn't come as too much of a shock to Lucas when the truth came out.

She opened a drawer and placed the proofs inside. At some time in the distant future, many years from now, someone might gaze at these pictures and wonder about the people recorded in them, what their lives had been like, their hopes and dreams.

When the finished photograph arrived, she must write the date on the back, to show that it had been taken just after the end of the Second World War. All the residents of Cwmbran House had been affected by that conflict, just as a field of corn trembles before a whirlwind, but they had come safely through and each of them could now go forward with renewed confidence and hope.

Ellen smiled at the thought, as she went to the kitchen to make herself a cup of tea.